HOUSE OF FAE AND MIST

SHADES OF RUIN AND MAGIC
BOOK 2

MEG XUEMEI X

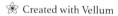 Created with Vellum

HOUSE OF FAE AND MIST

I have no intention of being anyone's bride, let alone fighting tooth and nail to get there. All the vicious catfights in the school nauseate me. I have bigger things to worry about, like being hunted by my father, who's getting closer every day.

Yet no one leaves me alone. The princes believe I'm playing hard to get, so they pursue me fiercely. When they realize that I'm not as ambitious or smitten as the other girls, they place a bet—whoever claims my virginity takes it all.

Their stupid vanity game paints a target on my back—all the bride candidates join forces to come after me, cleverly planning my demise. I might be an apex predator, but I'm one against a thousand of the meanest "coyotes."

To make sure I live through the game, Killian offers to train me. The chemistry between us cuts through every obstacle and tears down our own defenses.

We should know what's good for us. We should stay the hell away from each other. He's still forbidden fruit. If I taste him, we'll burn.

But I can't stop.

1

Barbie

It was the calm after the storm that vexed me more.

In the wake of the audience's roars came utter silence before shocked gasps and murmurs chased each other across the ice rink.

My hair grew like racing vines until the soft golden curls dangled under my chin. I was transforming in front of everyone after the brutal revelation of my true gender, helplessly responding to the chaos prince's whim, as if I were made for his dark desire.

No one would mistake me for a boy again. I looked every inch a girl who had passed her precious teen years.

Rage scorched me, my nostrils flaring, my shoulders trembling. I wanted to make Killian pay, yet terror sank its icy claws into my bone marrow, freezing me. If any of Ruin's agents were already in the realm, they'd have learned about my presence in Mist of Cinder.

Soon, my father would know where I was and come for me.

By exposing me, the chaos prince had brought unthinkable danger to his realm. I didn't even need to make my life's passion to destroy him; he'd done it to himself!

You're overreacting, Sy chimed in. *This isn't as bad as you think. You should make your life's passion to fuck the chaos prince. Murder can come after.*

"Come, Barbie," Killian commanded.

He extended a hand toward me, and I nearly spat into his palm. He pulled it back at my glare and dropped it to his side. A cruel smile formed on his lips, but it didn't reach his eyes.

Everyone was watching us.

Sparks of lightning flew out of Killian's fingertips, as if the chaos prince was daring anyone to challenge him or prevent him from taking me with him.

Silas seethed with anger, violence brimming in his amber eyes.

I'd made an enemy out of him by making him look like a fool in front of thousands of supernaturals. The tunnel-visioned shifter prince would regard my act as a betrayal, and he wasn't the forgiving kind. He hated Killian even more, though, for taking me out of his house.

Rowan kept his expression impassive, yet interest gleamed in his silver eyes. He sniffed the air again, sensing Sy yet unable to pinpoint her whereabouts. It was driving him mad.

Cade winked at me, trying hard not to laugh. I stared hard at him. Fine, he didn't hold me accountable for my deception, unlike the others, but how the fuck could this be funny?

Louis's reaction was the most unexpected. He was no longer angry. Seeing me as a girl had absolved his shame at lusting after a servant boy. I'd freed that fucker.

Heat and thirst replaced the harsh bitterness in his pale blue eyes. Tenderness grew in them as he watched me attentively.

Shit!

I shuddered. That was worse.

If I survived all this, I'd have to constantly ward off his thirst and advances.

I averted my eyes from the princes, only to be caught in the greedy gazes of Mistress Ethel and her druid. They coveted my power, their hearts as black as an eclipse.

"Move, Barbie," Killian ordered again as he glided on his jeweled skates toward the lift, expecting me to follow like a lamb. He was the lion. He'd made his kill today, and now he was collecting his prize.

I swallowed. I had no choice but to go with him. He had drenched me in humiliation, but he also offered me an exit.

At least his shadow and starlight still hovered around my breasts to provide half-decent coverage. His chaos power caressed me even in this dire situation, making my pulse quicken, my body heat up, and fury burn in my veins.

The spectators' boos swelled behind me as I stumbled on the ice after the chaos prince.

He skated like he was strolling in a park, yet with a lethal grace. Somehow, somewhere, he'd put on a shirt. He didn't spare me a glance as he reached the brink of the ice rink.

I spotted Bea standing with the guards and squires, who all glared at me. I glared back before dropping my gaze to avoid looking at Bea. I lowered my head further in shame and defeat.

"Barbie!" Bea shouted indignantly, rushing toward me.

Shit! She was going to slap me for lying to her. I guess I deserved it, so I didn't lift a hand to shield myself but waited for five fingerprints to leave their marks on my face. I even turned my cheek at a good angle for her convenience, so she didn't need to hit my nose. It'd be worse to have a bleeding nose under the circumstances.

The blow didn't come. Bea threw a blanket that I hadn't noticed in her hand around my shoulders. Killian glanced at her but didn't stop her. He beckoned impatiently for me to hurry up.

I swallowed back a sob as Bea wrapped an arm around my shoulders. I couldn't be seen to be vulnerable now, yet I started to shake.

"I got you, Barbie," she whispered. "I got you!"

I stopped trembling at her solid comfort, but I still hung my head as she led me out of the ice rink after the chaos prince.

Bea accompanied me, biting her lip nervously. She'd been trying to stay under the radar, but for me, she gathered courage and showed her support, despite knowing it would put her in the spotlight.

It was too late to push her away for her own good, but I vowed to protect her to the best of my ability. Anyone who wanted to get to her would have to get through me first. Yet it didn't lessen my fear for her.

Shades Academy wasn't like any other school; it had teeth, claws, and vicious magic. Any supernatural here could do a lot more damage than a human.

Killian's warriors, all in black, appeared out of nowhere and rallied around us in a tight formation. I'd never seen his sentinels before, but now I knew they were always around.

They were just damn good at blending into the background until it was time for them to show up.

We exited as a large group, with me trailing after the chaos prince reluctantly, my friend clutching me, and the sentinels from the chaos house preventing my escape. We left BattleStar stadium behind like a bad dream. I didn't even remember when someone had helped take off my skates, or maybe I'd done it myself?

The ivory tower of Skyward loomed in the distance like a beacon as we marched, its metal point glinting in the chilly morning sunlight.

The distance between me and the thousands of spectators couldn't dampen the roars in my head. Icy dread and fury coursed through my bloodstream. I vaguely registered that we were trekking between Infinite Library and Clockwork, where Sy had fucked the fae prince under the lime-colored tiled roof. How reckless! Sy grinned ear-to-ear at the memories and smacked her full lips despite my black mood.

A crowd gathered on either side of the path, watching our parade. Killian's warriors blocked the bystanders' view of me. No one dared to boo while the prince of the House of Chaos led our silent march and his warriors growled now and then.

Killian raised a fist to signal a halt, and his warriors stopped in sync, like a well-oiled machine. I nearly bumped into the chaos prince's back, dragging Bea with me. A large hand steadied me by my elbow, and I shoved it off with a hiss, only to evoke a low chuckle.

Killian turned to glance at me, but I refused to make eye contact with him, my jaw clenched. If I stared back, I was afraid I'd jump him, either to punch his teeth out or cling to him pathetically. Despite all this, my body still burned for him.

"Leave us, little witch," Killian ordered Bea.

Bea's slender arm shook around my shoulders. She didn't want to leave me with a pack of dangerous hybrids, but she couldn't refuse the heir's order. No one could. His every word was infused with power; even I felt its pressing weight.

"Her name is Bea, not little witch!" I said defiantly. I might be in bad shape, but I wasn't going to let anyone call my friend a little witch as if she was but a face amid thousands.

"Is it?" Killian purred, his eyes remaining on me, taunting and caressing at the same time. "Keep it up, little dagger. You'll need that spirit soon."

My heart fluttered at the endearment again, even though it was more of a mockery coming from the chaos prince's mouth.

"Please, Your Highness, let me stay for Barbie. She needs me," Bea pleaded.

"I can't allow you to go further," Killian said. "This is a house matter. Barbie will have to face the next challenge alone."

Shit! What challenge? Wasn't my humiliation today enough?

"Go!" I gently pushed Bea away. "I'll be okay."

Bea nodded while worry clouded her eyes. As soon as she departed, the opening in the ranks of the chaos warriors sealed again.

Killian resumed his lead.

"Follow closely and don't fall on your face, Barbie," he purred.

I wanted to tell him to eat shit. I wanted to kick him in the knee, but I didn't want him to take it out on Bea before she was out of range.

His team shifted their formation and formed two columns, revealing a large group standing in the granite courtyard and blocking the path to a violet building of steel and glass—the House of Chaos.

2

Barbie

The leading lady with ash blond hair was clad in red leather and tight pants, her slanted jade eyes trained on me in disdain, the corners of her dark red lips tugging down in distaste.

A troop of chicks dressed like Amazon warrior wannabes flanked her, glaring at me like angry bees ready to sting.

Shit! Was this bold chick Queen Lilith, the fiancée to Prince Killian?

My senses struck out to feel her magical scent. A Nephilim? Their kind were a bit different from demons, and they pretty much turned their noses up toward their local brethren.

Before I knew it, a jet of jealous fire shot through my hollowed chest.

Drag her down to the ground by the hair, then shove your

foot into her cheek, Sy hissed. *Show her our uncontested dominance! Let her understand who's superior!*

I might not like her at first sight, but I'm not crazy enough to go around attacking people without provocation, I protested. *Plus, I'm not a totally violent person. Remember our fighting rules?*

Don't throw the first punch, but always punch back harder. Sy grinned evilly. *Now let's punch that homewrecker much, much harder.*

She hasn't thrown a punch yet, I reminded her. *And someone might call us the homewrecker since she was there first.*

Everyone in the courtyard bowed to Prince Killian, then raised their heads to glare at me again.

"Princess Medea is going to be trouble," the giant warrior with chin-length blond hair sighed with resignation and sympathy for me.

But I let out an inaudible breath of relief. That cocky chick wasn't Queen Lilith! I could deal with this kind of trouble. I'd been afraid that I might come off too aggressive if I had to face the chaos prince's betrothed.

The giant warrior was the one who had stabilized me when I nearly bumped into Killian's back.

"Call me Rock." He winked at me, not minding me staring at him blankly. "May I call you Barbie, since you don't go by Little Bob anymore, I assume?"

Everyone was a comedian.

Everyone saw your tits! Sy said proudly. *More power to us!*

"I see, you're the silent type," Rock continued. "They say the quiet ones are usually the dangerous ones. Now that you're in the House of Chaos—"

"Slow down, Rock," said a warrior to Killian's right. He was shorter but more handsome than Rock, probably because his green eyes weren't as wide apart as Rock's. "That girl"—he jerked his chin at me— "who disguised herself as a boy and deceived everyone except our prince isn't out of the woods yet. She'll have to pass two house trials to be in the House of Chaos. Not even His Highness can break that house rule."

"Don't kid yourself, Archer," Rock said. "His Highness can break any rules. It depends if he's in the mood to do it for the new girl. He might though, since he's gone through enough trouble just to pry her out of the lethal claws of the other heirs..."

"Enough, Rock," Killian warned. "Don't confuse Barbie."

He'd seen my eyes dart wildly as I heard the unwelcome word "trials."

I'd entered three houses so far without any issue, since no ward could keep me out, but I hadn't had a chance to sneak into the House of Fae or the House of Chaos, since my previous employers had kept me busy and made me work overtime.

Drusilla, the half-vampire, had warned me to stay away from the House of Chaos, which played by different rules than the other houses. She'd also told me to avoid Killian, the heir who had the coldest heart in the realm, at all costs.

She'd been right. Look where I had wound up now!

"What trials?" I demanded in a shrill voice. "Why are there so many fucking trials in this realm? I'm sick of this trend!"

"Mind your language!" Archer growled. "You're in the presence of His Highness!"

"Now she talks." Rock smiled and nodded at the leading lady and her band, who insisted on blocking the path to the House of Chaos. "They're your first test."

"What?" I smirked. "You want me to kiss all of them? That's going to take a long time."

"Running your mouth again so soon, Barbie?" Killian said, his heated gaze darting to my lips. Instantly, my heart fluttered, and my pussy throbbed. "Better learn how to use it properly."

A few of his men chortled.

"After you get into the house, you can kiss anyone you want, of course, except our prince. How's that?" Rock asked with a wink. "But you'll fight a challenger first. Only after you win will you get to proceed to the second test. There's no need to waste time and energy telling you what test two is about before you conquer the first."

"For almost all the newbies who want to get into our house, there's only one test," Archer volunteered with a little sympathy. "Your reputation must've preceded you, Barbie, so you get a challenge. It isn't a bad thing though. Not everyone gets the special treatment. If you pass both tests, you'll become even more popular."

Sy perked up. *Let's do this!*

"Yeah?" I retorted. "What if I just turn around and get the fuck out of here instead of going through the lame tests?"

The warriors instantly formed a half ring to cut off my escape route. I narrowed my eyes viciously, seeking the weakest link.

"We went through this on the ice rink, Barbie," Killian sighed. "There's no getting the fuck out of here. The only way out is through."

"Yeah? What if I just fail the tests and go home?" I sneered.

Killian arched a dark eyebrow. "Go where then, Barbie?"

We have nowhere to go! Sy urged. *If you won't fight, let me out. I'll fight. I'll slash those pretty faces with my claws.* She giggled in bloodlust. *I'll sink my fangs into their necks and drink my fill, like the lovely vamp prince! Or better, let's fuck them, then eat them. Not necessarily in that order.*

"Whatever," I said, wrapping the blanket tighter around myself. "Let's get this over with. I don't have anything better to do at the moment anyway, and I'm hoping to have a place to sit down after this."

Too bad I couldn't swagger and swing my little cock around anymore. I didn't have one now. "Hey chicks," I called in my husky voice toward the hostile group a dozen yards away. "Who am I going to kiss first? I can't promise tongue though."

Princess Medea slanted me a look of utter scorn before nodding at a giant chick to her left. The big woman stepped out of the Amazon wannabes' ranks and gave me a crocodile smile.

Shit!

She was two heads taller than me. Her magical signature spelled a mixed descent of demon and Ice Giant. They said that Ice Giants were extinct. Well, we had a spawn right in front of us.

Medea shot a gloating glance at Killian, waiting for his reaction, but he was fixed on me, his face hard, his eyes colder. It was obvious there was no love lost between the prince and the princess.

What was she to him? A prince heir and a princess cohabiting in the same house. But then, from my experience, family wasn't just complicated. It was often overrated.

"Really, Princess Medea, you're unleashing Bellona on the new girl?" Rock stepped forward. "Aren't you setting the bar a bit too high for a new member, especially a very short new member?"

Princess Medea tilted her head, yet her jade gaze remained glued to Killian. "You're Prince Killian's attack dog, and Bellona is mine. Also"—she glanced at me, her tone acid— "I wouldn't call that mongrel a new member since she hasn't even gotten through the first test of the two-step authentication. Am I the only one who cares to enact the house rules set by the king?"

I snickered at her calling me a mongrel. The power in my blood was purer than any supernatural, probably except Killian. And my father was the only absolute pureblood, in a very evil way, though.

"You know Prince Killian can always rewrite the rules," Rock said.

"But will His Highness rewrite them for that new mouse girl," Princess Medea drawled as if she was in love with her own honeyed voice, "and arouse Queen Lilith's suspicion as to why her betrothed is so invested in another female?"

"Mind your tongue when you address me, Medea," Killian said harshly.

Medea bowed her head a little. "I meant no disrespect, Your Highness, but I have my duties. We'll have to work together to make our house stronger, even if I have to be the bad guy. Is your new pet so fragile that she can't take a little challenge? House of Chaos accepts no weaklings."

"Whom my house will accept is not for you to decide," Killian said. "After all, it's still my house."

"Exactly, Your Highness," Medea said, then turned to me. "If you don't want to go through the tests, peasant mouse, beg me and I'll let you run away with your tail between your legs."

"You should say haunches instead of legs, princess." I smiled. "Don't you read books? I do. I love reading. And I can tell you what my favorite books are if you want to be well-read as well."

Hushed gasps rippled across the courtyard, but Killian's men snickered.

"How dare you correct me?" Medea scolded.

"Will the next line be, 'do you know who I am?'" I asked innocently.

Medea marched toward me, her hair turning into numerous tiny snakes, hissing at me.

"What the fuck is that?" I yelped, stumbling back, pointing at her hair. "It's creeping me out!"

Rock stepped forward and stood between the princess and me, Archer backing him up. Brave men!

"Only His Highness has the right to punish his subjects," Rock said. "Remember the rules, Princess Medea. If you break any, Prince Killian can execute his right to banish you from his house, once and for all."

"The king appointed me to reside in his house!" Medea protested.

"Then try me," Killian said with a cold smile.

"You'll let a low mongrel defy me, brother?" Medea said.

Brother? Of course, he was a prince, and she was a princess.

"My pet is more important to me, *stepsister*," Killian taunted.

Medea's face turned purple with anger. "I'm done being nice." She nodded at her attack dog, who had been itching to swing her massive paws at me. "It's not against the rules to put down a mongrel, is it?"

"Love the friendly banter," I said impatiently. "But I have someplace to go, and it's been a really long day for me. So, let's get it done, shall we?"

I turned to Bellona, hooking two fingers and beckoning her.

Bellona marched toward me, her gait long and purposeful, her fiery gaze promising violence or even death. When she made two more steps, I backpedaled and raised a fist to stop her, my other fist gripping the blanket around me.

"Hold there for a tick!" I called, power infusing my words.

The giant paused and glared at me, not sure why she even listened to me.

"Bellona, right?" I asked. "At least let's exchange a few pleasantries and be polite before our dog fight." She frowned at me. "First, I have to say that you're big! Are you sure you aren't a dude?" Bellona hissed, but I nodded at her with a knowing smile. "I'm tiny compared to you, and I was still mistaken for a dick." I heard a few chuckles from the crowd. "I know the feeling of being constantly misunderstood. Anyway, I need to know the fucking rules of this duel before I let myself engage. I'm fed up with always being an underdog."

"There's only one rule," Rock replied for Bellona. "Fight to win."

"Aren't you helpful?" I shook my head, eyeing Deathsong in Killian's hand, my heart throbbing against my ribcage.

He'd disarmed me when I tried to stab him on the ice rink. Only now did I have the presence of mind to realize that he still held it in his possession.

The dagger was forged by the dark magic of a god, my father. The chaos prince wouldn't have figured out its origin or how deadly the weapon was, would he?

No one had ever met Ruin and lived to tell the tale. Everyone believed that the gods were dead. I wished that was the reality with all my heart.

Deathsong was sentient. It could whisper evil thoughts into the minds of its bearers. No one else could handle it except my father and me. It'd do some damage to the chaos prince's psyche or even control him if he kept it in his possession.

"Mr. Rock said to fight to win, high sir." I looked up at Killian through my thick lashes. "I'll need my dagger that you took from me. That big chick looks like she wants to bite me in two." I ran my lower lip between my teeth. "I'm still not convinced that she's not a dick."

"No one will bite you in two," Killian said. "I won't allow it. But the test must be carried out with either magic or hand-to-hand combat."

"Love hand-to-hand combat. Love touch-and-feel," I said sarcastically. "And if I win, will you return my dagger?"

"You can have many things if you win as my champion," Killian said.

He'd just turned this test into a pissing match with Princess Medea. But if I lost, his reputation would suffer as well.

A callous smile hung on Princess Medea's thin lips.

"Will I also get a hot bath and a late breakfast?" I asked hopefully.

Medea hissed. "Stop stalling, little mouse!"

"Have some spine, bug!" Bellona barked.

"Pardon me." I held a finger up at them. "But I'm not getting into any dog fight blindly without a proper bargain! That's not how I roll, ladies."

"Cami," Killian called. "Give Barbie your jacket."

A bronze-skinned girl with Viking braids pushed through the warriors' ranks and jogged toward me. I recognized her. She was on the Sinners team, Killian's right winger on ice.

She shrugged off her jacket and handed it to me. "You

also need a pair of boots. Being barefoot will put you at an even bigger disadvantage."

"You're very kind, milady." I pushed away her jacket. "But I'm good."

She narrowed her eyes. "That blanket isn't going to make you invisible!"

I wasn't ready to part with Bea's gift.

I smirked at Cami. "You have no idea of the power of a gift from a true friend, milady."

She shrugged. "Your funeral," she said and looked at Killian.

"Barbie—" Killian started.

"Let's do this, Bellona!" I shouted. "Get your fat lazy ass over here! Let's give them a good show!" I turned to run at half speed, giggling, my blanket flapping around my small frame in the wind. "C'mon, dude! Catch me if you can."

Bellona gave chase while bellowing, "Coward! I'll make you eat dirt!"

I giggled more. "And I'll make you eat a bag of tiny dicks!"

I heard Bellona picking up speed behind me. I halted, then ducked to the side, lightning fast, just as she stretched her long arm to grab my blanket. I let her pass right by me, then leapt high in the air before she could turn around.

Sy! I barked, and she pumped her speed and strength into me.

Not missing a beat, I freed a hand from holding the edges of my blanket and rammed my knuckles into an acupoint where all the nerves gathered on the nape of her neck.

"England, here I come!" I roared.

Bellona fell, her face smacking into the granite ground, and she didn't get up.

I alighted near her head, my bare foot kicking her to help turn her over, her face bloody. The bad fall had sent her to unconsciousness.

The crowd was shocked to silence.

A faint smile lingered on Killian's sensual lips. Rock grinned, and Cami blinked hard. Medea glared at me in pure hatred, as if her hate alone would undo me. She should not live in her illusion, which wasn't healthy.

"It's David and Goliath," I explained as I sat on Bellona's belly, brushing my curls from my face. I was tired, so I needed to sit down. "I took a page from D's book and tweaked it. D used a rock to defeat G, but you wouldn't allow me to use any weapons, so I had to improvise and use my knuckles." I raised my fist to show Killian my knuckles that had brought down Bellona. "Regretfully, I won't be able to duplicate the success since you've all seen this move. There're copycats out there."

Killian arched a brow. He looked so hot doing that, and my heart skipped a beat, my lips parting.

"Are you going to sit there all day and talk?" he asked, his amused gaze darting to my lips.

"No, sir," I said. "Bellona's belly isn't exactly comfortable. It's dirt hard. She must've spent all her spare time eating and shitting in the gym." I heard mixed chortles and disgusted growls. "And I'm owed a hot bath and a second breakfast."

"After you finish one more test," the chaos prince coaxed.

I sighed, getting to my feet.

Remembering something, I slid a hand into my pants, pulled out the socks I used to fake a bulge in my crotch, and tossed them into Bellona's face.

"Fuck it. Bellona can have it," I said. "I'm no longer a dick."

A few gasps were drowned out by Rock's laughter, then a few joined him across the courtyard.

"One strike, and she put down giant Bellona like no one else has done before. The new girl is super rude and foul-mouthed, but she set the record," someone said.

Medea stepped into my path. "You want to get into my house, mouse? You'll have to get past me."

"Love the warm welcome." I smirked. "Perhaps we should play cat and mouse and jackal, and see who's what?"

Medea raised her wrist, dark magic twirling around her. No magic, dark or light, worked on me, yet her magic didn't feel right.

Killian stepped between us. He had let me fight Bellona, but not his stepsister, which meant that he didn't believe that I could beat her. The princess had watched me defeat her top attack dog, yet she stepped out, looking for a fight. She believed that she would win, and I bet that she'd play dirty.

Within a day, I'd made so many enemies that I'd lost count.

Good job, Barbie! I thought in dismay.

Good job, Barbie! Sy echoed with pride.

"Don't want me to take out the trash?" Medea smiled darkly and seductively. "Then tell me, brother, why is this one so special?"

"Don't call me brother since you're no sister of mine, even if my father has named you second-in-line to his throne," Killian said, his voice devoid of any emotions. "The fight was over after your attack dog went down. I don't care what scheme you try to cook up but do it on your own time. Now get the fuck out of my way. I won't tell you twice."

"What will you do then, Killian?" Medea challenged.

Killian's eyes glowed. The temperature plunged. Frost

and darkness crept over the ground. Everyone shifted nervously, feeling the chaos prince's lethal, merciless power that was set to pounce.

Now I got why Bea had said that the prince of the House of Chaos didn't laugh. He'd only laughed at me because I amused him. If I knew what was good for me and didn't want to end up inside a body bag, I should start to kick some sense into myself and stop mouthing off to him.

Medea stepped away in a hurry, pouting yet gazing up at her stepbrother with lust. "Don't be a spoilsport, *brother*. I was only trying to have a little fun. Your pet still has to go through the guardians. The game isn't over. And everyone knows how terrifying and unbending the guardians are when it comes to the rules of the Passage. They even gave me a hard time when I was being initiated into the house, and I'm the princess!"

I snapped my head toward Killian in alarm, and his face darkened at the mention of the Passage.

It meant the next test was out of his hands.

Shit!

3

Barbie

I trailed after Killian to the top of the marble stairs. The
ivory door opened for him automatically. Killian
strode in, waiting for me on the other side while the
door remained ajar in invitation.

It felt like a trap.

I nudged the door open wider with a bare toe. I couldn't
just stroll in like I'd done in the vampires' house and then
the shifters' house, could I?

The temperature chilled, ice crystals framing the entry-
way. Two ghosts materialized.

What the fuck?

The female hovered beneath the ceiling and the male
leaned against the door, his pale arms across his chest, his
ankles crossed. The female ghost looked ageless in a white
gown that was obviously not from this era. Her elaborate
hairdo, pinned up atop her crown, was out of style as well,

yet not a single silver hair was out of place. The male ghost was clad in a trench coat, a longsword strapped on his back, the hilt visible. He waved a wand like a favorite toy, a cynical smirk on his pale lips.

The woman carried the magical scent of half-fae and half something else. It was hard to tell right away since she was too ancient, but the man was a warlock with probably one-tenth demon blood.

The two ghosts regarded me, the woman hostile and icy while hunger and a slice of fear simmered in her silver eyes. The warlock was younger. He might've died—murdered—a century or two ago, yet he still carried a curious, gleeful vibe on top of his sinister aura.

So, they were the terrifying guardians who guarded the Passage to the House of Chaos. I'd heard that one of them was a poltergeist.

They stared at me. I stared back, waiting for their move.

She can see us, the female phantom in white hissed.

She can also hear us. The warlock shrugged for her sake.

What is she? the female demanded.

The warlock winked at me. *Something bad. Something worse than us.*

Even ghosts were badmouthing me now? I darted an annoyed glance at Killian. He wasn't paying attention to the ghosts but gazed at me intently as if to remember my every line in case I perished trying to enter his house and he'd have to carry me out in a body bag.

Then it dawned on me that he couldn't see the ghosts. Everyone inside or outside the building was watching me, and none of them could see the woman in white and the man brandishing a wand.

Are you coming in or not, Barbie? the male ghost demanded. *Or would you prefer to go by Little Bob?*

He'd heard of me. The woman wrinkled her small nose in distaste. She'd heard of me as well.

I was hoping for a glass of low-fat milk. I pushed my thoughts out to them, especially the male. *It isn't too much to ask, is it, after a long day?*

Go get your own milk! the woman hissed.

The male laughed.

Let's just kill her while we can, the woman offered, blood-lust brightening her eyes. *She's trouble already. Her origin is unknown, and we don't like uncertainty.*

Not today, Lady Magenta, the male ghost said. *I actually like mystery. You know my penchant—I can never leave a puzzle unsolved.*

That's why you got murdered in the first place, Luther, Magenta snorted in glee.

I was right about him being murdered then.

Are you two just going to chitchat forever and bore me to death? I asked, not wanting them to study me like a bug. Killian might've revealed me as a girl, but my dirtiest secret was all mine.

Insolent brat! Magenta hissed again. *We can kill you right here and spit out your bones!*

She could try, but I wasn't willing to pick a fight with ghosts unless I absolutely had to. I didn't even know what exactly ghosts could do. It hadn't been on my study list.

Let's just let her in, Luther said.

Magenta narrowed her silver eyes. *Just like that?*

Perhaps we should do a riddle? Luther ran his slender fingers through his phantom hair. *Anyway, we can always harass her later.*

I pulled my lips back and smiled at them. *Come knocking on my door, and you'll get a warm welcome.*

"Why is this taking so long?!" Killian barked.

"I'm craving a glass of warm milk," I said, shifting my weight. "But Lady Magenta and Warlock Luther can't make up their minds on the percentage of the reduced fat."

Surprise flashed in Killian's eyes as he registered that I could see the guardians of his chaos house.

Don't say our names, you idiot girl! Magenta hissed again.

"Now Lady Magenta is mad that you made me say her name, sir," I said ruefully.

Don't block the door! Just show her in before she stirs more shit, Luther sighed, waving his wand lazily.

You're the one who blocks the doorway! Magenta scolded. *Stay back! I'm collecting the payment.*

"What payment?" I asked.

Everyone pays when they enter the House of Chaos, Luther said. *Just come in. We're closing business for the day.*

I stepped through sideways.

As soon as I entered the house's boundary, Magenta dove toward me from the ceiling and Luther lunged at me from the door, their intentions clear and vicious—siphoning energy from me.

"Bloody hell!" I yelped as I threw up both hands, faster than the ghosts' speed, and slammed the heels of my palms into their jaws, sending their heads snapping back.

I smirked. I could hit the ghosts like they were solid.

Both guardians stared at me in shock before Magenta hissed furiously and Luther growled. The house shook under their influence and anger, lights flickering on and off and making sputtering noises. The chandelier on the ceiling of the foyer swung back and forth.

The guardians faded in and out and in again. I had my dark wind shielding me, my eyes tracking the guardians closely, my knees bending slightly, and my hands raised in battle mode.

"What the fuck is going on here?" Killian demanded. "Magenta? Luther? Answer me. Were you two being difficult?"

He couldn't see them, but he'd learned their names.

The group behind the chaos prince and the group sealing the stairs behind me all gasped.

"Did the new girl just punch a guardian?" a dude called out. "She's dead! They won't tolerate it!"

What did you punch me for, Barbie? Luther flickered into existence first. *That wasn't very nice.*

She isn't a nice girl! I told you! Magenta appeared again. *Haven't you learned anything about females?*

We were only going to take a sip of you as payment to enter the House of Chaos, Luther complained.

"No one sips from me," I said. "Fuck off."

The vampire did! Luther pointed out bitterly.

And I'm done with that, I said. *Is that why you two became the guardians, so you can steal energy from every newbie? Does your prince know that you two are actually con men—and women?*

Magenta glared at me while licking her lips in hunger. *How dare you?*

I know hunger more than anyone, I said helpfully. *But you gotta control it, man, instead of letting it control you.* I looked around, then said it loudly to show my profoundness. "If you stare at the darkness for too long, darkness stares back!"

Words out of the baby's mouth, Magenta sneered.

If I let myself go, I'll drain you right here, I told her.

I dare you! Magenta said, but she floated some distance away.

I think she dares and she can, Luther said, rubbing his jaw where I hit. *We're outgunned this time. I say let's wrap it up before shit hits the fan, which happens often when Barbie is involved. The two of us can brainstorm this later, as guardians, and come up with a new plan.*

I strode ahead, ignoring them. I needed to sit down and get some food into my belly.

Wait! Luther called. *We must make your debut spectacular, Barbie! I have a feeling that you'll get a big promotion in this house.*

I don't want a promotion, I said. *Last time I got it, I had to watch the vamp fuck while he drank from me!*

Something red rained down from the high ceiling.

"Fuck!" I jumped back, only to realize a heartbeat later that it wasn't blood but rose petals.

Before I could swat the petals away from my face, a strip of red carpet appeared under my bare feet and extended to the end of the hall.

Ta-da! You're the house's favorite, Luther declared.

I shuddered at the hungry looks in both ghosts' eyes.

Shit! What had I attracted to myself this time?

Glowing letters reading *The Queen's Suite for Barbie* flashed across the air, and the guardians bowed out, vanishing behind the glass and wall.

Everyone in the hall looked aghast, staring at the glowing letters as if they couldn't believe their eyes, until the light winked out and the five words faded.

Shocked silence stretched before whispers rose all over.

I caught what they were telling each other: "The Queen's Suite has been vacant since the first queen of the house faded five millennia ago..."

"Not even Queen Lilith, our prince's beloved, has been invited to reside in the Queen's Suite..."

"No way would the house assign the Queen's Suite to the new girl, a lowborn...It was a prank..."

Killian swept his gaze across the hall before it alighted on me, his storm-blue eyes on fire.

The poltergeist guardian put me on the spot because I denied him a sip. What a petty dead man!

"Cami," Killian called.

The girl in dark Viking braids stepped out. "Yes, Your Highness."

"Barbie will stay in the extra room in your suite," Killian said.

"But—" Cami protested.

"Make sure she doesn't burn the house down, cousin," the prince said as he strolled away, not sparing me a second glance.

4

Barbie

We entered Cami's luxury suite on the sixth floor, fit for a royal.

Cami walked me through the living room, then a small gallery that opened to an archway. At the end of it was a room with a pale green door.

Cami turned the handle and pushed the door open. "This will be your room until Prince Killian makes another arrangement for you."

"What other arrangement?" I asked.

"When the house decides to give you another room," she said curtly.

"But the house already offered me the Queen's Suite, didn't it?" I asked with a smirk on my lips.

Playing meek wouldn't do me any favors, and I sensed that dark, sinister water was already stirring under the bridge of the House of Chaos, with many opposing players and power struggles.

In the vampires' house, everything had been straightforward—the vamps craved my blood. In the shifters' house, it was all about hierarchy, and Silas's attention was elsewhere since rumor had it that he was going to get challenged by his younger sister.

In this chaos house, I knew that Killian had a plan for me, but I didn't know what it was, and thus it made me sweat. Also, I'd made a powerful enemy. Princess Medea was a snake. On top of that, the guardians had also taken an unhealthy interest in me. They'd lurk in the shadows, waiting for a chance to pounce on me.

"Are you so eager to be killed?" Cami snapped.

I widened my eyes, playing dumb. "Who's gonna kill me?" But I skipped the endearment of babe, not wanting her to strike me.

"The Queen's Suite for someone like you?" She narrowed her eyes.

"Me?" I offered her another grin, knowing it'd irritate her more. "It's just a room, isn't it? What's the big deal?"

"Not a big deal? The Queen's Suite has been vacant forever! It's supposed to be reserved for Prince Killian's future true mate." She hesitated for a second. "Which is Queen Lilith, of course."

An unreasonable bolt of rage shot to my head, and I nearly stumbled at the dizziness.

"Then why isn't the queen taking up residency?" I asked in my most logical voice. "Why did the house assign that suite to me if it's reserved for her? Don't you lot rely on the house and its guardians to sort out this kind of stuff?"

She stepped toward me, and I ducked to the side then shot into the room.

She frowned. "You thought I was going to hit you?"

"You weren't going to smack the back of my head with your knuckles or box my ears until they ring?" I blinked. "Every usher tried that when I first entered their house."

"No!"

I smirked. "I got it. I'm a girl now. Sir Killian promoted me to a bride candidate. No one hits a candidate, right, since no one wants damaged goods?"

"Let's get this straight once and for all, Barbie." She raised a finger in front of my face. "First, remember your place. Don't talk shit if you want to survive in this house and even find a mate matching your station after all the princes have their pick. My cousin may have a soft spot for you, as he always collects strays, but everyone else here is merciless. If you stand in anyone's path, they'll remove you before maiming you. And if you stand in Queen Lilith's path, you'll be sorry that you were ever born."

"But what if I'm already sorry that I was born?" I asked. "And what's the second, or is there a second point since the first was so long?"

She stared hard at me. "One of the guardians is a powerful poltergeist. No one has ever gotten red-carpet treatment before, not even me. It was a bad joke at your expense! Assigning you to the Queen's Suite is the biggest prank the guardians have ever played. You should've had more common sense than to challenge the guardians. It's bad form to catch their eye."

I widened my eyes in dismay. "Shit! I knew it!"

Cami nodded. "From now on, keep your head down and try to survive the rest of the semester. Prince Killian went to a great deal of trouble pulling you out of the death trap and giving you a chance to turn over a new leaf. Don't waste it!"

I snapped to attention. "I won't, ma'am!"

She shook her head, turned on her heels, and left.

I turned to regard my new room, fully furnished with an ensuite, with a smile. It was bigger than any place I'd stayed. Even Sy was pleased.

I shrugged off the blanket and went to turn on the shower. In the marble bathtub, I scrubbed myself raw and pink, as if I could shed my past just like that. Despite all the humiliation and fighting today, there might be a new life here for Sy and me, even though I knew hope was a dangerous thing.

After a proper bath, I stalked toward the closet and let out a gasp. It was full of clothes my size, student uniforms included. Even the shoes and boots were all my size. Killian had set it all up before he'd revealed my true gender to everyone.

My heart thundered, and I didn't know what to make of this.

I'd been starved and tortured and threatened all my life, but the public humiliation that Killian had made me suffer was still a new low. Then he'd saved me, brought me to his house, and tried to give me a new start.

I shrugged on a long T-shirt that reached down to my thighs and padded to the narrow, arched window, only to jump back when the window started to expand until it covered one-third of the wall.

The sentient house wanted to give me a better view while providing me with a possible escape exit? The house had wanted me to take the Queen's Suite. It hadn't been a prank as everyone had thought.

"Thank you, good house!" I praised it, peeking out the window that had a partial view of the dark forest.

The window opened for me, letting in a flowery and lemony scent. I could get used to living here, like I might belong, but this life could be snatched away from me in two seconds.

"So dramatic!" a voice crooned loudly from behind me, making me nearly jump out of my skin and topple over the windowsill. "Aren't you going to wipe a tear from the corner of your eye, little Barbie?"

5

BARBIE

I wheeled around and found Luther, the ghost guardian, lounging comfortably on my bed, his phantom boots resting on one of my pillows.

"What the fuck?" I growled.

"Spitting fire! I can see why our prince is quite taken with you," he said with a smirk that I didn't appreciate. "But lower your voice. You don't want to get me fired, do you?"

I blinked, intrigued. "They can fire a ghost guardian? I thought it was a permanent position."

"There's no such thing as permanent," he scolded.

I nodded. "Only death is permanent."

"Rub it in, why don't you?" he said sourly.

I studied him. "How did you come to be employed in the House of Chaos?"

"Fake it to make it."

I narrowed my eyes. "Are you even Luther?"

"Name's actually Pucker," he said.

"So you're an identity thief?"

"I was also a clairvoyant and a gay," he volunteered, lighting magical weed with a skilled hand.

"Don't smoke in my bed!" I shouted. "And get your feet off my pillow. It's new!"

"Chill, Barbie." He spun his body, and now his ass sat on my pillow. "Better? Come sit by me." He puffed out a ring of phantom smoke. "We need to talk."

I narrowed my eyes with suspicion, not moving an inch toward him. "Is smoking weed even legal in the house?"

"You pissed off a lot of people, my darling," he started. "They plan to eat you alive. If you want to survive in this town, you'll need me."

"You need to work on your sales pitch," I said.

He tilted his head to regard me and sniffed. "A demigoddess?"

My heart pounded. I was more than that, but no one else had come closer than him to sniffing out my power, and that got my attention.

I remembered the conversation between Headmistress Ethel and her druid; the druid had suspected that one of the original gods was still around, and that he'd been hunting for a demigod. Thinking of the nasty duo only made my chest tighten with anxiety, especially as I didn't like how they'd stared at me greedily, sensing my power and coveting it.

I slumped into a chair by the window and stared at the ghost guardian on my bed. They said the dead didn't lie.

"Everyone knows that the gods are dead," I said, my face blank.

"Are they?" he asked. "No one has ever crossed your kind."

"Maybe everyone should go out more often, including you." Then something clicked. "You can't get out of the house, can you? You're bound to it as its guardian."

He peeked at me hopefully. "If you bond me to you, I can go wherever you go. All it takes is a sip of your energy."

"That's why you became the guardian, so you can take a sip from the students here, siphoning their magic and energy! Does Prince Killian know that your and Magenta's guardian business is a big sham?"

"Shush! I came to you as a possible ally. I'll be useful to you. Even though I'm dead, I can still glimpse a fragment of the future, and I saw yours coming."

"Then why didn't you see your own murder?"

"I understand you have doubts about me, even distrust," he said, sadness, pain, and vengeful anger flickering in his blue eyes. "My enemy knew me well, and seers usually can't see their own demise. I was deprived of the sight of my killers even at the moment of my death. They wore masks on top of their glamour. All I remember is those glowing eyes."

"I feel sorry for you, man, but I'm still not going to let you take a sip of my energy."

"You're tough," he said. "All this talk has made me tired and depressed! Now I have to go sip somewhere else to keep my mind active since you refuse to donate. I never bother to ask others when I take a swig."

"That's rude," I pointed out.

"It's the way of the realm—the strong take whatever they want."

"I'm stronger than you and I can spot you a mile away," I said. "I'll knock your ghost teeth out, and you won't even find a lousy dentist if you jump me. Don't say that I didn't warn you."

"What if I bribe you?"

"Huh? What do you mean?"

"I brought a gift."

He flicked his ghost wand, and a hologram streamed out.

My eyes bulged as I watched myself entwine with all four princes on top of satin sheets.

"It's an alternative scenario in your future, now that you've entered the Brides Selection," he said. "After all, I'm a clairvoyant. It's time for me to put my talent to use and get in the game again. And you'll need to get your head out of your ass and take the Selection seriously."

How could I take it seriously when I had to watch myself ride Cade while Louis, Silas, and Rowan had their hands all over my nude body in the hologram?

My face flushed. "Turn it off, Pucker!"

He smiled at me before he faded out of the door.

Aren't you naughty, little Barbie? Sy peeked out in glee. *Let's get popcorn and watch the free porn.*

6

Barbie

The four princes and the holographic Barbie were on a large bed in a penthouse in the streaming hologram.

Barbie straddled Cade, riding his hard length feverishly. He stared at her boobs, his turquoise eyes searing with lust.

Hissing in pleasure, the mage prince bucked his hips up and thrust deep into her. She let out a lustful moan, seemingly pleased by his ardor. Louis came around, his hands kneading her flaming red tits. Silas leaned forward to kiss her, their tongues entwining and lapping.

Rowan, however, hadn't joined them. Silas was bulky, Louis was all hard muscles, Cade was lanky, and Rowan was built like a scholar warrior.

The fae prince stroked his long hard cock while staring at Barbie with unnerving intensity, as if he could sniff out Sy.

The vampire prince took Barbie's nipple into his mouth and sucked.

The scene was getting steamier.

"I'm not that slutty," I murmured, my face flushing, my body getting warmer.

I'm fed up with your slut shaming! Sy warned.

"Pucker!" I called. "Come here and fucking turn it off!"

A loud bang made Barbie jump. Her eyes widened as Killian kicked the door down and charged into the room, his darkness and starlight lashing out at the other heirs and tossing them away.

The chaos heir grabbed Barbie and pulled her into his muscled arms, his hand cupping her round cheeks, his stormy blue eyes roaming over her naked body.

"You're mine, don't you know that?" he growled. "You've been a naughty girl. Now I'll have to punish you and fuck you in every way. I'll erase other men's stench from you. You're mine and no one else's, Bride!"

My pussy throbbed in aching need even though the chaos prince sounded utterly ridiculous in the hologram. Pucker was a terrible director.

Killian turned Barbie around, her back leaning into his hard chest. His massive erection pressed against the small of her back. She wiggled her ass shamelessly.

With a growl, he parted her legs and pounded into her.

Fuck! That was kind of hot.

Sy agreed, rolling within me in a flurry of excitement.

The other princes snarled and lunged at them, wanting a piece of Barbie as well, but Killian's magic kept them from reaching Barbie.

"You're more than welcome to watch how I fuck my mate, but none of you shall touch her," he growled, thrusting into her possessively with a rapid rhythm.

The wet sound of flesh slapping flesh was so erotic that the other princes watched, brimming with rage and desire.

"This little pussy is mine and mine alone," Killian declared again, *pounding into bimbo Barbie so hard that she made a show of seeing stars.*

It was the worst porn I'd ever watched. How the fuck did Pucker even get it made? Yet I couldn't take my eyes off it as I watched Killian fuck the holographic me with abandon. My throat felt parched, my heart raced, and my blood heated.

"You like it rough, don't you, my prince?" Bimbo Barbie *moaned like a feline in heat, and the chaos prince growled like a beast, his chest rumbling.*

A knock sounded on the door, and I jumped out of my skin again.

Fuck! Someone was at the door, for real!

How was I going to turn this group porn off?

The knocking grew urgent. It seemed whoever was on the other side of my door was going to kick it down at any second.

Pucker wouldn't return to help me out since he was a petty dead man and a terrible poltergeist. For all I knew, he might be watching behind the wall, laughing his ass off.

I charged into the hologram, punching Killian and bimbo Barbie, then wheeling and doing a roundhouse kick at the princes to get them off the program, but the hologram just kept streaming.

Holographic Killian drove into bimbo Barbie with long, rapid thrusts and roared in pure male satisfaction.

"What the fuck?" I hissed at him. "Stop bellowing! You're going to wake up the entire building!"

"What a delicious cunt," he purred, *spanking a meowing* Barbie. *"Look how well it takes every inch of my cock!"*

The door was giving in. Sweat beaded on the tip of my nose.

With a growl, I opened my mouth, the entire hologram streaming into my mouth until there was no magic left in it. Now I just had to keep it down until the crisis passed.

The door flew open just as I rushed toward it, slamming into a hard chest.

"Cool your tits!" I cried out.

A strong hand held me.

A familiar, intoxicating scent of powerful male blanketed me, making me want to snuggle against the chest and find my haven. I pulled back and found myself gazing up at the chaos prince's furious face.

The sentient house obeyed the prince. No lock could stop him, and no door would remain closed to him.

"I heard noises. Are you hiding someone in your room, Barbie?" Killian demanded, his eyes darting from my face to scan the room. "It's against the house rules!"

If I hadn't known better, I'd say his anger came from jealousy.

The heir attempted to walk past me to check out the room, but I stepped up, stood my ground in the doorway, and blocked him. I had to stick to my principles, though I didn't know exactly what that was. I was worried that if he slid in, the hologram would slip out of my control and play right in front of him, then for sure I'd be done for.

I wouldn't just suffer from utter humiliation. If anyone found out that I'd tried to fuck the heir of the House of Chaos, who was spoken for, I'd be dead.

"No one is here except you!" I croaked.

Killian let his gaze rove over me, so I gave him a bold onceover as well.

He was dressed in a designer black shirt and a pair of

slacks that showed off his muscled body. He was a large male with perfect proportions.

Sy peered out, drooling over the prince's cut chest and his exposed forearms, since Killian had his sleeves rolled up.

Ask him to turn around, Sy advised. *I want to check out his taut ass. I'm an ass girl!*

Fuck off, I told her. *He isn't here to make you horny. He's here to spy on us!*

Then we should give him something to remember, Sy insisted. *Thrust out your boobs! I've seen all of the bride candidates do that in front of the princes. You can do better! Now hold your bountiful boobs and pump them up to let him drool. He's been checking them out. Take this opportunity to demand he dump that queen bitch of his, or we'll do it for him violently! We need to constantly assert our dominance, Barbie, lest others forget!*

I didn't need Sy to nag me. I was already in trouble. My tits felt so taut and tender, in need of being sucked hard. My pussy throbbed achingly. I hoped that it wasn't dripping. I needed to cover my arousal, so I did my best by bending a knee and pressing my left thigh against the right, squeezing my sex to offer it some relief.

Killian followed my movement, a faint, mischievous smile lighting his sensual lips. The fucker enjoyed messing with me. Yet I couldn't help but gaze at his kissable lips and wonder how it would feel to have them lick me down there.

Now I'd done this to myself! I needed to pinch my sex, but I forced myself to relax my thighs and pretended to be at ease.

I crossed my arms over my chest awkwardly while I lifted my chin, defiance in my eyes.

"What are you doing here, sir?" I went on the offense. "I was just settling in!"

"I heard strange noises in your room." He narrowed his eyes, trying to detect if I was a liar. "It seemed you had boy visitors—"

"The only boy visitor is you." I cut him off. "If you count yourself, sir! I was in the shower. That was probably the noise you heard! No one showers quietly. I had to jump out of the tub to come to open the door before you huffed it down!"

The amused smile in his eyes deepened. "Is that why your face is so flushed?"

My palm flew to my burning face. "Yes. What? No!"

Anger rose in me. Who did he think he was that he could play me like a fiddle? Yet my face grew hotter as the images of how he'd fucked me and roared in satisfaction in the hologram flooded my head. It didn't help cool me down as another image of him fucking me from behind in the tub in that dreamland replayed as well.

He'd showed me that he liked it rough. Just thinking of it got my blood heated.

How would it feel if he fucked me in truth?

Let's find out now! Sy encouraged.

The chaos prince's nostrils flared as he sniffed, not subtly, his storm-blue eyes turning brighter and hungrier.

Fuck! No! He now smelled my arousal!

Yes! Sy hissed in glee.

The chaos prince had always liked my scent. From the first time he'd met me in the woods, he'd known I was a girl from my scent.

Killian glanced at my room again, and I couldn't exactly block his view since he towered over me. His gaze darted back to my face with a knowing smirk, and I realized what it was. I'd failed to fool him by denying the "strange noises" he'd obviously heard. His eyes grew hooded. He must've thought I was watching porn, since he didn't find any man in my room.

The high sexual tension was becoming unbearable. Sparks bounced between us. At any moment, I might combust, and then he'd retreat to safety while I had nowhere to go. Yet Sy had no such concern or modesty. She licked her lips with searing lust, her pheromones emitting into the air to trap Killian. She might burst out of me anytime to jump on Killian and fuck him. I didn't want her to touch him. I didn't want her to get any closer to him.

I called up my power and will to rein her in.

"I—I don't need to explain why my face was flushed, sir!" I said, desperate to diffuse the tension.

"You look good when you're flushing," he said in approval. "It suits you. No one will ever mistake you for a boy."

A jet of red-hot rage shot to my head and broke through my control.

"You had no right to expose me in front of thousands! Who wants that kind of fucking humiliation?!" I seethed.

"You like to play a boy?" He frowned at me. "I thought I did you a favor returning you to who you truly are."

"You have no idea who I am!" I couldn't help but raise my voice. He was messing with a monster with claws, fangs, and a black soul, and he'd regret it! "I was doing fine as a boy."

"Not that fine when Silas and Louis were going to punish you—you have no idea how nasty they can be. And the headmistress was going to toss you in the dungeon. If she'd done that, you might never get out. You're better off as a girl, and you get to be a bride candidate."

"Yeah, so the other candidates can eat me alive?" Pucker was right about warning me. "They'll all come after me!"

He let out a low chuckle to dismiss me. "You'll survive them. I have faith in you, Barbie."

My chest heaved up and down, my face still flushing from fury and desire.

"Here, you earned it back," he said, my Deathsong appearing in his hand.

The prince handed the dagger to me, hilt first. As soon as I took it, Deathsong came alive with a violent humming in my head. *Let's go slay someone!*

"Be careful with it," Killian added as he gave me one last glance before striding away.

"Whatever dark plan you have in store for me, sir, it won't work!" I growled behind him.

"I count on that." He chuckled sensually, not looking back.

I slammed the door shut, but the chaos prince was already gone.

In his wake, my fury and desire still throbbed.

7

BARBIE

I'd barely gotten any sleep, plagued by nightmares, as usual. Just when I finally dozed off, a knock banged on my door.

I struggled to open one eye, then the other. Sunlight streamed through the window and fell on my golden curls.

The knock grew urgent. I rolled off the bed, shot toward the door, and yanked it open.

A boy who was probably a year younger than me raised his knuckles, ready to knock on the door again. He had a cheerful face that hadn't seen many dark days.

"Who are you?" I demanded, annoyed at being woken up.

"I'm Bern." He grinned at me. "You missed your first class."

"Who cares?"

"His Highness cares," the boy said, tossing me a magical tablet, the same type I'd seen Bea use. She had showed me the ropes, so I knew exactly how to navigate it as soon as the new boy in front of me pulled up the touchscreen that displayed a page.

I browsed through the curriculum: ancient and modern magical history and classification, use of glamour, animalistic shifting and control, elemental conjuring, mind shielding, spell weaving, potions, magical combat, formidable dark magic for advanced users, etc.

I stopped flipping through the long list and frowned. "I'm not cut out for this. I'm too old for education."

"Those are basic class requirements for any freshman!" Killian's errand boy exclaimed.

"If you'll excuse me, I'll go back to sleep."

"I'm not going to excuse you," he said. "If you don't go to the class, His Highness's other squires will drag you to the second class. They're meaner."

I gave him side-eye. "I was a squire once upon a time, but I've never seen you before."

"That's because I'm a low-profile squire, and you, like other girls, have eyes only for the princes."

"Not me. I keep an eye on them so I won't get fucked."

"They say you were the worst squire ever."

I narrowed my eyes. "Who spread that rumor?"

"We can suss it out later," he said. "Right now, you need to get to the second class. I don't want to get fired for your tardiness."

"Where do I go?"

"I'll take you to the class," he said. "This is a one-time courtesy. Starting tomorrow, you'll need to attend every class and be on time. If you fail to comply with the rules of Shades Academy, there'll be discipline, like detentions, labor, or even solitary confinement."

"Do they provide meals if they discipline me?" I asked.

"Nope."

"Shit!"

"You missed the magical theory class already, if you care to know," he offered.

"The one taught by Professor Longweed?" I asked, and he nodded. "Then I didn't miss it. It would only be a waste of my time doing a replay. I was in her class when those little shits tossed magic at me to impress the vamp prince to get laid."

He chortled.

"Longweed spewed bullshit about getting the princes to find their fated mates in the Brides Selection. Whichever prince gets to fuck his fated first will produce the One who will bring back the magic of old and will be the High King. Shit like that."

"That sounds fun," Bern said. "But you might've missed the point of her preaching. We gotta go now."

"Give me a second!" I closed the door in his face, freshened up, and put on my school uniform and long stockings.

BERN GAVE ME AN APPRECIATIVE LOOK, and we walked out of the violet building of House of Chaos.

A schoolgirl with long bangs sauntered toward us, flashing Bern a cozy smile.

"Bern!" she said in a flirtatious voice. "I'll take Barbie to her next class."

"Are you sure, Imelda?" Bern asked hesitantly, his brows creased. "You're Princess Medea's lady-in-waiting."

Imelda tilted her head like a bird. "The princess thinks it's more proper for Barbie to have a girl guide. She's no longer a boy now, is she?"

Bern turned to me. "You good with that, Barbie?"

"Whatever." I shrugged. I was sleepy and hungry, so I

wasn't in the mood. And why did it matter who took me to the class? "Or I can just find the class myself."

Bern nodded at Imelda and gave me a warning look. "Any trouble, let me know."

Imelda winked at him. "I can handle Prince Killian's pet."

"I'm sure you're an expert." I smirked at her. "You flirt as easily as you fart."

Her smile dropped, and she looked aghast. Bern coughed into his fist before he fled.

"Just don't talk to me," Imelda said, raising a manicured hand as if to fend off a fiend. "You shouldn't even be in the Brides Selection! You're so crude!"

"Can't be crude anymore. I no longer have a dick. Can't even mark a tree." I smirked, and she glared at me, wrinkling her nose. "I'm a chick now, like you. And I'm in the same school as you, probably even in the same class. So, there's hope for me. There's hope for everyone. Don't you agree?"

She sneered in disgust, and we traipsed across the grass field. When I realized that she was leading me toward the BattleStar stadium. I started to sweat, my heart beating wildly.

Just yesterday, Headmistress Ethel and her druid had almost taken me to a dungeon, and then Killian had outed me. The shame of being exposed in front of thousands of students still hung on me like old dirty clothes. The last thing I wanted was to go back to the stadium.

"Shouldn't we go to Pathfinder where the classrooms are?" I asked, halting my steps.

"You missed the first class," Imelda snapped. "Your second class will be physical training. Are you too cowardly for a little combat?"

She was taking me to a fight. It'd come sooner or later anyway.

I'd been dragged onto the wagon, thanks to Killian, so I might as well get on with the ride and pray that the wagon didn't roll straight off the cliff.

8

Barbie

As soon as I stepped into the hall in the back of the stadium, I knew that I'd walked right into a trap.

I sighed as the door slammed shut behind me and over a hundred students turned to me like a pack of coyotes craving blood and flesh. A dozen of them rushed to guard the only entrance and exit like hounds.

The space was lit by the witch lights. The only natural light came through a narrow window close to the arched ceiling. A raised boxing ring, triple the size of a professional sports ring in the human world, dominated the center of the hall.

So, this was what the supernaturals called the Ring. It was different than the underground fight club, aka the Pit, run by Prince Silas. I also knew that while the mage prince had a few upscale cafés under his belt, his major trade was dangerous potions and spells. The vampire prince ran gambling joints, and Killian owned a chain of high-end nightclubs in both the mortal and supernatural realms. Rowan, however, hosted hunting games in the realm every solstice.

"Get on the ring!" Imelda ordered.

I looked around but didn't see Medea. However, America, the fae chick who had accused me of a crime even after I'd saved her from a Shrieker, parked herself at the corner of the stage. Well, it was refreshing to see the bullies from rival houses now working together to put down their common foe.

Pucker said that they'd eat me alive, but I might be too much for them to chew, and I wasn't someone who always brought good news.

"Where's your boss?" I asked. "It's interesting that she didn't show up, so if things go down the toilet, she can just wash her hands clean. Tell me, minion, who's the coward?"

"Shut up!" she said, her hand lashing out to shove me.

I sidestepped and slapped her hard in the ear. I didn't like anyone laying their hands on me.

"Oops, I was clumsy," I offered. "Did I hurt you?"

She covered her ear and stared at me in shock before pointing at the boxing ring. "Get in there and fight!" she said viciously. "Or you'll never get out of this room!"

I smirked. "Will you join me, minion, since you did a good job luring me here?"

"My name is Imelda of the House of Chaos!"

I jogged toward the ring. "My name is Barbie of the House of Chaos."

And my name is Sy of the House of Chaos, Sy offered giddily.

One leap, and I landed in the center of the boxing ring.

America stood stiffly in a corner, putting space between

herself and me. She had a whistle between her lips, playing referee.

"Hello, My Lady America, long time no see." I grinned at her. "How you doing?"

She glared at me. "You're a liar. You deceived Prince Killian!"

"My bad," I crooned. "He spanked me for that, so hard. Do you also want to get spanked by him, My Lady America? Pain and pleasure work wonders together, and it can get into your pretty head like a drug."

She licked her lips, probably imagining being spanked by the chaos prince.

Unfortunately, a few chuckles from beneath the ring jerked her out of her reverie. No one was rooting for me here, but it appeared that a lot of them didn't like her either.

"Think you're good enough for the Brides Selection? This is only the beginning!" she yelled at me.

"I might just be good enough. But are you, My Lady America?" I asked sweetly.

These privileged brats with a capital B thought they could stomp anyone beneath them. They were worse than the prince heirs.

"Don't let that low life, good-for-nothing goad you, Lady America. We're all sick and tired of her talking!" Bellona's voice boomed, and on cue, the boxing ring lit up.

The descendant of an Ice Giant leapt into the ring, glaring at me, hate in her ice-blue eyes. Her face had mostly healed, as supernaturals recovered faster than humans. Now only a faint purple patch was left on her big cheeks.

"Ooh, it's Christmas!" I cheered, turning my head left and right to admire the light show. "Do you like Christmas, dude? I do. Lots of candies."

That's Halloween! Sy corrected. *Christmas is eating turkeys with gravy!*

"You think you're funny? You're ridiculous!" Bellona spat. "I want a rematch, and you're going down!"

"All the way down?" I consulted her. "Could you kindly explain to me the rules of engagement?"

"Fight until you're dead!" Bellona shouted, charging me without fair warning.

I dodged two of her swings, left and right, before I rolled under her attacking arm that was larger than a tree trunk and darted to her back. My leg kicked out, making contact with the back of her kneecap. She stumbled but didn't go down.

"You're tough, dude!" I called.

Bellona wheeled to face me, snarling, shock slamming into her face at my speed. I'd defeated her just yesterday, but she must've thought I'd gotten lucky.

She raised her hands, an ice spike appearing between them.

"Don't use magic, Bellona!" America shouted her warning. "It won't work on her, and she'll only turn it back on you!"

They'd studied me, and they knew magic, except Killian's, was useless against me. They'd taken notes before organizing the ambush.

Sy, I called.

Let me take over, she growled. *I'll open them up!*

Very graphic, but not today, I said.

Sy grunted unhappily, but she loaned me her speed and strength right away.

"I'll maul your face, bug!" Bellona barked, her leg sweeping with brutal force, aiming for my face.

"When was I downgraded from a chihuahua to a bug?" I asked.

Instead of rolling away this time, I swung my arm toward her attacking leg. My fist punched her ankle before her foot could connect to my face, and I heard the cracking sound of her bone splintering. She yowled in pain and dropped onto her side.

"No pain, no gain," I offered.

"You! Little Bob!" I squinted and spotted Javier from the House of Shifters coming toward the ring, pounding his chest. I used to sneak into his and Luna's apartment to shower when I'd taken the role of a boy squire.

"It's Barbie to you now," I said. "You should keep up with the updates; good for your brain."

"Suck my dick!" he spat.

"No thanks," I said humbly. "It's too short. Even you yourself can't reach it to suck it."

A couple of male students chuckled but stopped quickly at an animal snarl.

Javier shifted. A large black panther leapt into the air and alighted in the ring, its small eyes glowing as the shifter marked me as prey.

Shit!

The animal's height reached over my shoulders. If he stood on his haunches, he'd be eight feet tall.

My pulse spiked, adrenaline rushing through my bloodstream. The panther lunged at me, and I leapt into the air, twisting my torso, and landed on his back. He touched down on the other side of the ring, pausing in surprise, then thrashed to shake me off. I refused to let go but adapted my pose like I was riding a bull. My hands grabbed his ears hard, my sharp fingernails digging in, courtesy of Sy. The panther cried like an angry baby.

"Javier, your fur is too rough," I shouted out my complaint. "It's not comfortable for anyone to ride on your back. You need to be better at self-care! At least go to a grooming service or a dog spa once a month, for fuck's sake!"

He snarled, dropping to the ground, ready to roll and pin me beneath him. It was a good tactic, but it was just his luck that he happened to be dealing with me. I didn't put up with tantrums.

I'd already leapt off him. Not missing a beat, I booted him in his ribs when he was down, sending the panther of over three hundred pounds flying out of the ring. That was how strong Sy was.

The panther uttered a surprised, enraged yelp, which couldn't stop him from crashing into the queue of minions who were waiting in line to challenge me. I didn't spare Javier another glance as the panther struggled to stand on his paws while a couple students pushed him off them, groaning and bitching.

"Now, now." I rolled my neck. "Which of you little shits is going to help me stretch?"

"Shut up!" America pushed a whistle between her lips and blew like a maniac, as if that would make me fall in line.

I was in her face the next second, tearing it out of her mouth. She blinked hard, fear flitting by her eyes.

"How dare you be rude to a noble lady, your better?" she hissed.

"You might be a noble in this realm," I said, "but you aren't my better, babe. And you never will be. No one here is my better."

No one! Sy roared, pounding her chest with pride. *We're the best!*

"Is that so?" a familiar voice answered coldly from across the boxing ring.

I turned to face Dixie, blood draining from my face. I didn't owe anyone anything, except Bea and Dixie.

"What are you doing here, Dixie?" I asked quietly.

"No longer using your little boy's voice?" she asked. "I brought you to the House of Shifters. I offered you a shelter, and Luna befriended you. How did you repay us?" She paused as pain coated her eyes. "You got her killed."

Guilt rained down on me. I bit my lip. If I hadn't come to this realm, no lives would've been lost. There were five deaths in total, murdered by the Shriekers. More death would come, even if I left Mist of Cinder.

And when Father finally came, it would be the end, unless I could get stronger and stop him.

"I'm sorry," I said.

"Your sorry means nothing! Luna is gone!" she spat. "Fight me."

"I'm not going to fight you," I said.

Dixie swung her fist at me.

The first punch landed on my check. Pain bloomed in me. She didn't hold back. Her next punch hit my nose, shattering my bones. I tasted my own blood as it poured out of my nostrils.

Power pulsed in the air as my blood was spilled, and everyone felt it, yet no one could understand the shift in the room, only silence falling as Dixie rammed her fist into my ear, making it ring.

I was thankful that there were no vampires except Drusilla, who was a dhampir, in the hall, or the scent of my blood would drive them into a frenzy.

As if summoned by me, Drusilla jumped into the ring

too. She went straight for me, and with a devil's kick to my jaw, she sent me to the ground.

Drusilla was in love with Prince Louis. The last time I saw her, I'd sent her to tend to her prince after I stabbed him in the chest. She now came to punish me on his behalf.

"You should never have entered the Selection!" someone shouted, and the others agreed.

"A bug wants to be a bride," Imelda snickered. "Have you seen her drool over Prince Killian, even though he's spoken for."

"Little sluts think I'm their competition," I murmured amid the blaring pain as a dozen students jumped into the ring and kicked me brutally.

"You were never our competition," America declared. "This is the reckoning."

The crowd cheered.

From the cracks between my arms, which I had wrapped around my head, I caught half of them raising their devices toward me to record my beating. I didn't think they'd be bold enough to put the show on Spinchat, but I had no doubt that they'd share it in their private group.

Fight back, Barbie! Sy shouted. *Or I'll do it for you. I'll shred them with my fangs!*

Hold back, I said. I'd let Dixie vent her anger this one time, and then my debt to her would be paid. *It'll be over soon. Don't blow our cover. I can take a beating. We're good at it. Cracked ribs are nothing new. Black eyes and split lips and bruises over my fat cheeks? It's peachy compared to what Ruin did to us.*

Dixie kicked me in the ribs again and again. Then more lackeys jumped into the boxing ring, surrounding me like a pack of jackals, kicking me and cheering.

I curled into a fetal position, my arms covering my head to protect it.

Sy yowled in rage. *Get up!*

If I continued to lie down here to die like a loser, her survival instinct would overrule everything, and she'd take over and go on a killing spree. Sy had no brakes, and I was the only one who could hold her back, most of the time.

If we shifted in front of everyone and revealed who we truly were, every supernatural would come after us, and I wasn't sure that Killian would be kind enough to just rip off my breast bindings.

I spun on the ground in the center of the ring, my legs lashing out with a roundhouse kick in a low arc. Several minions dropped in a heap, yipping in surprise. Then I was up, spitting out a mouthful of blood and wiping more blood from my nose.

My fists struck out, precise and powerful. Every blow hit an eye or cuffed an ear.

"It hurts like a bitch, right?" I smirked as blood still dripped from the corner of my mouth. "It'll ring for a long time, babes."

"You aren't made right!" America yelled at me, remaining a safe distance from me.

I laughed. "Are any of you? Now it's time to take care of the gentlemen of your species."

My boot rammed into at least three guys one by one, making solid contact with their balls until they bent over, cursing in pain.

I'd caught them by surprise. No one had expected that I could still fight back after I'd been down and beaten like that. They should know by now that I was never good at staying down, and no one here could match my speed.

But I wasn't foolish enough to linger and fight in my

current condition. I had a few broken ribs and internal bleeding. I needed to get to Underhill, the only place where I was truly safe and where I'd hole up to regenerate. I needed to get there fast before I lost control and drained this land that I'd grown to care for.

"Love to stay and make friends, but I'm a busy girl," I told them.

I flipped into the air, shaolin Kungfu style, and alighted on two bystanders' heads. They were watching the fight in the ring with their mouths agape.

They yelped, throwing their hands up to shove me off, but I'd moved on and stepped on another head, then another, while they shouted and cursed in panic and anger, never having seen awesome moves like this.

I turned, locking my gaze with Dixie. I'd thought of her as a friend, but she'd marked me as her enemy after her lover died. Grief was a dark beast that fed on hate.

"I don't owe you anymore, Dixie," I said. "Fight me again, and you'll have to pay to see a bad dentist."

I leapt off the last head and dashed toward the door. No one was guarding it since everyone was gathering around the ring to watch me being beaten.

"She's getting away!" America shrieked, and the mob gave chase.

I could drain them all, and once I started, I wouldn't be able to stop. While they cornered me as their prey, they had no fucking idea how close they were to death's door, playing with an apex predator.

Before I reached the door, a force tore it away.

Shit!

Whoever blocked me would be the catalyst of a disaster when I finally snapped.

9

Barbie

Violent wind wrapped in starlight slammed into my face, passing through me like cool liquid. With a snarl, I crouched into a tight ball, ready to launch an attack.

"Stop!" Killian commanded, cold rage and power rolling off him and crackling in the air.

The mob froze behind me, halting their pursuit, and gasped for air.

The chaos prince's elite warriors, including Rock and Cami, flanked him and stepped into the hall after him. Bern lowered his head in shame before looking at me, worry in his eyes.

Killian's murderous gaze pinned me down. I hissed in return, still in my crouch, a hand planted on the ground, about to unleash violence. Sy hissed within me like a mad kitten.

Hadn't the chaos prince already humiliated me a great deal by ripping off my clothes just yesterday? What worse could he do to me? Punish me more? He'd have to get in line.

Killian's storm-blue eyes dipped to my bloody uniform before returning to my face. I knew I was a sorrowful sight without staring into a mirror. My left eye was swollen so badly that it failed to open. My cheekbone had been shattered, and a red cut split my left cheek. The bridge of my nose was broken too, blood still dripping from my nostrils. And my bottom lip was split.

What he couldn't see was the pain I hid and a few broken ribs concealed by my ruined uniform. I wasn't doing too hot now. In fact, I was fighting to keep from passing out.

In this realm, weakness was unforgivable. The supernaturals weren't made or taught to protect the weak but to prey on them. Too bad that I looked like a loser in front of everyone, especially in front of the chaos prince.

"Barbie," Killian uttered.

"I ain't shaming your house, sir." I smirked at him in defiance. "I got a talent for taking a beating. So don't count me out. When they come after me again, I'll make sure to come up swinging. You have my word, sir."

His glacial gaze skipped me and zoomed in on the mob behind me.

"Anyone from my house who was involved in attacking my newest member is banished from the House of Chaos. Effective immediately," he ordered, his voice sharper than an icy knife. "Cami, strip the offenders of their house marks. They're no longer permitted to enter my house. Should they try, they will meet death."

Gasps broke out from the crowd.

Cami stepped out from behind the chaos prince and sauntered toward Bellona first.

"You can't do this!" Medea pushed forward and bypassed Killian's warriors.

"Say that again?" Killian said, his voice calm, yet menace gilded every word.

"Even you have to obey the rules of the Brides Selection, Prince Killian," Medea shouted. "One of the clauses says that no head of the houses shall intervene with when and how the candidates compete."

"Educate her, Rock," Killian said.

"You misinterpreted the rules, Princess Medea," Rock said with a low chuckle as he gestured at the mob. "This has nothing to do with competition. The first rule decrees that culling isn't allowed before the second trial of the Selection."

What was that? There'd be official culling after the second trial?

"That notorious servant boy-turned-candidate is still breathing, isn't she?" Medea said bitterly.

"If she's dead, you'll be dead," Killian said.

My heart clenched, and warmth swam in my chest. Had he just said that?

Ask him to repeat it! Sy nudged. *He looks delicious saying that!*

Medea blinked hard. "You'll defend a street urchin against your own kind?"

"Make no mistake, *Princess*," Killian said. "If you happened to be in the room when the beating was taking place, you'd be kicked out too."

"Make no mistake, *stepbrother*," Medea sneered. "You can't touch me. I'm not only the second-in-line to the throne. I'm also assigned to be here to represent Queen

Lilith's interests and make sure no females try to tempt you. If you remember that, we'll get along better."

"Make threats all you want," Killian drawled. "But if you step out of line, you'll suffer my wrath."

Medea drew a sharp breath. "The king will hear of this. His Majesty will know how you threatened his beloved daughter."

"Stepdaughter," Killian said. "Now get the fuck out of my way."

Medea tilted her head and smiled, a little vicious and a lot more seductive. She wanted to play with the chaos prince.

"Say please," she purred.

Killian lashed out, his starlight and darkness smashing into her. She threw up her shield, but it couldn't counter his might. His strike sent her flying into the ranks of her minions. She brought down several of them with her.

The princess lay on the ground, stunned. She'd overestimated her own charm. If the chaos prince had used his lightning on her, she'd have been dead.

Medea raised her hands, about to toss her magic at him, and Killian smiled at her like a big mean cat at a rodent he'd cornered. Medea dropped her hands.

She rose to her feet slowly. "I'll remember this."

"Please do," Killian said, his smile merciless. "See, I said it."

Medea snapped her attention toward me, venom filling her eyes. Her hair turned to snakes, hissing at me. Killian had beaten her since he was stronger, and she had accepted it. Yet she needed a channel to vent her frustration, so she thought I'd be the easy pick.

She'd have a rude awakening if she came at me now. I

had an anger issue as well, especially after a brutal beating on an empty stomach!

I'd braced for another humiliation, even severe punishment, from Killian, but he surprised me by ruthlessly defending me—the lowest member in his house. Perhaps I should hate him less. I could just ask him to grovel more and then forgive him.

Then a dark thought slid into my mind. What if he was using me for the power struggle between him and his stepsister? Either of them could afford the fallout, but I'd be the one to suffer through the damage left in their wake.

The mob scattered as screams rose amid them. Cami threw up her hands, a dozen crimson threads shooting out from her fingertips and seizing several students from the House of Chaos like claws.

"I now strip the mark of the House of Chaos from you," she announced. "You're no longer one of us."

"No, please!" Imelda pleaded, and Bellona whimpered.

Cami yanked the crimson threads mercilessly, tearing the crest of seven arrows of different lengths in a radial pattern off Bellona's left wrist.

Five students were stripped of their house mark. They dropped to their knees, sobbing.

"It's done," Cami said without emotion.

Bellona struggled to her feet, her chin lifting in defiance. "I don't need to have a house to serve Princess Medea."

"As long as you don't come near the House of Chaos," Cami answered coldly.

America cowered in a corner, watching wide-eyed, not wanting to draw Killian's attention while he was full of wrath.

The show was over.

I limped toward the door and tried not to wince, every

breath burning my lungs now that the adrenaline had run out.

Killian nodded toward Rock. "Carry Barbie to the house. She'll need a healer."

"I can walk!" I protested. "I'm a big girl."

"You have three broken ribs," Killian said. "Your left ankle is also shattered. It's a wonder you can still stand."

At his unkind reminder, my legs gave out.

Killian's starlight shot out and cushioned my fall. Then Rock was there.

But I vaguely remembered that it was Killian who tucked me in when we got to my room.

10

Sy

I bit my nail. Barbie was out cold in bed. She probably didn't even register that the chaos prince tucked her in and caressed her chubby cheek with his thumb before he left. His gentleness had surprised me. No one had ever taken care of us like that. I hadn't thought the cold-eyed prince had it in him.

While my other half slept, I was restless. When she slumbered, I always stayed up as her sentinel. There was no rest for the wicked, but I wasn't wicked. I was a powerful three-quarter goddess, or at least, I shared the goddess's body.

There were barely any demigoddesses still roaming the earth, and Barbie was more powerful than any. But to beat Ruin, she'd have to find a way to unleash her core power.

The healer had made Barbie drink a healing potion, but it wouldn't work on her. She'd taken it only to fool Killian and the others since he was watching the process like a hawk.

The chaos prince was a control freak.

Barbie would regenerate on her own, with my help, of course. It meant that I would need to feed tonight. When the night grew darker, I would sneak out and fuck some supernatural. I shook my head. It didn't sound too appealing. Ever since I had a taste of fae male, I could barely stomach anyone else, but maybe the other powerful heirs would do. Uptight Barbie had strictly warned me not to fuck the other heirs, especially the chaos prince.

I would seek out the fae prince tonight then. With that goal in my head, I took over and shifted.

Moonlight shone through the window. I pushed open the panes, ready to leap to the windowsill and jump from the sixth floor. The space between the red trees with fern-like leaves would be my landing spot.

Just then, I heard the faint sound of the door to the living room opening, then quiet footfalls coming in my direction. I pricked my ears, and my superior hearing confirmed that someone was approaching Barbie's room.

Anxiety flooded me.

Fight or flight?

If I took off and they found Barbie's bed empty, it'd cause a riot. The chaos prince would send out a search party to hunt us down.

I cursed in frustration. I had to wait and act later. I'd go out after midnight.

I returned to bed swiftly, lying down and sinking back under Barbie's skin just as the door flew open.

Killian stood in the doorway, his presence so loud and clear you didn't need to look in his direction to feel him. Whenever he was in the room, everyone could feel his brutal power, even though he leashed it, just as Barbie always did.

Barbie's pulse quickened. She sensed him.

Before I could nudge her with a fair warning, she'd flashed open her two-toned eyes and rolled out of the bed in one smooth move, as if she'd never been injured.

Barbie crouched on the ground, Deathsong transporting from beneath the pillow to her hand in a tick, her gaze fixing on Killian as if he were her prey while she ignored Cami, his cousin, behind him.

Killian let out an amused, sensual chuckle that could make any girl's toes curl before he scolded, "Barbie, shouldn't you be in bed resting instead of crouching and huffing like a bad kitten?"

Sexual tension and tangible desire between them sparked to life like a livewire. It happened every time they were together. These two wanted to fuck each other so badly, yet they both tried so hard to hide their blatant lust. It was laughable.

"I *was* resting, and then you nearly broke my door!" she said.

Somewhere along the way, she'd learned to use anger to hide her arousal and embarrassment.

"Did I?" The chaos prince's brow arched. "Now put away that knife. There's no need to hurt yourself."

"I'm not going to hurt myself. I don't plan to! I..." Barbie said exasperatedly, but at least she rose from her crouch. The movement was so sudden that she swayed on her feet, dizzy from the beating and internal bleeding hours ago.

"I don't share your confidence," the chaos prince said. He was at her side in a heartbeat, holding her and supporting her. He seemed to want to pull her against his chest, and she leaned forward an inch or two, very much wanting to snuggle against him.

But she pulled back, and he let her, fighting the same pull. These two liked to make everything complicated. What harm could a good fuck do? It'd lift their spirits, not to mention the pleasure and energy we could harvest! So stupid!

The chaos prince scooped her up easily and put her back on the bed.

"Stop fooling around. Stay in bed until you're fully recovered!" he ordered.

Cami watched them with a strange, disapproving, and worried look on her face.

"I need to hear your side of the story," Killian said, pulling a chair near the bed. "Tell me exactly what happened."

"Your Highness." Cami stepped forward. "I can take over the interview. You don't need to be concerned with such a trivial matter."

"A trivial matter?" Killian gave her a sharp look. "A new member of my house got attacked on her first school day, which reflects badly on the house! I have every intention of finding out who's behind it firsthand."

"We all know who's behind it, cousin," Cami said.

"I still need to get to the bottom of this and take in Barbie's narrative," Killian said, "so there'll be no fucking filter."

"You never paid attention to any other members before," Cami said, despite the prince's warning look. "I'm sorry to say this, Your Highness, but you can't really prevent the competition between the bride candidates."

"Things are going to change," Killian said, his jaw

clenched in displeasure. "You're excused if you don't wish to be here."

"I'm staying," Cami insisted.

Barbie darted her glance between the two as they argued but mostly focused on the prince.

"Tell me what happened right from the beginning, Barbie," Killian commanded.

Barbie widened her eyes and batted her eyelids. Whenever she did that, she was up to no good. "I can't remember much since I'm too weak from lack of nutrition."

Killian stared at her, his lips twitching into a faint smile. "You're recovering well if you're hungry."

"I'm hungry." Barbie nodded eagerly and sat up. "I gotta go to the kitchen now. I'll seek you out after I eat something. Deal? Only then will I have the strength to remember and speak."

"Stay here," Killian said. "Cami, send someone to bring Barbie food. Enough for three."

Cami frowned. "Are we going to eat with her?"

"Let Barbie eat for three. She used to eat for two, according to Louis," Killian said with a hint of amusement. He'd learned about that from the vampire prince. "Just bring her all sorts of dishes and lots of cakes. Don't forget ice cream as well."

Cami grunted, but she took off.

Barbie beamed at Killian, seemingly forgetting to hate him for ripping off her clothes in front of thousands of students.

I can always hate him again after my belly is full. Barbie dismissed my ridicule.

"You'll need training, Barbie," Killian decided.

"Thank you, but no, high sir," Barbie said, jerking a

thumb toward her swollen face to stress the point. "This is what happened to the training."

Killian leaned forward and traced a thumb over her cheekbone, as if trying to ease her hurt. Barbie held her breath, gazing up at him, confusion, need, shyness, and desire mixing in a cocktail of emotions. Barbie always felt too much.

I waited for the fuse to be lit and the fireworks to go off while they gazed at each other, forgetting the world around them.

The heels of boots clicked on the floor as Cami rushed back. She was reluctant to leave these two alone with each other. Killian jerked his hand back as if burned and leaned back against the chair, his ankle lifting to cross over his knee to cover up his slip.

"Uh, sir," Barbie said in her husky voice, her face flushing. "I just need to lie low and not attend classes. Perhaps I can go back to being a squire, like a low-profile one in the background, someone like Bern?"

"That ship has sailed," Killian said. "You'll start the training with me after you're completely recovered."

"It'll take a long time to recover though, sir," she lied. And I knew she'd pretend to be unwell.

"Cousin, you can't be serious," Cami said, reaching our room in no time while panting from running. "What will others say?"

"Say what?" Killian asked. "And since when do I care what others say?"

"If you play favorites," Cami warned, "word will spread, and then Queen Lilith—"

I felt Barbie's rage shoot to her middle at the mention of Killian's betrothed.

"I know what I'm doing," Killian cut in roughly. "It'll be private training."

"But I just said that I don't need more heavy training, high sir," Barbie said. "I can fight all right. I just need to be more vicious and bite harder, so my opponents will back off."

"You have enough viciousness," Killian said. "But you lack discipline. Street fighting isn't going to get you through the rest of the year. You'll only end up being everyone's dish and a laughingstock, supposing you don't get yourself killed. If my newest house member heads to her grave too early, it'll shame my house."

"But sir, you just said you don't give a fuck what others say," Barbie protested, then over the prince's hard stare, she caved in and changed her strategy. "What I'm saying, high sir, is that my classes are very demanding. I've had a chance to look at the schedule, and I'm not afraid to admit that I'm shocked at how super loaded they are! I just don't have time for extra work, like extra training. I sincerely appreciate your concern and kindness, but I wasn't built like a machine, good sir. Also, I have a social life!"

"Social life?" Killian frowned, and Cami rolled her eyes. "Where will you go?"

"Here and there," Barbie offered. "But I'm not going to be too transparent. I value my privacy."

The prince let out a low chuckle. "You're at the bottom of the food chain, do you know that?"

I could feel Barbie's face flaming in humiliation and indignation at the prince's condescending tone. Barbie was always sensitive. To survive and do well in this dangerous school, she needed to develop a thick skin, even in front of the ones whose opinions she cared about.

"I've made a couple of friends!" she said, exaggerating.

She had only one friend, the little outcast witch!

"Have you?" he asked, studying her, and Barbie lifted her chin.

"You stupid girl," Cami snapped. "Prince Killian has never offered to train anyone before. It's a great honor that His Highness even glances in your direction!"

"Yeah?" Barbie gave Cami side-eye. "Then why don't you take my place and go training?" Then over Cami's angry face, she backed down. "What I'm trying to say is that I'm not cut out for this life. In fact, I don't want to be anyone's bride." She shook her head, her golden curls bouncing. "That's just too heavy and too much responsibility. And I'm too young to be tied down!"

"How old are you again?" Killian asked, his lips tugging up in a smile.

"Uh, I usually don't reveal my age."

"You revealed that you'd be twenty in four months on the ice rink where thousands of spectators heard you," Cami chimed in.

"You don't want the other bride candidates to eat you alive, do you, Barbie?" the prince asked tersely, as if she was testing his patience.

"No, sir," Barbie answered.

"No more whimpering," Killian said. "No more pathetic excuses. You'll train with me, starting Monday, little dagger."

11

Sy

I need to feed tonight, I told Barbie.

She gazed out the window. A blanket of stars hung low in the sky.

Let's sneak out of the Veil and find someone for you tomorrow, she bargained. *I'll be stronger then. We're due for patrolling the Veil to prevent any Shriekers from getting in anyway.*

It has to be tonight, I said, digging my toes in. *I have nothing left. Killian sent you a feast, so you forget what hunger does to me!*

Fine! she snapped at me. *Let's go hunting and find a dude for you outside the Veil later tonight after my nap.*

I don't need you to find anyone for me, I gloated. *I know where to look.*

She rubbed her temples as if I gave her a headache. *We agreed that the fae prince is off-limits, Sy.*

You decided it alone, and I never agreed. I have a say in whom I fuck and feast upon.

He's too close to home! She pursed her lips. *It's too dangerous. Rowan is dangerous!*

No more dangerous than your prince. And when aren't we in danger? I challenged, refusing to let her walk all over me. I was fed up with her deciding everything for us. *Rowan is the only male who can sate me, and you won't let me try your chaos prince!*

Fine, go fuck Rowan. She bit her lip sullenly.

Mostly, she caved so easily because Killian had gotten her all worked up by calling her little dagger before he'd left her room. This pent-up lust had become too much for her to handle, so she would let me vent for both of us. I was her dirty secret that did her dirty work!

We need to be careful and extremely smart! she warned. *No fucking on the campus grounds! I don't care how you do it. Just lead him to Underhill.*

That I agreed. My heart leapt at the prospect of seeing the fae male again, my blood heating at the image of his cock buried deep inside me.

With an annoyed sigh, Barbie retreated, and I surfaced.

Whenever she took over, it was instant. But when I shifted, we'd be vulnerable for three long seconds. I steadied myself by the window, my gaze lingering on my gorgeous reflection in the dark glass.

I was no longer a short humanoid girl with sapphire and green eyes and a full head of soft golden curls. My bright molten-amber eyes stared back, savage, untamed, and wicked. I swiftly braided my lush hair that reached down to my ankles. I could easily pass as fae in this realm, so there was no need to cover my pointed ears or even wear a pair of sunglasses.

I wondered if the fae prince would be happy to see me. No matter. I'd seduce him and take what I wanted. I adjusted the cuirass breastplate that covered my breasts but exposed enough skin to my liking. The short skirt down to the top of my thighs would provide convenience for Rowan when he bent me over to fuck me.

He'd appreciate it.

I leapt onto the windowsill, taking in the surroundings as I calculated my best moves to leave the building without been seen. I'd jump onto the top branch of the red tree below, grabbing a small branch and swinging onto the roof of the side building. From there, I would leap over thirty feet onto another rooftop. Then I'd cut across the path through the back side of Clockwork, where Rowan had fucked me against the wall the first time.

If I didn't see him around, I'd head south to the House of Fae to lure him out.

"So, you're out," a cheerful voice boomed in the room.

I nearly fell over the windowsill.

"Shut up, Pucker! Shut the fuck up!" Barbie's voice tore out of my lips.

I snapped my head toward the ghost guardian, hissing as well.

Pucker laughed. "How delightful! I caught you!"

"You're going to wake everyone," Barbie said. "Then how are we getting out?"

"Why are you going out?" Pucker asked.

"For a snack, of course," Barbie said sullenly.

Pucker rushed to the window to peek out, and I slashed my claws at his cheek but found they passed through his phantom form.

"Barbie is much nicer," he said, jerking his head away from me instinctively. "What's your name?"

"Don't fuss over Sy," Barbie said. "I want you to cause a distraction for us to sneak out, Pucker."

"I don't do favors, Barbie," Pucker crooned. "You know I only trade."

"Let me kill him and then eat him for annoying us!" I offered, my voice smokier and harsher than Barbie's.

"And I shudder," the ghost said.

"He's already dead!" Barbie said before she let out an exasperated sigh. "Fine, you can take a sip of my energy after we return. Now go to the hall and make noises. We need a good distraction."

Pucker grinned. "That is my specialty. I'm a chaos guardian."

He shot toward the wall and phased out.

A few seconds later, we heard Pucker singing the *Phantom of the Opera* offkey somewhere away from us, the entire building vibrating with his terrible voice. As the ghost guardian drew all attention and curses to him, I jumped, following the route I'd mapped out.

Remember, do a quickie! Barbie warned.

Of course! I was going to draw it out as long as I could and enjoy every second of it.

12

Sy

The violet building of steel and glass that was the House of Chaos blurred behind me. The ivory Skyward stood tall as my guiding tower, radiant under the starlight in the north.

I sprang toward Clockwork, its curved, lime-colored structure and tiled roof looming ahead. Last time, Rowan had fucked me against the wall. I licked my lips, remembering the delicious feeling and wanting to have it again.

A blur of movement dashed toward me; a flow of silver hair whipped in the wind. A pair of silver eyes gazed at me in longing and rage. He'd been waiting for me, and he was angry that I'd only popped onto his radar now.

I contained a wicked smile and veered toward Underhill. The fae's cruel lips tugging up, he gave chase.

Game on!

I kept luring him toward my destination. Underhill was

the safest place for Barbie and me, but the wild magic might not welcome the fae prince. I'd fuck him at its border then, since Barbie warned me not to foul the forest of Underhill.

The wind loosened my braids, and I let my hair stream free under the starlit sky. I felt so free as I raced against the fae prince across lush green, passing by bushes, blossoms, and uninhabited cabins along the slope, toward the dark forest and rolling hill.

Despite my long legs and amazing speed, Rowan was gaining on me, to my delight. On the entire field, it was just him and me running with the wind and each other under the night sky. It was a sight to watch. I hoped Barbie would appreciate it, but she was being gloomy and difficult. She didn't share my excitement at meeting the fae prince.

Before I reached the black maple tree upon which hung a sign: *Underhill! Enter At Your Own Peril,* the fae leapt at me.

It was about time!

I was down, and he was on top of me, caging me with laughter and gazing down at me like I was his prize.

I let out a low purr and giggle. "There you are!"

"Is this a game for you?" He narrowed his eyes, anger and lust searing their color to winter gray. "I've been waiting for you every night, Sy!"

He remembered my name. I preened. And I liked how it rolled off his tongue sensually and intimately.

"So you say, princeling." I showed him a mouthful of fangs. "Sorry that I didn't get your memo. But I'm here now."

"You shouldn't come to this dangerous place," he said. "Don't you know it's forbidden?"

No supernaturals dared to enter Underhill. Uninvited, they went in, and they never came out. The creatures inside the dark forest were unlike any beasts in the mortal or immortal realms. They were shadow beasts with teeth, claws, and magic.

They loved Barbie and they wouldn't harm me. Underhill regarded Barbie as kin.

"Can't blame a girl who wants to live on the wild side," I purred. "Are we going to waste the whole night arguing?"

"Where are you from? Where do you live?" he demanded.

Barbie wouldn't like it if I gave away that information. The last thing I wanted right now was for her to harass me. So I pulled the fae male's head toward me, my mouth catching his to seal his questions.

His resistance fell away. He kissed me back fiercely and lustfully, his lips molding around mine. I opened my mouth, and his tongue invaded inside. I inhaled his clean, minty breath and let his scent wrap around me while I propelled my hips toward him to urge him on.

"Can't wait to get fucked, little monster?" he asked, his voice silky and rough at the same time, which made my pussy ache.

"I want to get royally fucked, princeling!" I panted in glee and desire, writhing beneath him.

His control slipped. His hand slid between our bodies, palming my bare pussy, and he took in a sharp breath. "You did not wear underwear?"

"Never," I offered.

"What if other males saw you?" he growled.

"You're the only other male," I smirked.

"Next time wear something more decent!" he ordered.

"Should I return to my place and come back with an elaborate kimono? It'll be most modest, and it'll take you an hour just to reach my panties. Is that what you want?"

He grunted and shoved my skirt up, which was unnecessary since it was short enough. My hands got busy too as they yanked his slacks down. I wanted it to be fair, as I didn't want to be the only one naked.

So there!

His large erection sprang free. Then its thick crown aimed between my plump folds. Rowan lifted his hips and drove down. His rock-hard cock pushed inside me and sheathed itself deeply.

Letting free a gasp of pleasure and a peal of giggles, I arched my back to receive all its length. Without wasting a second, he started to thrust, in and out, long thrusts, then rapid short dives. He wasn't a patient man.

I moaned, loving us fucking like animals. The wet, erotic sound of flesh slapping flesh only made me want more. I spread my legs wide, even though he'd completely settled between my thighs.

I lifted my head to watch how my flesh gloved his cock tightly and how his massive cock drove into me vehemently. In and out. Yes, slamming hard, sugar man! His cock was a hard bridge between his body and mine, and then it vanished into my pussy, with no space left between us.

It was amazing!

He drilled into my depths over and over, invading, dominating, and intending to claim. He pulled out a few inches before thrusting back in. I shifted my weight and hooked a leg around him, then I was on top, riding him.

I heaved my hips up and drove down, my pussy clamping around his cock, sliding along its hard length without mercy, without care, only wanting the maximum frictions and pleasure from him.

He growled in approval, his large hands grabbing my bouncing, heavy breasts. Lust twisted his face, giving him a beastly look, which only turned me on more. He moved a hand to rub my swollen clit, the sensation undoing me.

I fucked him wildly with my incredible strength. This was a male who could take all I threw at him. My hair flowed in the wind, getting on his face. He swatted it off while bucking up his hips to meet my plunges.

We both panted hard.

Then he lifted me and placed me on the ground. I was on all fours, and he got behind me between my thighs. With a powerful thrust, he drove into me.

He was so skilled that it made me wonder if he took pleasure from other females all the time.

"Do you fuck a lot?" I asked.

"Yes, I like fucking," he said roughly, his hand grabbing my hair and pulling my head back as he pounded into me. "I fucked all sorts of women in the past, but it was nothing compared to fucking you. Your tight cunt is made for me, woman. Now tell me, Sy, would you get off watching me fuck others?"

I felt horny when I watched the vampire prince fuck two at a time, but I wasn't sure if I would like to watch Rowan fuck others. Yet, imagining how he would fuck others made my blood race fast while rage burned in my veins.

"I like fucking very much too," I said. "And I fucked a lot, but my pussy was never this wet compared to fucking you."

He growled in possessive rage, and I giggled, but not too loud.

Barbie insisted on me shutting my big mouth during sex since there were a few unfortunate incidents in the past. My fucking pals ended up passing out in the middle of banging when they saw my mouthful of fangs, caused my feeding to be undone and Barbie to curse profanely.

But Rowan's cock wouldn't go limp inside me at the sight

of my fangs and claws. He liked them. He cherished what I was. He had fangs like mine. One of these days, I was going to take a playful bite at him as foreplay.

"What a hot mess you are," Rowan growled, his voice full of heat. "Your cream drips all over my cock. Now I must punish you, dirty girl."

"To live up to my reputation," I let out another round of giggles, "I should try a foursome with the other princes as well, or even a fivesome, if Prince Killian is up for it."

I didn't mind all five prince heirs fucking me at the same time. They were all so powerful. Think of the energy I could glean from that kind of feast.

"That's not going to happen!" Rowan snarled, his fingers gripping my hips, so tight it hurt. I turned my head to gaze at him over my shoulder, the jealous fire in his silver eyes mesmerizing. "I'll kill any male who tries to touch you!"

He pounded into me, so brutal that my face nearly hit the ground. He pinned me down, fucking me faster and harder, which was meant to punish. Yet I got turned on just fine.

Then the dam broke, and I screamed as his next thrusts pushed me to reach the pinnacle. His energy poured into me like liquid flame, filling up my well. He started to feed on my lust energy as well while thrusting hard into me, riding the waves of my orgasm. My pussy milked him until he turned rigid behind me, his body utterly taut. The fae prince let out a rough groan and emptied himself in me.

"No one has given me as much as you," he said, bending over me, his fangs grazing over my neck.

I felt his hot seed and my cream dripping down my legs.

Universe, give me strength, patience, and tolerance. Barbie roiled in me before she barked, *What did I say about a quickie, Sy?*

I ignored her.

Rowan pulled out of me and carried me to the black maple tree. His cock jutted forward, remaining steel hard. He pressed me against the bark of the vast tree, hooked my leg on the crook of his arm, and thrust into me for round two.

While he fucked me more lazily this time, the branches shivered, leaves drifting and falling over our heads.

Underhill was watching. The wild magic didn't come to me though, not like when it saw Barbie. It always twirled at her feet and chased her like an overeager puppy. They talked to each other.

Rowan gave the dark forest a wary look before turning to me. His lust overruled his sense of safety. I liked his ruthless side, and it satisfied me that he couldn't resist me. When danger came, we'd deal with it. I also appreciated that he'd put up a shield, frosty vines forming a circle around us while we fucked.

A wolf howled from the other side of Underhill, which was the shifters' territory. Beastly growls responded from within the dark forest. Neither Rowan nor I slowed down as we fucked faster and harder.

"I need to see your face when you come," Rowan said, his silver eyes full of scorching lust as they traveled from my face to my breasts, then dipping down to watch our joined flesh as he thrust deep into me.

I grinned. "You'll have to make me come first."

"Is that a challenge?" he snorted, his cock growing even harder, driving into my molten depths and eliciting a series of moans from me. "You won't remember any male after this, little monster!"

Are you done yet?! Barbie chimed in with a big yawn and

a bad temper. *And must you guys talk? Just wrap it up already, for fuck's sake!*

Just go back to sleep! I pulled my lips back and hissed at her.

"Fierce," Rowan said. "Now you made my cock harder!" He showed me his fangs too before he traced the column of my neck with them.

It felt so damn good that I shivered and giggled.

I wonder if he'd freak out knowing that Barbie was watching us through my eyes, annoyed and aroused. Thousands of supernaturals had seen her perfect perky tits on the ice rink after Killian helped her gain popularity, yet she was still spitting mad at him. Sometimes I didn't get her.

Rowan pounded into me, sending waves of pleasure to my nerve endings. No one had fucked me like he did. Barbie was afraid that I'd grow attached to the fae male, but I was already addicted.

My appreciative gaze roved over his strong frame—his broad shoulders, cut chest, the hard plane of his stomach. His mighty thighs propelled toward me with such vigor as he impaled me over and over. His cock was most fascinating! The fae prince was trying to imprint me so I'd fuck only him and no one else.

While I admired his savage beauty, I felt a connection I'd never felt with anyone, except Barbie. A thought started to root in my mind. Rowan could be my mate, the One for me.

When I saw the way he looked at me as if he also sensed the same, my chest ached and swelled. My claws sank into his shoulders. He hissed in pain and pleasure and took me so hard that I saw stars, in a good way. I was on the brink of coming, yet I held back, wanting this to go on forever.

"Yes!" I moaned. "Try that swirl again, my sugar fae male!"

"Call me Rowan, little monster!"

"Rowan sugar!" I cried and moaned as he rocked his hips against me to give me what I wanted. "Fantastic! I'm close. So close!"

He stiffened against me, tension in his every line, while his body caged me against the tree.

Fuck! Barbie shouted.

Chill, girl, I chuckled. *What do you think I'm doing? You enjoy it too, don't you? I told you it'd be worth it—*

Someone's coming. Predators! Barbie screamed a warning.

A tick later, I felt the approach of a formidable presence.

13

Sy

"We have company," Rowan hissed in my ear. "Hold still. I'll send them away."

A band of supernaturals were heading in our direction at top speed, only to halt a dozen yards away at Rowan's harsh warning.

Killian was taking point. No wonder Barbie panicked.

Rowan and I snapped our heads toward the intruders while our bodies were still locked together. Rowan tried his best to block the view from the incoming party by angling his giant figure to shield me. I was a tall female, yet he was still a few inches taller and much broader.

The chaos prince's cold gaze fell on me for a breath, just to make sure I wasn't whom he was looking for. I caught relief flitting by his eyes while rage ebbed from him. I had a hunch that he was searching for Barbie. He must've noticed that her room was empty.

We can never let him find out that we're the same! Barbie warned.

But we're not exactly the same, I said.

Just stay quiet and lie low! Killian is cunning! Barbie hissed.

"Look away," the chaos prince told his men, and they obeyed.

"Killian, what the fuck are you doing here?" Rowan demanded harshly.

"I could ask you the same, Rowan," Killian purred.

"Now you are in the business of watching others fuck?" Rowan growled in displeasure.

Killian chortled lowly, spreading his arms as if he was being forced into this situation and inconvenienced by the fae prince. "And of all the places, of all the people, you had to come to the restricted area to fuck? Is your bedroom getting so boring that you have to sneak out for a snack?"

I hissed. At that, Killian darted a glance at me before training his eyes on Rowan again. "What are you hiding?"

"I'm not hiding anything!" Rowan snapped. "Leave, Killian. Leave me alone!"

"Are you giving me an order, Rowan?" Killian crooned. "Now my interest is piqued."

"You don't want to antagonize me, Killian," Rowan said. "One of these days you will want a favor. You have enough enemies already, even within your own house."

"Thank you for pointing out the obvious, but I did not come here to catch you. So relax, man," Killian sighed, worry sinking into his voice. "I'm looking for someone. A new member of my house is missing."

"I guess you're looking for Silas and Louis's former squire?" Rowan asked. "Barbie, right? She came to the realm only a short while ago, but trouble seems to follow her every step."

"Did you see her?" Killian pressed, his voice menacing.

"No!" Rowan said. "If I spot her, I'll send her your way. Now fuck off, Killian. I'm busy here."

"I won't leave until I find her," Killian said in determination, and I groaned. Barbie sat up on high alert. "I'm going to sweep the whole area. I suggest you take your dessert somewhere else if you don't want us to get in your way or keep going for all I care. I and my men will just keep searching."

"I don't think so, Killian," Rowan disagreed. "I demand you leave with your men right now or come back an hour later!"

The two princes were going to clash while Rowan still had his hard cock buried deep in me. I could tell he wanted to thrust badly, and I wanted him too. I writhed. I didn't mind anyone watching, especially Killian. I wanted Barbie's male to see me too and desire me.

Barbie's rage burned through me.

Get the fuck out of here! she screamed at me. *Go!*

Barbie was more ruthless than me when she was pissed. Getting on her bad side was like courting a swarm of hornets. Whenever we got into a serious fight in the past, I'd always been the one picking up the pieces.

Reluctantly, I glided back from Rowan's hard length to extract myself. It was painful to leave him and put space between us, but I did it. I let out a frustrated breath while patting down my skirt.

"Wait here," Rowan ordered me. "I'll make sure those jerks leave soon. I'll take care of you."

While he clenched his teeth and pulled up his pants, I stepped out of his space. Flashing him a sultry look and blowing him an air kiss to remind him of our good time, I broke into a run in the opposite direction of the chaos prince and his party, along the perimeter of the dark forest, and vanished into the shadows of the deep night.

"Wait, Sy! Sy!" Rowan gave chase, then halted and cursed at Killian. "Look what you've done, asshole!"

"Your secret fucking buddy is already gone," Killian offered without sympathy, his voice reaching me in the wind. "You might as well help me search for Barbie. There was an incident in the morning class. A bunch of candidates roughed her up. I don't want her to be scared away. Louis mentioned she tried to run away from him twice!"

I leapt over the shrubs that blocked the entrance to Underhill and took off toward the lake, one of Barbie's favorite haunts, as she demanded. No one could track us down in the dark forest since the wild magic would cover our scent.

"Then you shouldn't have gotten her into that chaos house of yours!" Rowan barked. "You also did a good job of scaring away my woman!"

"If she were your woman, she wouldn't have run away," Killian said lazily, and a few of his men chuckled.

A force slammed into me like a punch in the jaw as Barbie surged up and took over our form. She was annoyed with me, blaming me again for leaving a mess for her.

Maybe Rowan and I were star-crossed lovers? Every time we got together, something bad happened.

The wind blew through the ancient trees under the thick canopy as Barbie raced through the forest. Wild magic chased her like an excited kid.

A misty light hovered over the lake. Underhill might be menacing and dangerous to others, but it was a fairytale home to Barbie. Stripping swiftly, she tossed her attire onto the branch of a tree and leapt into the lake. The pure, icy water splashed around her. She sucked in a gasp at the chills but swam a few laps before reaching for the bank. She found a soap bar she'd stashed here and started to scrub herself, not wanting to leave any trace of the fae prince's scent on her.

While she was still lathering the soap up her leg, she stilled, tension rippling off her. At the same time, I felt two powerful presences before Rowan and Killian emerged into the clearing. Their gazes snagged on Barbie at once, and both princes came toward the lake in a stride.

There was nowhere for Barbie to hide, not even under the clear water. Underhill usually wouldn't allow anyone else in. There was a truce between Underhill and Mist of Cinder. However, Underhill also had a penchant for drama when it came to Barbie. It loved to see her caught in the act.

So, it allowed—it lured—Killian and Rowan in, eager to see how Barbie would respond to a love triangle situation.

Barbie swallowed a curse as the chaos prince's deep, rich voice pierced the night, and the shadow beasts within the depths of the forest growled in response. They didn't attack, leashed by Underhill.

"Barbie, you shouldn't—" Killian started.

"Uh?" Barbie paddled in the water, her arms covering her tits. "Don't come closer! I warn you. I'm not decent! And I'm still a...virgin!"

If she could call it that, she might be the dirtiest virgin ever.

The forest was utterly silent for long beats, as if the V-word had special magic.

Both princes froze before Killian growled at Rowan, "Do not look at her!"

"Then why are you looking at her?" Rowan raised an eyebrow in challenge. "Who gave you the exclusive right? Plus, it's too late to play a knight in shining armor now, isn't it? Weren't you the one who stripped her in front of thousands just yesterday?"

Barbie glared at the chaos prince at the reminder.

"Barbie, how long have you been bathing here?" Rowan asked.

Killian narrowed his eyes. "That's house business."

"Will you stop being a jerk for once?" Rowan growled. "I just want to ask if she saw my little monster—no, a fae woman run this way!"

"I'm not sure, sir. I lost track of time," Barbie said, deceptively innocent. "I must've fallen asleep. I kind of heard noises though, like someone running away before you two high sirs charged in. Underhill usually doesn't let anyone in. I don't know why it showed you two courtesy this time." She gestured at the princes dismissively, as if she wanted to shoo away two ducks, then over their scathing looks, she added hurriedly, "No offense, high sirs. I was just surprised."

"How come Underhill let you bathe in the lake?" Rowan wanted to know.

Barbie smiled coyly. "Didn't they say I'm an Echo, so no magic or ward works on me?

Rowan narrowed his eyes in suspicion. "You aren't an Echo. However—"

Barbie made a show of shuddering in the icy lake and rubbing her forearms as if she had goosebumps all over her skin due to the chills.

Killian noticed her shudder right away and turned to growl at Rowan. "Are you going to freeze her to death with your long-winded questions?" He stepped toward the lake and ordered, "Get out of the water, Barbie! I don't want you to catch cold and pass it to the entire house."

Rowan frowned at Killian. "Only mortals catch colds or STDs. You know that."

"Since when are you an expert on mortals?" The chaos prince glared daggers at Rowan. "And don't we have humans in the realm too? They might be servants, but all lives matter!"

"Barbie is a supernatural, so she won't catch cold," Rowan argued just for the argument's sake. "So there's no chance of her passing it to the human servants in your house."

"You can't know that!" Killian said in a clipped tone.

Kick them out! Barbie urged Underhill telepathically, chiding it for letting in the princes while she was bathing. *I've had enough!*

But this is fun. I haven't had fun for a long time, Underhill cooed in delight. *I want to see how things wrap up. No one likes cliffhangers.*

You're as bad as Sy! Barbie complained. *If you let everyone in to sabotage me, this place won't be a haven for me. Then I'll have to stop coming here altogether. In the future, I might just hole up in the House of Chaos and go nowhere else.*

Underhill bit its claw-nails. *What will I get if I do your bidding?*

They got into a bargain, and both agreed that Barbie now owed Underhill a favor. That was a terrible deal for Barbie, but she was desperate. But she wouldn't take any criticism from me right now. She'd initiated the silent treatment toward me.

Without warning, the forest shifted. Dark wind rippled across the icy lake. Trees and bushes moved around, sealing the old paths and opening new ones. The landscape changed completely. Underhill pushed the lake further into its depths, and at the same time, the shadow beasts dashed to guard the lake while Barbie stayed in the water.

Rowan wheeled in shock. Underhill sifted him out like a

weed. One second, he was still interrogating Barbie and arguing with Killian, then the next, he was out of the forest, bellowing his protests out of sight.

Killian leapt toward the lake to grab Barbie. He almost got her, but Underhill plucked him up in the air. He sent out his starlight and darkness, his magic crashing with the wild magic that took the form of an icy flame.

The forest rumbled, the beasts howled, leaves and dirt swirled in the air in attack mode. Underhill tossed Killian out of its domain and closed all entrances.

Barbie watched with her mouth open, eyes wide, and I did the same.

Underhill was a wicked force!

"Barbie!" Killian roared from outside the forest, fighting to get in.

I gotta go, Barbie said, wading toward the bank.

You better! Underhill answered. *He won't give up until he has you. Be careful with him.*

Barbie leapt out of the water, the wild magic drying her right away and bringing her clothes.

Killian was still roaring, his power slamming into Underhill over and over.

Go calm him down! Underhill urged. *I don't want to battle one of the most powerful beings in the realm for the whole night. I might like to stay up for a late show, but I need my beauty sleep too.*

Barbie jogged out of the forest, eyeing Killian, Rowan, and a band of chaos warriors, who all stared at her with an identical strange expression on their faces. No one could ease in and out of Underhill like the new girl Barbie.

"Are we returning to the house, high sir?" Barbie asked, shivering in the cold wind. "Or if you want to kick me out, I'll just go back to Underhill and finish my nap. It's better you expel me than punish me, sir. I'm not equipped to take another beating—"

"I'll kill anyone who lays a hand on you in my house," Killian said as he shrugged off his jacket and wrapped it around her shoulders.

The warriors watched quietly, and Barbie rubbed the jacket with two fingers to get a feel of its fine material.

"It's good leather, sir," she murmured and beamed at Killian, her golden curls bouncing in the wind.

He looked like he wanted to brush her curls off her soft face.

"If you get sick, you'll waste more of the house's resources!" he chided.

"Sorry. I hope the kitchen is still open," Barbie said hopefully.

She was more relaxed now, as we'd just averted a disaster.

"We gotta do something about that damn poltergeist guardian," Rock complained. "I hope he's stopped singing when we get back."

"Uh, I think I can talk Pucker out of singing that damn song the whole night," Barbie offered, not sounding guilty at all.

Killian frowned at her. "Pucker? His name is Luther."

"Uh, his real name is Pucker," Barbie said as she gave Killian then the other chaos warriors a meaningful nod. "And he likes pretty boys."

14

Barbie

I jogged toward Jubilee Haven for breakfast, then I'd go to class. Sy had offered me half of the energy she'd gotten from her sex feeding, and my bath in Underhill had also given me a boost. I was good as new.

Just as I passed the gold and amber building of House of Mages, Bea stepped out from behind a sphinx sculpture in front of Infinity Library.

"Barbie!" she called.

"Bea!" I beamed at her as she rushed to me, panting. Mages didn't work out much. They relied too much on their spells. "Did you see me coming in your tea leaves?"

She hadn't seen my beating from yesterday, though. And she hadn't seen Killian tear my clothes off in front of thousands. Her predictions seemed selective.

"You need to skip breakfast!" she said. "They're waiting for you in Jubilee Haven."

"Who are they?"

"Princess Medea and her army." Bea winced. "They got there very early just to wait for you."

"Really?" I smirked. "In my honor?"

"You don't get it, Little Bo—Barbie," she said and shook her head. "It'll take a while to get used to you being a girl."

"You can still pretend I have a small dick," I said. "I don't mind."

"I'm serious, Barbie," she said. "They want to kick you out of the Brides Selection."

"All the better," I said gleefully. "I want out, too, so we'll have a gentlewomen's agreement."

"It's not that simple. You aren't from here. You don't know how things really work around here. Just avoid them, okay? They won't be gentle! Let's go somewhere else for breakfast. I'm buying."

"No way are you paying when we can get free food," I said. "I still owe you from last time. Prince Silas and Louis still haven't paid me. Now that I'm not a squire, I can't even ask Prince Killian for minimum wage, let alone a dental plan. Don't worry, though. When I'm a little more established here, I'll chase Louis's vamp ass for a week's pay. He won't get away with it! He's lucky that I might not demand a bonus for the extra hours he made me watch him fuck."

Bea's eyes widened, face flushed, and I nodded a confirmation. "And second, I don't run away from a fight." Sy and I only ran away from the fights we couldn't win, mostly from my father. "In a nutshell, I want my free breakfast."

I strode across the courtyard with Bea in tow.

"I really think we should go somewhere else, Barbie," Bea started again, wringing her hands together. "I have a horrible feeling about what's coming."

"You worry too much, my friend." I grinned at her to comfort her, not pausing my steps. "You need to live a little."

Even before Killian had tossed me onto the wagon of the Brides Selection, shit had always chased me. That was the story of my life.

"I heard about yesterday, Barbie. I'm so sorry I wasn't there for you."

"You never need to say sorry," I said. "And I'd rather you not get caught in the crossfire. You're a better friend than I deserve. You were there, standing by me and offering me the blanket when thousands of students shamed me, when the authorities were about to arrest me. You painted a target on your back for my sake, even though I lied to you."

"I understand why you did what you had to do, Barbie. I'm not an entitled shit who demands anyone hand over her trust. Everyone has a secret or two, and they have the right to keep them their own. Your secrets are yours, Barbie, yours to own. Truth will set you free? Fuck that lie!"

It was the first time I'd heard her curse. I was finally rubbing off on her.

"You deserve my truth, though. I won't think badly of you if you walk away from me any time. We can be secret friends, so there won't be a target on your back."

Bea looped her arm around mine.

"Man, do you smell bacon and Portuguese sausage?" I asked, quickening my pace. "I'm hungry."

She laughed. "I used to think that you were hungry all the time because you were a boy."

A sense of danger hit me as we approached the russet building of Jubilee Haven. A few students milled around the perimeter, their eyes lighting up at the thrill of the hunt as soon as they spotted me.

Those were scouts. Two lackeys immediately lowered

their heads and typed on their tablets, probably posting something on Spinchat, the supernaturals' social media.

Through the large windows, I saw a full house in the dining hall. That was a first. It appeared that everyone had gotten here a lot earlier than usual, just as Bea had told me.

This was another ambush.

"We can still run," Bea whispered.

"I'm done running," I said.

It was a pun Bea wouldn't get. Mist of Cinder would be where I stood my ground, if or when my father came calling.

I jogged toward the door but halted five paces from it. The warded building allowed anyone from any house in, but someone had added a few nasty spells above the door, holding a bucket of blood, probably from pigs.

If I pushed the door open, the blood would drop on me. These supernaturals weren't exactly creative, as they obviously borrowed the trick from Stephen King's *Carrie*. I'd watched that movie twice.

So far, I hadn't seen anyone go in or out of Jubilee Haven. That nasty surprise was for me, but my antagonists didn't know that I could see through glamour.

Bea halted with me, her wand out, ready to work to disarm the offensive spells.

"I got this," I said.

Offensive spells came in three colors—gray, brown, and crimson. They entwined and locked tight. It'd taken the casters hours to get them right. I almost felt bad to frustrate their plans.

I tossed out my dark wind that could eat magic and spells, but I didn't eat the offensive spells this time. Instead, I pushed them further until they reached their original spell casters through the link. Now the magical bucket of blood hovered over the heads of the casters.

With a can-do attitude and a friendly smile on my face, I shoved open the door.

The hall was so silent that even a single whisper would be heard. All eyes were trained on me, faces smirking with viciousness, waiting for a disaster to hit me.

The spells were triggered, then released.

Nothing landed on my head. Confusion and dissatisfaction spread across the hall, only to be interrupted by a loud *pop*. The bucket of blood plunged from midair down to the table, where a few witches sat with Bellona, Imelda, Jarvis, and the fae boy who had tried to take Bea's wand in the courtyard. They were America's and Medea's first army that had beaten me in the ring at BattleStar stadium.

Killian had kicked Bellona and Imelda out of the House of Chaos, but the duo remained in Shades Academy and stayed in the Brides Selection program. I didn't know where they lived now since I hadn't had time to find out. They were all rich kids, so they'd never need to worry about being homeless.

Everyone leapt away from that table, a second too late. The pig's blood enveloped the heads of two witches and a mage, dripping down their faces and painting everything red, just like the brilliant scene in *Carrie*.

The blood also spattered onto the dishes in front of the other minions. There was so much blood that drops and blobs spilled onto the next table, where Medea, America, and other royals and nobles were seated.

In Shades Academy, even seating was a game. The elite bride candidates took the center tables. At the very center, a royal table was forever reserved for the heirs if they decided to come down from their throne seats upstairs. No one dared to sit at the heirs' table, not even the royals like Medea, America, and Cami.

When I was Louis's squire, I used to attend him upstairs, and I'd seen those candidates parade themselves in the center space of the ground floor to try to catch their eye. It was comical, though none of the candidates thought it was funny but took the mating game very seriously.

Dixie shared the table with America and Medea. She used to sit at the shifters' table with her shifter friends, but now she'd joined them.

Hate was easier than grief, and it changed a person. There was no one else for her to blame except for me, so she clung to that, especially since everyone knew that she'd vouched for me and brought me to her house.

My throat tightened for a second. I grieved for Luna too, and I blamed myself for her death, but I wouldn't take another beating from Dixie, as I had low tolerance to pain. If she came at me again, I'd punch back.

Too bad that Dixie had joined the ranks of my foes and shared their table; now she had a splash of pig's blood on her student uniform as well.

Cami, however, was spared the spectacle since she had her own table, surrounded by members of the House of Chaos. Like the rest, Killian's cousin had been waiting for the pig's blood to drop on my head.

I was sure that despite her loyalty to Killian, she hadn't told the chaos prince about this ambush. No one wanted to be labelled as a snitch. Besides, she wasn't happy with me drawing Killian's attention. She also blamed me for last night's drama when Killian led his elite team to hunt me down then tucked me in.

Everyone had whipped out their magical tablets, ready to record my humiliation and wailing and share it to Spinchat. Only I had disappointed them again.

Shocked silence dampened the hall until I shouted out loud, "Is there a gala here? Yes, there is! Looks fun!"

Everyone snapped out of their stupor and outrage broke out.

America shrieked, Medea snarled, and Dixie stared at me coldly. Their minions rushed to wipe the blood from their masters' uniforms, but the princesses shoved them away.

Their magic shot out, cleaning up the mess. I thought of snuffing out their magic and leaving them in a bigger mess, but I let it go. I didn't need to bring a full war down on me. I should always caution myself not to go too far, so it wouldn't come to the point where there was nothing to come back to.

These clowns didn't know what kind of disaster they were courting, but I knew better. No matter how nasty they were, they belonged to the realm, and I'd vowed to protect it. Also, I had to take Bea into consideration. She stuck close to me like a shadow, her wand trembling in her hand.

I jogged toward our usual corner table.

"Behold the slut!" Medea rose and shouted.

Instantly, a large hologram streamed in midair, playing the scene of Killian stripping off my clothes with his darkness and starlight. I'd been bare for all to see, my tits the color of flame. My face had flushed, horror, fear, and humiliation flashing in my sapphire and green eyes. The camera had caught it all.

"*Take off Barbie's pants! Let's see if she's got a cunt!*" some dude had bellowed off screen, echoed by the spectators.

I'd thwarted my foes' Carrie stunt and turned it on them, but they'd moved to step two by forcing me to relive yesterday's public humiliation, tearing off the Band-Aid before the wound was closed.

"Shame the slut!" America called for action like a hound on a blood hunt.

Every finger pointed at me, every eye flashing malice, every mouth laughing and mocking. The hostility was stunning and brutal. The lower-class supernaturals weren't any better. They'd found someone even lower to stomp on.

Killian might've prevented the candidates from ganging up on me to beat me to within an inch of my life, but even he couldn't stop this social media war against me, led by the two most elite bride candidates, who made it their personal mission to destroy me.

I didn't bow to Medea. I'd beaten her champion before entering the House of Chaos. I, a servant boy-turned-bride-candidate, shone brighter than her, and Killian had defended me against her in the open. The princess would do anything in her power to put me in my place.

To America, I'd been Little Bob. Even as a servant boy, I'd made a fool out of her on the ice rink in front of all the princes, the most coveted bachelors.

I hadn't thought yesterday's bad smell would follow me everywhere, like a permanent stain on my forehead. I was ill-equipped at supernatural social media wars, and my foes held the power.

Bea stared at the looping hologram in horror. She waved her wand to weave spells, aiming to take down the hologram. But I grabbed her wrist, turning the tip of her wand toward the ground. She'd only paint a target on her back. And even if she could get the hologram down, it wouldn't change anything. It'd only give my opponents the satisfaction they were seeking.

"Let's get out of here," my friend whimpered.

"Not before I have my breakfast," I insisted.

As I passed by the tables, I tried to ignore the holographic display of the topless me looking utterly helpless and lost.

Many students thrust their devices in front of them, recording me being shamed. Some stuck out their feet to trip me so they could film me falling on my face if they succeeded.

"Slut! Slut! Slut!" they chanted, pounding their tables.

"Shut up!" Bea screamed, pressing her hands over her ears.

"Slut! Slut! Slut!" the crowd bellowed louder, laughing.

Only a few tables didn't join in.

Cami and the chaos members at her table remained silent, picking at the food on their plates while watching me. To my surprise, Dixie remained sitting and didn't chant with Medea, America, and the rest of the nobles, but it didn't mean she hated me less. She was just not a follower. After all, she was a royal beta in the House of Shifters.

Some supernaturals from the corner tables also weren't enthusiastic about going with the flow. They looked like geeks. They were talking to each other while watching me.

I could no longer fly under the radar like when I was a servant boy.

"Take off your pants, Barbie!" It sounded like Javier, and his friends shouted with him, having a hell of a time.

Shame me? These clowns hadn't the slightest idea of how to really do it well. They didn't know what material I was cut from. I wasn't built like the supernaturals. I wasn't raised like them. They would get under my skin only if I let them. I was no one's prey, especially not to the lesser beings, who thought they were more.

Living on borrowed time helped me put things in perspective. I shifted gears the next instant. In this wonderous realm where magic welcomed me, I could have three free meals a day, I had a soft bed to sleep on at night, though nightmares plagued me, and I was relatively safe behind the Veil inside the warded academy grounds.

And I got to go to classes to learn magic. I might've whined to Killian about the overwhelming schedule, but it was only a show. For the first time, I felt grounded. I had a role to play and a possible future ahead of me, even though everything could be snatched away from me in a breath.

I was no longer drifting. While Killian had humiliated me in front of thousands, he'd also inserted me into this new life. Being publicly humiliated and bullied was peachy compared to my former life with my god father.

On top of all the perks, I made a good friend.

So, bring it all on! Shame me all you want.

"Slut! Slut! Slut!" the girls chanted.

"Take off your pants, Barbie!" the boys demanded.

I turned on my heels. They wanted a good show?

I strode toward the heirs' table in the very front and center of the hall.

"No, Barbie! You can't do that!" Bea called, her face paling as she realized what I was about to do. "The heirs will end you, and no one will be able to save you!"

Yes, let's do it! Sy hissed in glee, even though I was giving her the silent treatment after her last stunt.

"Please, don't do this." Bea tugged my sleeve. "For me, please."

"Don't ask me to act like a weak ass, because I'm not," I said, "no matter how good your intentions are. But you should go, Bea. This isn't your fight."

I leapt onto the heirs' table.

"You dare!" Medea hissed. "You're dead!"

America was so shocked that she just stared at me and utterly forgot to lead the chant.

I stood tall on the royal table and made a show of cupping my ear. "What did you say, sheep?"

"Slut!" they shouted.

I laughed. "That's the best you can do? Let me show you how to do it properly." Then I roared "Slutttt!" and my voice drowned out all the chants. "You little shits, shout like you mean it!"

I wheeled for good measure, laughing, then I stomped on the table in a rapid rhythm, starting a buck-and-wing-style tap dance. I'd learned this flashy dance that combined Irish and British clog with African rhythm a while ago.

I finished my fast footwork with three rapid kicks, a sudden sense of danger slamming into my face like a broken brick, and I wheeled around. My roar of "C'mon, give me your worst scream. Sluttt—that's how you roar, you little cunts!" pounded the suddenly vast, silent hall just as four princes—Rowan, Cade, Silas, and Louis—stood in front of their royal table, staring at me incredulously.

Oh, shit!

15

Barbie

All the students, most of them still standing with their mouths agape, waited with bated breath for the prince heirs to strike me down.

The hologram that featured my tits still streamed in midair, not far from me. Pig's blood still dripped from a couple of tables. The three casters of the "Carrie spell" were still partially covered in blood.

"Do you fucking know whose table you're standing on?" Silas's menacing voice boomed through the hall, his alpha stare set to pin me down.

He should've known that it wouldn't work on me since he'd tried his power stare on me twice now. This was the third time.

Why did people keep doing the same thing over and over and expect a different result?

I stared back at him before making a show of blinking in

confusion. "Pardon, sir? No one sits here, so I took the liberty of educating and entertaining the crowd." I gestured around, including the hologram that was still showing. "As you can see, they're so bored."

Silas fumed. Of course, I knew that his question had been rhetorical.

Cade waved his wand at the hologram, and it vanished with a deflated hissing sound. "Haven't you seen enough tits?" He shook his head, surveying the crowd briefly with distaste.

"Thank you, sir mage." I nodded my gratitude. "The filming wasn't good. Those amateurs didn't even get the angle right. The tits looked too red and big. I don't like it."

Louis narrowed his eyes at me. Ever since I had turned out to be a girl, I confused him.

"Explain better, Barbie," Cade said, an amused smile tugging on his lips.

"Go on, little Bo—Barbie," Louis snorted. "Let's hear what kind of creative excuses you'll come up with this time, and I might just let you off the hook."

"It started with these royal bimbos," I offered, jerking a thumb toward Medea, America, and their minions, "pulling a *Carrie* cliché."

Medea stared at me, death in her eyes. She should meet Dad, and he'd teach her what death truly was.

"Be careful what you say, peasant mouse," she threatened, her voice laced with venom.

"What *Carrie* cliché?" Rowan asked.

"It was based on Stephen King's book," I explained. "Those high school bullies poured pig's blood onto their classmate Carrie's head to publicly humiliate her, and thus woke her power, so she razed the entire school and killed all the bullies, including the teachers, in the ballroom." I waved a hand in an arc. "Those copycats didn't know that I knew about the *Carrie* move, so I avoided the hit. Worse, their spells backfired, so the casters were dipped in the pig's blood instead." I thrust a finger toward the minions' table. "Prince Cade, look, they're witches from your house; one of them is Fake Blonde. Not everyone can fake it and make it."

"Which one is Fake Blonde?" Cade squinted at the table I pointed at, and the two witches and the mage dropped lower, attempting to hide.

"I've heard enough of your excuses!" Silas barked. "Get the fuck off the table, Barbie! Now! Whenever you're involved, shit hits the fan."

The shifter prince held a grudge against me. I'd shoved him off on the ice in front of thousands of students and faculty, revealing my strength and humiliating him. Of course, me making a fool of him by disguising myself as a boy wasn't going to make him my fanboy. He despised me even more than the vamp prince. Yet there was undeniable heat in his gaze, now that he knew I was a girl through and through and had seen my perky tits.

"The table you are dancing on is our table," Rowan chimed in mildly, as if to educate me. "It's reserved for heirs only."

"I could kill you just for that offense!" Silas added acidly.

Excitement from the crowd rippled across the hall. They all wanted my blood.

"Let's not kill anyone today, shall we?" Cade said as I lowered myself, my hand planting on the edge of the table, and slid off the other side, with the wood between the princes and me, as if that could stop them. "Killian won't be pleased if his new member gets killed so soon."

Rowan nodded, but Silas snorted. "Who gives a fuck if Killian is happy or not."

"Well," Cade said with a dreamy smile. "If Barbie is slain, Killian will have to bear the reputation that he can't protect anyone in his house, and then he'll become even more unreasonable. I bet money he'll even start a mini house war to satisfy his violent nature. No one wants trouble in paradise, Silas, especially before the fun of the first Bride Trials starts."

I turned toward the door, ready to sneak the hell out of here while the heirs got into a debate.

"Where the hell are you going, Barbie?" Louis called, snapping his fingers at me.

Gunther and his team instantly blocked my path in a half ring. My old nemesis had no love for me, since we hadn't parted on friendly terms after I'd burned his eyebrows and hair. He was wearing a wig now.

"Apologies, sirs," I offered in a sigh. "I didn't want to interrupt your intelligent discussion, so I thought that I should see myself out, even though I haven't had breakfast."

"You won't wiggle out of your shenanigans easily this time," Louis said. "Go upstairs, Barbie. We'll continue this interrogation at our leisure while drinking and sitting at our usual table."

"What are you waiting for? Go on!" Silas barked at me, backing up the vamp prince for the first time.

Shit!

My heart sank. Nothing good would come out of this.

The princes turned, heading toward the stairs, chatting and laughing at an inside joke. They didn't bother to look back at me, expecting me to follow.

I seized the opportunity and bolted toward the door.

Gunther dashed into my path, his team following suit to cut off my exit. At the same time, the mixed guards of shifters, mages, and fae moved to surround me. What I'd told Sy was true—these supernaturals weren't nice folks.

The crowd whispered to each other excitedly, like hounds scenting a blood trail.

"The princes summoned you, *Little Bob*, aka *Barbie*!" Gunther barked smugly. "Get going!"

"But why?" I spread my arms. "I'm not a squire anymore."

"Exactly," the vampire captain snickered. "You're now a bride candidate, so every prince from every house can summon you at Their Highnesses' pleasure. You're open season, ripe for the picking. Good job, Barbie. Now go reap what you sowed!"

I opened my mouth, but he raised a finger. "No fake bathroom break! No more crude comments that turn my stomach! Man up and go stand before the princes to receive their righteous judgement! If you're lucky, you might get a month of solitary as a punishment with no meals and no drinks!"

He really took it personally that I made him bald.

I dragged my feet, trailing after the princes with my shoulders hunched in defeat. But I vowed to find a way to get out of this without sacrificing my next meals.

Bea tried to follow me, her face paling with worry and fear, but one of Cade's mage minions stepped into her path to block her.

I waved her away, not wanting to drag her further down with the sinking ship, but mouthed hopefully, *Chocolate bars! Save me two chocolate bars!*

16

Barbie

The princes lounged on the chairs half-circled around a golden table with star charts adorning the edge. From their high seats on the patio, they could overlook almost the entire ground mess hall.

I was led to stand on the opposite side of the royal table, my back to the hostile assembly beneath. Hunching my shoulders, I stared at the princes, waiting for an inevitable conviction.

While I was being placed for the trial, I bitterly watched the princes enjoy their comfort. Cade had his ankle across his knee, relaxing.

Rowan leaned forward, his large hand cupping his chin as he regarded me like a tiger inspecting a deer. Sy peeked out, drinking him in with longing and leaking pheromones, and I snarled inwardly at her to rein her in. The last thing I wanted was for her to act impulsively, blinded by her lust, and leave me no room to wiggle out of this bad situation.

Louis rested a muscled arm on the back of his throne chair, his blond hair in a manbun, his legs wide apart, as if he very much hoped for a blowjob. Good luck with that, as it wasn't going to happen here despite his pale blue eyes and aristocratic face.

Silas narrowed his amber eyes on me. He was a hard to please type. He always carried a swaggering attitude, as he was fully aware of his physical beauty and royal status and wanted everyone to remember it. Too bad he didn't really stand out among the other heirs. To distinguish himself, he had tattooed giant paws on his temple.

My gaze shifted to Rowan as I continued to read the room to find a way out. Maybe the fae prince could be it? He didn't seem as pissed off as the others. The fae prince's beauty was otherworldly. His pointed ears were like Sy's. Right now, he wasn't showing his fangs. His silver eyes held mine as he sniffed subtly. He felt Sy but wasn't too sure about it.

"Why are you pouting, Barbie?" Cade said with a chuckle. "I kind of miss calling you Little Bob. You fooled me, but then you fooled everyone, except Killian."

Cade was also gorgeous. His bronze skin was as smooth as dark marble. When his wine-red hair was ruffled, it gave him a bad boy vibe, just as he intended. He had great fashion sense and a thing for scarves. This time, he had a silky golden scarf to go with his designer shirt.

"That wasn't my intention, sir high mage," I protested. "Sir Louis called me Little B, and I had to roll with the punches."

"It's always someone else's fault, isn't it, Barbie?" Louis snorted.

"When you came to my house seeking asylum from the vampire house," Silas barked at me, ignoring Louis's growl at demeaning his house, "you should've come clean, and I'd have shielded you, so you wouldn't have ended up in the House of Chaos and gotten a bad beating the second day there."

"Sure, sir," I said flatly. "A few shifters from your house initiated the beating and broke two of my ribs."

"This is one of Barbie's passive-aggressive tactics," Louis commented.

"Raise your head and look at your better when I talk to you!" Silas growled.

I raised my head, my eyes rolling back and gazing up at the ceiling.

Silas bared his teeth, and Louis snickered.

Before the shifter prince rose to strike me, Cade cut in, "Let's focus on Barbie's most recent misdeed." He beamed at me. "We'll have to dole out a punishment. You understand that, right, Barbie?"

"I don't understand, sir," I said.

"You see." His smile grew wider. "If we don't set an example, everyone will try to usurp our table."

"But it was empty when I got on it," I protested.

"Exactly," Cade said. "It's a symbol of power, and you don't stomp on a symbol of power."

"But I didn't know that, sir." I widened my two-toned eyes innocently. "No one told me about it. There's no name or sign on the table, and I'm new on the scene. Perhaps you can let it go this time and I'll appreciate it?"

Cade looked at the other princes. "We should consider it.

"See how shrewd she is? She'll pull the wool over our eyes again if we let her," Louis snorted, but there was admiration in his voice. Vampires were cunning creatures. Like calls to like.

"We'll punish you, Barbie!" Silas said, wanting to pump fear into my heart. "And it won't just be a slap on the wrist."

"Let's play a game before we punish Barbie," Cade said, fixing his blue gaze on me. "Now, Barbie, you must answer all our questions truthfully. And if you lie—"

My heart skipped a beat. What if they sniffed out my dark past or my lust toward Killian? I took a deep breath to calm my heartbeat, telling myself that I was a good actress and an excellent liar. I'd handle all the shit these cruel princes threw at me.

"If I lie, I'll accept the punishment and down the booze," I offered. "No problem."

Alcohol didn't affect me.

"The booze is for us, but you'll drink a truth potion," said Cade. "I've been testing the new potion, and I was thinking the other day about who'd be the best test subject. Ha, there she is!"

The mage prince pulled a vial from his pocket and opened the lid, the odor wafting toward me.

I winced. "But it smells terrible!"

Cade laughed gleefully. "Of course. Truth always stings."

I eyed him warily.

"You'll dance for us while we throw questions at you," Louis ordered, "so you'll be too busy to think of lies or excuses."

I blinked. "You want me to dance here?"

"Why not?" Cade gave the vamp prince a playful punch on the back. "That's an excellent idea, Louis."

The vamp prince grinned back.

"You seem like a girl with layers of hidden talent,

Barbie," Louis suggested with lewd menace. "I bet you're good at striptease."

There were secrets between him and me. He'd kept the fact that I'd stabbed him out of the public light. He also never mentioned our confrontation in Underhill to a soul. He'd glimpsed the relationship between Underhill and me, and Underhill had given him a taste of its teeth and claws.

Give them a damn good striptease, one they'll never forget! Sy chimed in, even though I'd been ignoring her.

"I don't do striptease!" I said testily. "I'm not a squire anymore. I'm a bride candidate, and I know my rights, sirs."

The Selection gave me a level of protection, and no one was allowed to kill me outright. But the powerful heirs could always get away with murder. After all, "accidents happened."

"Do you now?" Silas's amber glare fixed on me, the threat sending a bad shiver down my spine.

"A lap dance then." Cade waved his wand at me, as if he was doing me a huge favor.

"I'll be the first to receive her dance," Louis said. "I'll know if Barbie takes any shortcuts."

My superior hearing caught jealous murmurs from the ground floor. A good many students were using magnifying spells to eavesdrop on us.

We won't take a shortcut, Sy said. *We have pride!*

"You aren't going to be the first, Louis," Silas said. "No one wants your leftovers."

"I won't do either dance," I said. "I don't get paid enough for that! Just give me a good beating already and get it over with." I flashed a taunting smirk at them. "If you don't know, my best talent is taking a beating. Who'll do the honors, sirs?"

The princes stared at me, heat in their eyes. My defiance

actually turned them on. What kind of world had I stumbled upon?

"Just let her do the same dance as when we came upon her stomping on our downstairs table and kicking her legs rapidly," Rowan said. "It's nice. I liked it! I want to see more. What kind of dance is that, Barbie?"

"Tap dance, high sir," I said. "It was buck and wing mixed with contemporary hoofing. There're many other styles, like soft-shoe, classical, jazz, Broadway, and funk tap, which is a new age thing. Soft-shoe is lighter; one of its routines is *Bugs Bunny Rides Again*." The princes gaped at me, and I nodded. "Its beauty is in simplicity. My favorite, however, is classical tap. Some call it sensual swing tap, made popular by the Nicholas brothers—"

"Just do the sensual swing!" Silas interrupted me rudely. All he'd heard was the word sensual. "No more talking!"

"Proceed, Barbie," Rowan agreed with him.

"Shall I dance here, sirs?" I gestured at the floor.

"On the table, so we can all see your every move," Louis said.

I was about to jump onto their royal table, but he raised a finger to stop me.

"The buffet table," the vampire prince said and motioned for the servers to remove the dishes covered by silver cloches.

I looked at the dishes longingly. "Maybe I should grab a bite first so I can pump more energy into my dance, so customer satisfaction can be guaranteed?"

"This is your punishment!" Silas yelled. He just couldn't help being so rude! "We didn't summon you here so you could have a feast! As usual, you forget your place!"

There was no point arguing with a douche. Last time I'd done that, Dixie had cut in between us to prevent the situation from escalating. But now she was my enemy as well.

In no time, the buffet table was cleared of all the dishes, the embroidered linen removed too. I jogged to the table as if I owned the stage, but I gave the princes a wide berth. I'd never forget that they were predators, no matter how white their teeth were.

One wrong move from anyone, and they'd pounce.

Planting a hand on the red oak table, I leapt onto it smoothly, my ass alighting before I did a twirl, rolled onto my knees, and rocked to my feet, all in one seamless act. Then, I was dancing.

My boots clicked and tapped on the wood, toes landing first, then I shifted my weight to the heels as I warmed up with a jazz tap, throwing in a few basic acrobatics for an appetizer.

I was in the mood for class acts. I started swinging my torso sensationally while tapping my toes. Tar-ta. Tar-ta! It was a nice rhythm. A few rapid beats later, I got to rock my hips, less sensual at first, then more sensual in design.

The princes traced my moves, hunger and heat growing in their eyes.

"Put your hands together, good sirs!" I urged.

If I got them to have fun, they'd forget about doling out punishment.

"Why not?" Cade laughed and started to clap.

To stay in beat with his claps, I swayed wildly while kicking my legs and tapping the wood at high speed.

"Let's do this!" I called to the other princes. "C'mon!"

I stomped the table harder. Dong-bang-bong! Ta-Ta! The wood groaned and rumbled beneath my boots. I twirled, my legs kicking high. Dong-bang-bong! Sha-sha!

Louis started to pound the table to meet my beats, then

the others joined in, clapping and pounding and laughing like big kids.

Who didn't like music, dance, and fun?

I started singing—

"I'm good, yeah, I'm feelin' alright
Baby, I'm having the best fuckin' day of my life
And wherever it takes me, I'm down for the ride
Baby, don't you know I'm good? Yeah, I'm feelin' alright."

I HAD an angelic and sultry voice—not Little Bob's voice but the true Barbie's. My singing not only held the princes mesmerized; the entire hall went silent, listening, even though almost every student hated me.

"You know I'm down for whatever tonight
I don't need the finer things in life
No matter where I go, it's a good time, yeah
And I, I don't need to sit in VIP
Middle of the floor, that's where I'll be
Don't got a lot, but that's enough for me, yeah
'Cause I'm good, yeah, I'm feelin' alright..."

"WILL we still chastise Barbie after this?" Rowan asked in puzzlement. "I find it quite interesting that we can't make up our minds when it comes to her."

The spell broke just like that.

Silas growled, remembering his supposed meanness toward me. That fucker should paint a growl on his face permanently, even when fucking.

"She almost got us," Louis said.

"That might not be her intention," Cade said. "Now, Barbie, everyone seems to have lost trust in you. It's time for you to redeem yourself. I noticed that you eye us judgmentally, evaluating each one of us in your head. I want to hear what you truly think of us. Louis brought you to his house first, and you spent a lot of time with him as his squire. So, what do you think of him? Truth only, Barbie! May the truth set you free."

I raised a hand as if to swear on the Bible. "May the truth set you free," I parroted.

"Not us, you!" Cade barked, shaking his head. "Don't stall. While you answer a question, you'll keep tapping. Miss a beat and Silas might react badly." He winked at me, then at Silas, despite the shifter prince's scowl. "You don't want Silas, the meanest son of a bitch among us, to come after your ass, sniffing or pouncing, do you?"

"No, I don't want him near my ass, sir," I answered, shivering, just picturing...

Silas growled, and Louis chortled in delight.

My boots hit the redwood table without missing a beat as I mimicked a duck's moves for comical effect, so I could get the princes to laugh. I needed to win over at least two princes, so they could vote in my favor in the end.

Louis and Silas had set out on the path to give me grief, but Rowan and Cade weren't a lost cause.

"Say the truth about Prince Louis," Cade ordered.

"Prince Louis is a man whore," I offered sincerely. "He sticks his dick in any hole that will fit."

All the princes stared at me, jaws dropping in shock. No one expected that answer, but didn't they want the truth? Yeah, sue me! Truth stung.

The entire hall became deathly silent before Louis bellowed in rage, shattering it.

"What the fuck?!" the vamp yelled, dark fire lighting his

pale blue eyes. He probably had never heard anyone saying that about him.

Silas pounded on the table, his other hand wiping a tear of laughter out of the corner of his eye.

Cade doubled over, laughing his hat off, and untied his scarf to breathe.

I tapped on the table rapidly, Ta-ta-ta. dong-dong-dong-ta. "But you said the truth sets you free, sir." Over his vicious glare that promised retaliation, I put on a meek face and hurried on. "I have no choice, Sir Louis. If I lie, sir mage is going to make me drink his truth potion. I can't deal with it since I don't think I have a strong stomach. It smells so terrible and makes my eyes water even from here!"

"Well, we told her to speak the truth," Cade said, straightening now but still laughing.

"But that's not the fucking truth!" Louis barked in anger.

"Everyone knows about your blood orgy parties," Silas snickered.

"That's how the game is played, princes," Rowan said matter-of-factly. "You can't expect the truth not to hurt. What was in Barbie's mind fired off right away, since she was trying to avoid drinking the truth potion."

Cade snapped his fingers, and a lovely human girl rushed to the heirs' table, kneeling to pour whisky for Louis. He gave her slender neck a glance before he raised the shot and downed it. Resting his hungry and vengeful gaze on me, he slammed the shot on the table.

I performed a perfect split. "I have more truth to share about Prince Louis." I beamed. "May I, high sirs?"

"Fuck no!" Louis shouted a profanity. "Nothing nice or sweet has ever come out of your mouth! Even when you were my squire, you never said anything positive!"

I pouted at his negativity while I spun and tapped my toes and heels on the table with spirit. Boom-Ta. Boom-Ta.

"Let's move on to Silas." The vamp prince sneered. "How do you like Silas then, Barbie? Didn't you attack Silas on the ice before Killian recruited you to his house?"

He was stirring shit for me.

I swayed my hips, my boots pounding vigorously, as I started to hum 'Dirty Orchestra.' "First, I'm afraid that I have to say all you high sirs are Ass-holes with a capital A. You don't know how to treat women right." The entire hall, downstairs and upstairs, went deathly quiet, except the words flowing out of my mouth and the *dee-dee-tar, dee-dee-dong* sounds generated by my boots. "I keep wondering why those chicks fight to be your brides if they have an ounce of self-respect. I just don't get it. What are the perks of hooking up with any of you—"

The princes stared at me, stunned. They'd stopped clapping their hands, tapping their feet, or pounding the table.

A snarl tore out of Silas's twisted lips. "Pause!"

He was quick to jump to his feet and raise a finger to stop me as if I were a record that could stop playing at his whim.

The shifter prince dashed to the glass rail of the patio and stared down at the masses. Every eye trained on him, the girls gazing up while thrusting their breasts out to give him a fantastic view.

"Out!" Silas bellowed. "Everyone out! Now!"

17

Barbie

The shifter prince's command carried the power of compulsion, and the students started to flee. All the heirs had the same power, but they didn't know that it wouldn't work on me. Yet I was going to take this chance to make my exit as well, pretending that I was under the same influence.

I leapt off the table, ready to rush downstairs and merge into the exodus.

"Where are you going, Barbie?" Rowan asked.

He didn't speak much, but he watched me closely. It was always the quiet ones that were more dangerous.

"Uh." I blinked as if waking up. "Sir Silas said everyone out."

Silas snapped his head toward me. "Not you! We aren't done with you. Think you're a *bride* candidate so you're untouchable? You're still fair game to us. Get back on the table and keep dancing!"

I had a dark feeling that he was going to do something nasty to me. That might be one of the reasons he sent everyone out, so there'd be no witnesses except for the other princes, who were in this together with him. And I'd thought I might get Rowan and Cade on my side.

I was about to defy Silas's order and bolt, only to find Louis parked at the top of the stairs, smirking at me, his muscled arms folded across his chest.

He'd expected that I'd try to run, so he'd zipped to the spot before I could.

Amid the exodus, Medea, America, and their friends remained at their table.

"Out!" Silas snarled at them.

Medea opened her mouth to protest but then submitted to the shifter prince's alpha stare. The group took their leave at the rear of the crowd. Cami, however, stayed at her table with her tight circle from the House of Chaos.

Silas pointed at her. "Didn't I say everyone out, Cami?"

"I don't take orders from anyone but my prince," Cami said coldly. "And it's not your right to dole out punishment to one of the members of the House of Chaos, Prince Silas."

I squinted. Was I being duped?

Silas trained his potent alpha stare on Cami. In the end, she dropped her eyes, but she still kept her ass glued to her chair. Silas shook his head in disgust, but he gave up the pissing contest with Killian's cousin and shifted his amber glare to me.

He jerked his chin at the heirs' table. "Didn't I tell you to get on the table?"

"But you said one should not trample on the symbol of

power, sir," I said, my heart beating harder, bracing for his nastiness.

He darted a menacing glance at Cami then at me. Now he wanted to punish me with Cami as an audience.

"Not when I order it," he purred, his compulsion brushing me. "Now, climb onto the table like a nice girl."

I blinked as if trying to wake up from a dream as I pretended to be under his influence.

I trotted to the heirs' table, stepped on the chair that Silas had been sitting on despite his scowl, and got on the table. I started a new tap dance, not putting in any effort. The fun was over. Hunger pangs pulsed in me, and thus my anger mounted.

Sy wanted to eat Silas.

"Be a good girl, Barbie. Strip," Silas commanded. At the same time, he whipped out his tablet, ready to record. The tablet glowed with a faint green light.

Louis dropped back into his chair, his arm resting on its back, his ankle across his knee. He watched eagerly, heat gleaming in his eyes.

"That is a bit of a stretch, Silas," Cade said, his brows creased. "We don't want to go too far."

"Killian stripped her," Silas said. "And he took her from my house. Now it's my turn to have a little fun."

"Barbie didn't agree to a strip dance earlier," Rowan said. "It's not our way to force any female. That's the line that we should draw."

"Barbie made a fool of all of us." Silas pointed at me like I was a criminal on display. "Don't buy her innocent looks. Even the druid was sure she was hiding a dark secret. Killian only revealed part of it. He didn't rip her clothes off entirely. I'll finish the job he started. Let's get every inch of her bare and make her confess."

"Let's just call it a day, man," Cade said.

"I agreed to teach her a lesson and bend her will," Louis said. "You might be different, Silas, but I don't want to carry the reputation of forcing a bride candidate against her will."

"You all can leave. I'll see it through," Silas said.

No one left.

Silas grinned. "You all want this, but you don't have the guts to be the bad guy. Fine, let me be your fall guy since I'm always the one who gets the job done."

"I'm staying, but there'll be a limit," Cade warned.

"Careful, Silas," Rowan said. "The girl is under Killian's protection."

That only incensed the shifter prince.

"Fuck Killian!" Silas bared his teeth. "He pulled the rug from under me first. What is he going to do about it when he sees her strip then suck my dick on Spinchat? Enough talk, princelings. Let's get the ball rolling." He snapped his fingers at me, his power slamming into me like a hard wave. "Strip and dance like your life depends on it, Barbie!"

I tilted my head at him while I tapped on the wood, harder now, as I intended to put a dent in the heirs' table. Sy pumped strength into me.

"But my life doesn't depend on it, shifter sir," I said. "If I go bare like a turkey ready for Christmas, I'll catch a cold. I'm vulnerable now since I haven't had my breakfast, as I was dragged here to dance to entertain you princelings. You don't want me to pass a bad cold to every bride candidate, do you, sir, since it'll be on you? Your command of 'strip and dance like your life depends on it, Barbie' was based on a false statement, sir, and I obey only the truth. As sir mage said, 'The truth will set you free.' Has it set you free yet, Sir Silas?"

Louis started laughing, whipping out a silky handkerchief from his pocket to wipe a tear from the corner of his blue eye.

Cade smiled. "That's what I was waiting to see. Barbie isn't susceptible to compulsion."

"She's more than an Echo," Rowan agreed. "No wonder Killian was eager to recruit her to his house."

"Maybe Silas didn't put in enough effort?" Louis said in delight.

"I enjoy a little challenge." Silas clenched his teeth. "I'll show her the truth!" He returned to his seat. "Tell me, Barbie, are you a bride candidate?"

"Yes, sir, I believe I am," I answered.

"Every candidate wants to land one of us. Don't you think?" Silas asked.

I'd just said that I didn't get why the candidates even wanted to be a bride, but the shifter prince was too full of himself to listen to anyone.

I made a show of thinking hard by blinking three times. "A lot of them fight so dirty. Princess Medea will do anything to be in the lead. You should ask her to suck your cock, but I don't think she's into you. Everyone can see that she wants to screw Prince Rowan badly, if they haven't fucked already."

Sy hissed in rage. Medea now went to the top of her to-eat list.

Rowan stared at me before narrowing his eyes in displeasure.

I nodded at the fae prince. "If she can't get into your pants, she'll settle for Sir Silas. The rumor on the campus is that the shifter heir will take anyone who'll have him, doggie style."

Louis looked at the sour and enraged expression on Silas's face and guffawed. Cade leaned his forehead against his palm and chuckled. Even Rowan shook his head while chortling.

I tapped the table with the heels of my boots. Dang-dang-dang. Tar-Ta! I found the warded table was too solid to make a dent in it, and I didn't want to put in all I had or I might break it and fall through.

"Let's not get sidetracked again, Barbie!" Silas barked, fuming. "I'm going to give you two tasks. Let's start with an easy one. Pick a prince among us for your first date!"

He sent another wave of compulsion my way, decreeing for me to pick him. He wasn't only petty and cruel; he was also a cheater.

"Must I really do that?" I asked, batting my eyes at him to give him false hope.

"One of us prince heirs has the first pick of any bride candidate to find a potential mate," Cade sighed, as if it was a chore for him to pick a date. "You belong to the House of Chaos, so your prince, Killian, should be granted the first pick, but then he's the only heir who's spoken for, so the heirs from other houses can step in. It'd be bad form for us to fight over you, so we'll let you do the picking, and you'll get to go on a date with one of us."

The princes believed that any woman would be thrilled should any of them send a glance her way. They expected me to act the same.

I decided not to play their games anymore. I stopped tapping and dropped to sit on the table, my legs crossed, my pose slouched, as none of them deserved good posture.

"I'm tired, man. Sirs," I said. "I need to go to class. I don't want to be late all the time. The teachers bitch a lot."

"Decide, Barbie!" Silas barked.

"I will if I can get two donuts to go with a pumpkin spice latte," I bargained.

"You'll have your donuts and coffee after the pick," Silas said.

I smiled at him, all teeth. "Prince Roman—pardon—Prince Rowan will do."

Silas fumed in frustration, Louis narrowed his eyes in displeasure, and Cade shook with laughter.

"I appreciate it, Barbie," Rowan said. "That settles it. She needs to go to class."

Silas grinned viciously and tossed another wave of strong compulsion my way. "Not before I get what I want. Crawl to me and suck my dick, Barbie!"

I brushed off his compulsion like I was swatting away a fly. "Too bad for you. With all your power, you can't make me do a damn thing that I don't want to. And I ain't the kind of chick who bends a knee to anyone. So I got words for you." I flipped him the bird over my head. "Suck this, sir!"

Cami roared with laughter from downstairs, and her companions from the House of Chaos joined her.

I drew a drop of power from each prince; with it, I left my handprint on the surface of the heirs' table for them to remember me by.

"You dare!" Silas shot to his feet, intending to come swing at me.

I shot to my feet as well, ready to kick him in the teeth.

"Cool your jets, Silas!" Cade chuckled with the others.

Before Cade and Rowan could reel Silas back, a wall of darkness and starlight swirled to life, erected between Silas and me.

Killian strode toward us, his gaze fixing on me and making me hot and cold at the same time.

18

Barbie

"Some bird told me that you busy bees were having a party, and I wasn't invited," Killian crooned.

He wore a gray shirt that fit his physique perfectly, the sleeves rolled up to show off his muscled forearms and part of the tattoos on them. His slacks hugged his powerful legs. Everything about him spelled sex and might.

His face was striking, framed by his medium-length hair that had grown darker. His icy storm-blue eyes roved over me, but they didn't freeze me over. His gaze dipped to my lips, so I let my eyes skim to his carnal mouth as well to return the favor.

Before I knew it, heat pulsed in me, and my pussy ached with need. Fuck! I'd give anything to cover up my arousal. No other male could do this to me, but Killian was flame, destruction, and sin incarnate.

I would not let him be my downfall!

"You aren't an eligible bachelor like us, Killian," Silas snickered. "So don't blame us for not inviting you for a little fun."

A wave of rage rolled off the chaos prince, the air crackling with electricity. The other princes all tensed.

"Is that so?" Killian drawled. "Do you think that with my absence you can take advantage of Barbie since she doesn't know any rules of the Selection?"

"Nothing happened, Killian," Louis said.

Killian ignored him but fixed his predator stare on Silas, and the shifter prince met it with his alpha glare.

"What are you? Her daddy?" Silas snorted.

I licked my lips. That sounded dirty.

"Barbie belongs to my house, and no one shall touch her without her consent," Killian said.

"I don't remember you being that possessive toward any other members of your house," Silas said. "In fact, you don't even know the names of half of the members of your own house. Why is this one so special to you?"

The shifter prince was drawn to my power as well, but he regarded me as a low creature, far beneath him, so he set out to humiliate me and bend me to justify his shameful attraction to me.

"You know why, but you'll never get it," Killian said coldly before he turned to me. "Go to class, Barbie."

I slid off the table; the princelings had yet to find my handprint on their royal table. "Thank you, Highness. I'm just going to grab a donut before I go. I'm starving."

"You starved her?" Killian scanned the princes, his face terrible. "You know what hunger does to her!"

Did they know?

Silas's face remained hard and unremorseful, but the other princes looked uneasy.

"Look, Killian," Louis said. "Barbie is going to get her breakfast. I won't deprive her of her food. The dance was taking a bit too long."

"She danced for how long? An hour?" Silas said. "What's the big deal? She should feel honored that we even paid her attention—"

"Go after her again and you'll be sorry, Silas," Killian said, his voice as hard as an icy blade. "And if you hurt her, I'll hurt you back tenfold, as I always protect what's *mine*."

The princes traded glances.

"She isn't *yours*," Silas said, his jaw clenched. "One of the Brides Selection rules indicates that all four of us, except *you*, have the first pick of any females in the pool."

Killian ignored him but beckoned the servants, six of them lining a sidewall. A woman and a man scrambled to him right away.

"Your Highness." They bowed.

"You got hamburgers?" Killian asked.

The woman nodded in reverence. "Yes, Your Highness. The cuisine includes dishes favored by humans."

"Pack three donuts and two hamburgers in a box with French fries," Killian said. "And a cup of pumpkin spice latte to go, if you have it."

"We have it." The servants bowed again, rushed away to fulfill the order, and returned quickly.

"Give it to me! Appreciate it, folks!" I zoomed toward them, snatching the elegantly packed takeout bag filled with burgers, donuts, and coffee before they could hand it over to Killian, startling them.

A faint, amused smile tugged at the corner of the chaos prince's lips.

"Thank you, high sir!" I beamed at him. "I'm going to class now! I won't shame the house."

I shot toward the stairs before anyone could stop me.

Silas's tart voice chased me before I reached the base of the stairs. "In my house, a shifter only offers his female food. Aren't your engaged to another, Killian?"

"Good thing I'm not a shifter like you," Killian said coldly. "I do whatever I please."

"Are you sure, Killian?" Silas retorted. "And you don't own that Barbie girl. She'll go on a date with Rowan, then the rest of us. We'll all date her one by one, picking on her for fun. There's nothing you can do about that but watch, bro."

I bit into a strawberry donut, moaning in pleasure while I mapped out my defense. As the princes singled me out with their unhealthy interest, they made me a walking, talking target. And by shielding me, Killian evoked the shifter prince's primal need to win the challenge. Silas would use me as target practice to get to Killian.

Well, fuck it!

19

Barbie

The classes had been exhausting, especially the potion class. Just naming, identifying, and collecting the ingredients took forever. And who had the patience to waste an hour brewing the herbs that smelled so pungent? My hands got sore just stirring the potion in the cauldron. And I didn't need Professor Moor, a middle-aged pointy-chinned mage, to call me lazy.

I dozed off only twice, and he banged my head with his black wand to jerk me wake. My classmates snickered gleefully. Those little shits didn't have a single empathetic bone in them. If I hadn't been able to resist magic, the spells from Moor's wand could've caused permanent brain damage.

I could learn things quickly, but this organized study wasn't working for me. What did I need potions for? Forcing the Shriekers to drink them?

As soon as I returned to my room in Cami's suite, I put

down my school satchel near the door and rushed to my bed to take a nap, only to find it was occupied.

"What the hell?" I yelled at Pucker.

The ghost guardian lounged on my bed, his phantom shoes on my pillow again. Last time I'd demanded he remove his feet from my pillow, he'd sat his ghost ass on it.

"Join me?" he offered.

"This is my room!"

"I know! Hey, I heard that you landed a date!"

I squinted at him. "What date?"

"With the fae heir, Prince Rowan!" He rubbed his phantom hands enthusiastically, as if he were the one who would go out with Rowan. "Everyone is talking about it," Pucker cheered. "It's all over Spinchat!"

"Shit!" I said.

"Excellent shit, Barbie!" Pucker beamed at me in pride. "Even though the hashtags named you loser, slut, little whore, lowlife, and many more. Anyway, you've achieved the impossible! No one, not even the nobles and princesses in Shades Academy, has such popularity! A servant boy who turned out to be a girl got invited by all the princes on her first day as a bride candidate and secured a date with one of the most coveted bachelors!"

Sy lifted her chin in pride.

"Technically, it wasn't my first day," I said. "In fact, I got ambushed and beaten on my first day! The second day, I got ambushed again and was publicly humiliated, and then the princes doled out punishment and made me dance for two hours nonstop without food and drink." I exaggerated a little to show Pucker how cruel those princes were and how bad my days had been! "On the third day, which is today, I had to endure the boring classes and watch out for many, many traps. Several students tried to trip me. One time I almost fell on my face. And a teacher hit me with his wand, trying to fry my brain like an egg!"

"Don't be a negative Nancy," Pucker said dismissively. "You must look at the big picture. You've found a way to draw attention to you and secure yourself a date with an heir. You're the underdog who won the bet, and everyone loves the victorious story of the underdog."

"Not here," I said. "Not in this realm where the weak are despised."

"But you don't despise them," he said. "You see strength in the weak, and if you use them as a resource—"

"I'm not going to use anyone, certainly not the repressed and the weak," I said, showing him a big yawn without covering my mouth, so he'd get the hint and leave.

"That's rude, Barbie," he said. "I might be a ghost, but I demand the same respect you show the living!"

"I don't even pay the living respect," I said. "They don't deserve it any more than the dead."

"That's true." He nodded. "But you need to manage your anger issue."

"Will you fuck off now, please? There, I'm being polite. I need an uninterrupted nap before a big dinner."

"Life's good here, isn't it?" he said. One second, he was in my bed, then the next, he stood close to me, gazing at me in hunger. "I haven't tasted food for a very long time."

"I'm too tired to feel sorry for you right now," I said. "Bye, Pucker. Next time, knock first or you might not like the warm welcome."

"It's cute when you threaten a ghost, Barbie." He chuckled. "But I have to give it to you for your distraction. Going on the offense as soon as you spotted me, pointing out my faults, and then issuing a warning to throw me off track, so I'd leave with my ghost tail between my legs and utterly forget my purpose here. You know I came to collect a payment."

Shit!

"What payment?" I asked roughly, still trying to put it off. "You want a lock of my curls as a souvenir?"

"They're soft and have the color of real gold," he said in admiration.

"I can cut a strand for you to keep," I offered. "That's the best I can do for your help, since I don't have anything else to give."

"Oh, you have a lot to give." He grinned. "You have more to give than anyone else." He sighed as if it pained him to say what he must say. "I won't beat around the bush anymore, as I'm getting hungry. You owe me a drink."

"Not a drink, dude," I snapped. "I promised a sip. You see, my other half, Sy, is frugal, and she has a temper." Sy chose that moment to growl, giving the ghost guardian pause. "Have I told you that Sy can eat anything, including ghosts? You met her, and right now she wants out to play. So, a deal is a deal. A sip only."

Pucker lunged at me, his phantom fingers sinking into my shoulders, and my energy flowed into him.

"Goddess, three-quarters, more powerful than a demigoddess." He threw his head back and sighed euphorically. "Your energy is even purer than I expected."

He latched onto me, trying to take more.

I rammed my fist into his jaw. "That's fucking enough!"

He jerked back, eyes wide, his hands dropping off me, and our connection cut out.

"You can hit me like I'm solid and even cause me pain?" he asked incredulously.

"I'm a three-quarters, dude," I said, really hating leeches of any shape and size. "When I say stop, you stop!"

"Sorry, Barbie." Pucker smiled. "And next time, after another sip, when you say jump, I'll ask how high."

"There'll be no next time if you value your teeth."

"You can't know that, girl. I'm much more useful than you think. I can be your familiar. If you keep feeding me, I can even spy for you. Your power will also allow me to travel outside the bounds of the house. I've been bound to the House of Chaos for hundreds of years! I long to roam all the lands."

I eyed him, pondering. Maybe I could use him.

Those meanest bride candidates didn't worry me, though I had no doubt that they'd try to make my life hell. The princes worried me a bit more, but I could still find wiggle room and probably turn them against each other. Yet the prospect of more Shriekers getting into the realm haunted my every waking moment, and not just for my own sake.

I took responsibility for every death caused by them, which was eating me up. And I was even more terrified of my father finding me. I had a lot to lose now. No matter how dangerous this school was, I felt at home, as if I'd been looking for a home all this time and kind of just found it, even though I'd resisted locating this last pure magical realm when I was under Ruin's thumb.

For the first time, I felt I belonged.

I peered out of the window that overlooked part of the forbidden forest of Underhill. Even now, it was aware of me, calling me.

And the room was a lot more spacious than when I'd first arrived. The house had wanted me to take the Queen's Suite. When Killian denied the arrangement, the magic started to make adjustments to my room without me asking.

The chaos prince had seen the changes, but he hadn't said anything or objected to it.

Yesterday, the house magic shifted more of the structures in my room. The sidewall had been replaced with a floor-to-ceiling window with a French door in the center since the house knew Sy could only leave through the window to avoid being discovered.

Even with the window closed, air still flowed in, carrying the scent of jasmine, pine, and lemon, so I could feel I was outdoors even in sleep. I wondered if the house magic could read some of my memories, knowing that I'd slept under the sky for years. But it was treating me like its mistress.

"You'll need me, Barbie!" Pucker persuaded urgently. "We'll do great things together."

"I don't buy it." I eyed him suspiciously for show to pave the way for a favorable bargain. "Whenever someone sets out to do great things, they often do more damage. Hasn't history taught you anything? And what great things? Make Mist of Cinder great again?"

My true thoughts were actually the opposite while I ridiculed the ghost guardian.

If Pucker could roam the academy grounds, he could be my eyes and ears. I could send him to patrol the Veil, and no one could even see him. The Shriekers had been thorns in my side. With the loaded class schedule, mandatory dates, and training with Killian, I wouldn't have a lot of time to guard the Veil. And if I was seen hanging around the Veil too often, it'd only bring suspicion down on me. I already had too many foes who wanted to take me down at every chance.

The sentinels of the academy had taken up the task of patrolling the perimeter of the school. All five princes had also assigned their own teams to monitor the Veil. Silas and Louis did it for the sake of rivalry.

The supernaturals were powerful, but none of them understood the Shriekers and their weaknesses. I had seen that their magic couldn't kill the abominations without me being there to tweak it. And the only weapon that could deal the Shriekers a fatal blow was Deathsong.

I wondered if Killian's lightning could kill the Shriekers, since his power wasn't entirely of this realm. That was probably how he'd caged me with his power in the first place, another matter I needed to study and take care of.

So, yes, the ghost guardian would be my perfect minion to monitor the Shriekers' activities since I couldn't be tied to the abominations. Last time they'd led to me, my breast binder had been ripped off and burned, and thousands of students had seen my tits!

No longer a nomad now, I needed allies, useful ones.

When Pucker became my familiar, he'd be bound to me —not that it would do him any good in the long run, but then he was already dead. What more could my father do to the dead, even as an evil original god?

All I had to do was give away some of my juice to Pucker, which was utterly different from being fed upon by my father.

"You're a cynic at such a young age," Pucker said with disapproval. "What got you so wound up, my goddess?"

Well, anyone else who had suffered at my father's hands would be damaged goods, not just a little cynical. Pucker would weep with joy that I wasn't an utter sociopath plus psycho if he could catch a glimpse of my past.

"You're naïve to want to do great things at your age and being dead already," I said. "However, I'll give you a chance to blow shit up by my side. But you'll need to prove your worth first, and I'm not talking about pranking the students as a poltergeist and singing off-key opera in the dead of night. And don't call me goddess."

"I'm not really a poltergeist," he protested. "It's a ruse. But that's not important. And before you assign me any task—yeah, I can read the room extremely well, despite you pulling a blank mask over your face. The first order of business is to make sure you survive here, since we don't need three ghosts in the house, which would be crowded. To prevail in this realm, you need to survive the Brides Selection. The official Bride Trials, which will be magically televised for the entire realm to watch, start in three months. Our time is tight, since you'll need a lot of training."

My eyes flew wide, my heart pounding as a swirl of dark foreboding closed in on me.

"Shit!" I squirmed. "I thought I only needed to go to class, fend off other candidates during three meals, and go on a couple of dates with the princes and be done with it."

Pucker laughed in wicked delight. "They all think you're a lamb among the wolves, not realizing a big bad she-wolf in a sheep's skin is lurking among the sheep."

I frowned at him. "I don't like the analogy. It's not flattering."

"How about a she-fox in the chicken coop?"

I shook my head. Even a ghost didn't have a single nice thing to say about me. Ever since I'd come to Shades Academy, I'd first been branded as Little Bob with a tiny dick. After I'd been outed as a girl, I'd been slut shamed even though I hadn't even had real sex. And now my future familiar was calling me a she-fox.

"Just tell me about the Bride Trials," I said. "It doesn't sound good."

"Now you're talking." He smiled. "The Bride Trials are the *culling*."

"Are you serious?" I asked. My heart skipped an icy beat.

"Oh yeah." Pucker grinned wider. "Right now, every candidate is just warming up for the trials, and the princes fool around by fucking as many candidates as possible. They can't even put the names with the faces of those they fucked. So don't get cocky that you landed a date with one of the prince heirs, though it's somewhat impressive. You're still far from the finish line. They're interested in fucking you, sampling you, then putting your name or face on their lists of conquests, which are long. Before long, they'll forget all about you."

I hissed. "Motherfuckers!"

"Nope, they aren't fucking their mothers. That won't be tolerated. They just fuck naïve girls like you, who will do anything to be a bride to a prince."

"You're confusing me with the other supernatural chicks." I sneered at him. "But I'm right about the princes treating women like sex dolls! They think they have the looks, money, and power, so they can just do whatever they want!"

Pucker nodded. "That's the gist of it. That's how things are run here."

I thinned my lips. "You're morally gray, Pucker!"

He grinned. "Thank you. I was never a black-and-white sort of guy even when I was among the living."

"You know," I shook my head, "the last thing I want is to be anyone's bride."

He narrowed his eyes. "You can't be serious!"

"I am, Pucker. I am!" I said firmly.

He studied me for a long moment. "You sure you don't want to move up in rank by banging a prince?"

"What good will it do me?"

"People with no ambitions always worry me."

"I have ambitions."

"Such as?"

"To stay alive. To breathe the next breath of fresh air, then the next. And I don't want to just stay alive, I want to have quality of life, like drinking clean water and eating gluten-free hamburgers. I'm planning to get on a healthy diet program next."

"Are you sure hamburgers are gluten free?"

I stared at him. "Why don't you find out for me?"

"You don't have big plans for the future." He shook his head in dismay. "That's depressing, and I don't like depressing stuff. Death is already dreary, and I faced it daily, until today I got a sip of your goddess nectar." He perked up. "I haven't felt so alive for centuries!"

He inched toward me, intending to get another sip when I let down my guard. His form had turned half solid after getting a drop of my juice.

I raised a firm fist to stop him. "Remember what I said about knocking out a tooth or two if you jump me?" I warned.

"You're the only one who can actually hurt a ghost," he sighed. "That's why Lady Magenta, my colleague, stays away from you."

I wasn't the only one, but I wasn't willing to tell him about my father. My future familiar might've detected my godly bloodline, but he didn't know which god. If he'd known, he'd have run, ghost, dead, or whatever.

"Hmm," I said noncommittally.

"No one likes to smell desperation on others." Pucker reevaluated me like a ghost hawk. "Your not-giving-two-shits attitude might just work in your favor, giving you an advantage at winning."

"But I just said that I didn't want to be a bride."

"Exactly!" he exclaimed happily. "That's the best strategy, Barbie!"

What I'd said was falling on deaf ears. But then, who could beat a dead horse, or worse, a dead warlock?

"This conversation is getting sidetracked and taking too long," I said, and my stomach grumbled its complaint as well. "Just give me the bullet points on the rules of the Bride Trials before I go grab a bite since my naptime is gone!"

"The whole purpose of the Brides Selection is to find fated mates for the heirs," Pucker drawled. "It's crucial to preserving peace in Mist of Cinder. The rivalry between the houses could lead to war at any time, and every house wants to secure the strongest bloodlines in the next generation. Every heir fights to find the strongest female to mate. The heir who finds his fated mate first is most likely to produce the prophesized One, who will bring back the old magic, and thus ascend to the High King's throne. One king rules them all."

I smirked. "Like one ring rules them all?"

"I want you to take this seriously, Barbie," Pucker snapped. "This is no joking matter! The prince heirs are all in their third year now, yet none of them has found his true mate. That's why all five kingdoms agreed to the Bride Trials. Time is running out; the pressure is high."

"That's why the realm rounded up every eligible supernatural and put us in the academy, and the princes are the foxes in the chicken coop," I said in understanding.

"If you have to put it that way," Pucker sighed. "Soon there'll be a trial, the culling. Many will die. Two hundred candidates will enter the second trial. The rest of the candidates who don't make the cut will be allowed to stay and continue their education in Shades Academy, but they won't be elevated as privileged bride candidates anymore."

My eyes brightened. "I'll join the rest and go with the flow."

"You'll be kicked out of the academy unless you can pay for the expensive tuition," Pucker sneered. "Don't expect free meals and boarding anymore!"

My eyes bulged at the bad news. "What the fuck? That's unfair!"

"Then you'll be motivated to win, yes?"

"No one told me there's a catch!"

"There's always a catch, dearest," Pucker said without sympathy. "No strings attached is an illusion. Freedom is an illusion. Having a choice is an illusion. You see, Barbie, you've entered the Brides Selection, and now you're facing a whole different game. You've proved to be a surprise to all, and the other candidates are royally pissed that a *nobody* like you joined their ranks."

"If they think I'm a nobody, why does it matter if I'm in or not, as the chance for me to win is slim?"

"They regard it as an insult to their perceived status. While instinctively they know that you're *the* threat. You're the unknown factor, and they've seen all the princes are taken with you. Mark my words, the candidates will come after you, day and night. They'll cut your throat in your sleep if they can. And I bet poison will be the most popular method for them to kill you. Those candidates look all pretty outside, but they're all little monsters inside."

We're the bigger monster, and we'll eat all the little monsters, Sy vowed, as if that could calm my nerves.

"Killian will have the last laugh when those monsters kill me," I said bitterly.

"That's why you'll need me to watch your back," Pucker said.

After he'd had a taste of my goddess energy; he'd been trying damn hard to whore himself out to me.

Why do you need him to watch your six when you have me? Sy demanded, getting territorial. *Are we stooping so low as to take advice from the dead? If he was that good, he wouldn't have ended up dead. If we keep listening to him, we'll end up just like him!*

"If I announce my withdrawal from the Brides Selection—"

"No one gets out of the Selection, not before the first trial," said the ghost guardian. "And the more you play hard to get, the more the princes will want you. Like it or not, you're trapped in the middle of the mating game."

I slumped into a chair like a deflated balloon, but Sy perked up. *I got this! Mating is my specialty!*

"The only way out is to win," Pucker said excitedly, as if he could live through me as a bride candidate. "Don't you worry, you got me! I'll be the brain behind this operation! After the second trial, the numbers will be cut in half. The top twenty-four that survive the third trial will have wealthy sponsors in the realm, and each of them will go on a one-on-one date with the princes." He snapped his fingers, and I straightened from my chair before I slouched again. "I can tell your eyes are starting to glaze, Barbie! You need to pay attention. As soon as the trials start, it's not illegal or uncommon for the candidates to murder each other in cold blood."

Chills slithered up my spine. I wasn't a stranger to violence, but I never enjoyed killing. When it was kill or be killed...

I let out an uneven breath. I'd worry about the first trial

when it came; right now, we needed to take care of the Shrieker business.

"Listen," I said. "Here's what I need you to do, Pucker. The stakes are higher than the mating game—"

We both snapped our heads toward the door as quiet footfalls crept closer.

20

Barbie

I yanked the door open and found Rock, the captain of Killian's security team, standing by it, his knuckles frozen in the air. Pucker had phased out through the wall to do only gods knew what a poltergeist would do for fun.

"No door for you to knock on now, Rock," I offered.

"How?" he asked. A lock of ashy blond hair flopped over his eye, and he shook it away. "I was as quiet as a jungle cat."

"I heard you a mile away, like a big rhino coming," I said.

For a giant warrior, Rock had surprisingly quiet footfalls, but Sy could be quieter and sneakier than anyone. At my praise, she preened. Sy loved to be flattered and never took any criticism well.

Rock shook his head and chuckled. "You got me, girl."

"I'm going to Jubilee Haven to grab a bite," I said. "You coming?"

With Rock watching my back, everyone would think twice if they thought to sabotage my dinner, and I'd eat my meal in peace.

"It's not even dinner time," he said. "Dinner will be served in an hour."

"That's why I said I was going to grab a bite. After a few bites, it'll be dinner time," I said confidently.

"No bites," Rock said. "His Highness summoned you to his office."

"But I didn't do anything wrong!" I protested. My heart pounded as I remembered stomping on the heirs' priceless table then leaving a permanent handprint on it.

Rock arched a brow. "Are you sure? Let's go to His Highness's office. The sooner you sort it out, the better you'll sleep tonight."

I followed Rock out of the suite, traipsed down the hallway, and climbed up the stairs, my head bowed in defeat, my shoulders slumped, my mind running all sorts of scenarios and excuses.

"It won't be too bad." Rock chuckled. "Prince Killian has a soft spot for you."

"Thank you, but I don't share your confidence." I bit my lip, then I thought of something. "Hey, Rock, did the high sir fire Bern, his former squire?"

Rock's expression hardened. "Bern failed in a simple task, which ended up with you getting ambushed and beaten by the mob."

"I don't blame him though," I said. "He was duped, and that Imelda chick is sultry."

"Sultry?"

I nodded.

"It doesn't matter. His Highness isn't forgiving when it

comes to executing his orders. One strike, you're out. No second chance."

The rumors weren't wrong about the chaos prince being cold-hearted.

We reached the seventh floor. Rock paused on the top stair, towering over me. "Go right ahead. His Highness's penthouse is the third to the left. You won't miss it. Just don't bump into the second room with the red door to the right. That's the Queen's Suite." My heart skipped a beat. The house had wanted me to take that room. "The house magic guards it. No one can get through the door, not even—" Rock swallowed the rest of his words and waved me forward. "Off you go. You don't want to keep His Highness waiting. He's in a bad mood today."

"Shit!" I said, then spread my arms. "But when is he ever in a good mood?"

Rock nodded and chuckled lowly. "Just don't say it to His Highness's face."

And then he was gone like a shadow.

I HADN'T MEANT to stop in front of the Queen's Suite, staring at the red door.

But the magic beckoned me toward it, even after I jogged along the luxurious hallway and passed it by.

Inhuman voices whispered behind the sealed door, chills filling my head like icy fog. I sensed a dark force within the walls, contained yet wanting something from me.

Flight or fight?

"The Queen's Suite has been vacant forever," Cami had said. *"It's supposed to be for Prince Killian's future true mate, which is Queen Lilith."*

Then why hadn't Killian's mysterious betrothed taken up residency? Where the fuck was she?

Rock had also had a slip of the tongue minutes ago: *"The house magic guards it. No one can get through the door, not even—"*

He didn't finish the words but swallowed the rest of them as if he was gagged. Had he meant to say not even Queen Lilith? Again, if she was Killian's fated mate, why wasn't he with her? Why was there such intense, unnatural attraction between the chaos prince and me when we could never be together?

I shook my head, not wanting to dwell on the dark puzzles and the impossible affairs of the heart, which would only mess up my head and ruin my day.

I wanted to see Killian every second, yet I was dreading seeing him. What if one day, I lost my shit and just jumped him? I was vulnerable in his presence. I remembered how I'd been at his mercy on the ice rink when he ripped off my clothes!

So why did I allow myself to freeze like a fool in front of the room reserved for his fated mate?

Barbie. Multiple voices rose behind the red door. *Magic fades. Mist reveals, and Ruin comes. The chosen one—the cursed and the blessed—comes before him to bring tides. She's the darkness in light and light in massive darkness. Find the buried living flame and hope kindles. Turn the wheels of the Fates and the vicious cycle stops. Time is running out. Beware of the hanged. Join the Brides Selection, Barbie! Be the BRIDE, one and only...*

"Fuck!" I jumped back.

It crept me out that those were the exact words that had flowed out of Bea's mouth when her eyes turned all glassy and milky white.

"Are you going to stand there cursing all day?" a deep, rich voice boomed through the hallway.

I shrieked, startled.

I didn't know what exactly happened, but Killian was suddenly there, and I was leaning against his chest, my fists grabbing the front of his shirt, hanging on.

He dipped his gaze to me, then darted it toward the red room, his expression unreadable.

"You okay, Barbie?"

I released his shirt and stepped back. "Uh, sorry, sir. I'm a little jumpy today."

He turned in the direction of his penthouse. "Come."

The entire seventh floor was Killian's except for the Queen's Suite.

I sprang after him to match his long strides, as I needed to get on his good side, and I couldn't wait to get away from the red door and the creepy whispers behind it.

The prince led me to his study, his master bedroom on the other side. One of these days, I was going there to snoop around.

While I took in the setting, admiring the pristine room with expensive, tasteful furniture, Killian went to sit behind his mahogany desk carved with runes on its shiny surface. There were also artistic details of a battle dragon on the edges of the desk.

On the other side of the study was a grand sofa set and exotic plants. Two glass shelves pressed against the wall displayed priceless antiques.

The chaos prince propped his feet on his desk—his leather shoes spotless, his hands clasped behind his head, and his storm-blue gaze regarding me. Now he was waiting for me to open my mouth.

I'd dealt with this kind of intimidation technique

enough times to know when to keep my mouth zipped. Silence didn't unnerve me. It wouldn't make me talk and thus give my opponent an advantage.

So, I stayed silent and still, staring back at him, not even bothering to inquire why the fuck he'd summoned me.

A smile slowly ghosted his sensual lips. He needed to learn soon that no pretty man or his charm could make me lose my cool head.

"Don't you have something to say for yourself, Barbie?" he asked, his gaze roving over my uniform. There were wrinkles here and there.

"Pardon, sir? And say what, sir?" I asked passive-aggressively, even though my body heated at his scrutiny. "I don't know why I was summoned before dinner."

Sy moved closer to the surface, peering out at the chaos prince. She longed to reveal herself to him, and I could virtually hear her silent shouting, *Look at me, princeling! Here. I'm Sy.*

"You made a spectacle of yourself today," he drawled, his voice darkly sensual.

"I still don't know what you mean, sir!"

"Didn't you get enough attention on the ice rink? You had to dance like that for the princes of the other houses? Don't you know you're a sacrificial lamb in those fucking wolves' eyes? They're toying with you, only waiting to get bored before they sink their jagged teeth and claws into your tender flesh. Do you hold this dream like every girl that you might be the special one to them, and that they'll realize you're their one true love? They're predators to their fucking bones. They aren't like the harmless mortal boys you used to hang with."

My hackles rose, and dark fire swirled to life in my eyes.

I'd almost gotten over him stripping me in front of thousands of students, and he had the nerve to bring it up again and blame it all on me. He didn't have an ounce of remorse for what he'd done to me. He was no better than the other princes. In fact, he was much worse! He was never going to grovel for the harm he did to me.

Powerful fuckers thought they could do whatever they wanted to whomever they chose!

"Yes, I had enough on the ice rink," I spat. "And guess who the fuck put me in that situation? Shit keeps rolling my way ever since you forced me into the Brides Selection!"

"Would you rather be a vampire's blood slave?"

At least he didn't say blood whore. He might be thinking of it!

"What if I did? You don't get to decide my path, bodice-ripper!"

"Do you understand the real meaning of bodice-ripping?" he asked, arching an eyebrow. I flushed. "When I truly rip your bodice, you'll beg for more."

"Never!" But my body told a different story. All I wanted was for him to rip my clothes off, put his hands on my breasts, then bury his face between my thighs before I let him impale me with his massive cock over and over.

The sexual tension built higher and higher between us, the heat in his eyes scorching me, and I had to squeeze my thighs to ease the ache. He tracked my moves with predatory hunger.

"If you're as smart as you think you are, you shall not flirt with the princes in the future." My temper rose higher at his accusation, my eyes on fire. "They're too dangerous for you to handle."

As if he wasn't dangerous. He was the most dangerous and ruthless of them all!

"The pot calls the kettle black," I murmured under my breath.

"What did you say, Barbie?" he demanded.

"If you hadn't gotten me into the Brides Selection, I wouldn't have to deal with all the shit!" I shouted at him. I didn't care if he struck me. I'd kick him back super hard and give him a taste of my true viciousness! "You tore my clothes off in front of everyone. You greatly humiliated me in front of the entire school! I'll never forgive you, even if you grovel!"

My rage drowned out his, and now he just stared at me, heat brimming in his storm-blue eyes. My fury had turned him on.

"Would you forgive me if I'd ripped your binder off in private?" he purred, his anger gone, in its wake dark amusement and lust glinting in his eyes.

"What?" I glared at him. "No! How could you even say things like that?!"

"Tearing your clothes off is but a small thing," he sighed. "Over half of the bride candidates would kill to get that treatment. Under the circumstances, I had to make a quick statement to counter Ethel's moves by showing everyone who you are in order to get you into my house, then properly enrolled in the academy so you'd stay. The shock effect worked, didn't it, before anyone could sweep you away? You'll just have to live with that, Barbie."

"You put me in a worse danger! Don't think I don't know about the coming Bride Trials! Thanks to you, sir, all the mean coyotes will come after me. They'll try to tear me apart!"

His look darkened, but it didn't stick, as determination surfaced and gleamed in his eyes.

"You'll survive," he said quietly. "You must, Barbie. That's why I'll be training you and getting you into fighting shape."

"No fighting shape can prepare me against a thousand bloodthirsty bride candidates!" I yelled at him, forgetting myself.

"Are you done throwing a tantrum?" He arched an eyebrow, his voice sensual and hoarse at the same time.

Even though I was spitting mad, I shuddered with need, my pussy aching. The sexual tension between us was like a storm brewing, waiting for the first lightning to strike.

I'd be at its mercy.

This was a helpless situation. It was always like that when I was in the chaos prince's proximity. Now that we were alone, who could stop the storm?

Any moment now...

A plan took shape in my head—jumping on Killian while he was off guard, straddling him, and forcing him to surrender. As soon as he gave in, I would tear his pants off with my three-quarter-goddess strength and fuck him aggressively right there on the ground.

Pounding him while giggling—

I blinked, waking from the trance, and shoved Sy down. She'd been manipulating me, fueling my lust. But I couldn't tell which idea was hers and which was my own.

Killian gazed at me, dark fire in his eyes, his heat radiating to me so intensely even from behind his desk that he might pounce on me first. My lips parted, inviting him, then clamped down. My jaw clenched, I shoved down my lust and let my rage surface.

That's better.

"We're done, sir!" I spat. Let him strike me.

"We're far from done, little dagger," he crooned. "You're dying to fight me, even punish me in your head, aren't you? I can see it all in your eyes. And you aren't good at covering your feelings, which are always written all over your pretty face. If you want to come out of the trials in one piece, you need to work on it. Supernaturals are fierce creatures, and they're always hungry and cruel, but they also learned to cover their emotions as children. But you're lacking training and education, obviously, considering your questionable background." He chuckled. "I can smell the smoke and see the fire in your nostrils when you fume like that. You can't tone it down even standing before your superior, who holds your fate in his hand."

"You aren't my superior," I spat once more. "No one is, and no one ever will be."

"Then prove it, little dagger." He hooked a middle finger at me, beckoning me forward. Another insult! "C'mon, I'm giving you a chance to work off your frustration and—"

I lunged at him, faster than a flash. A blink and I had alighted on his very expensive desk, smooth and cool beneath my ass. One leg anchored on the wood, I kicked out with the other toward the chaos prince, only to hit an empty space.

He wasn't behind the desk anymore.

"Where the fuck did you go?" I demanded.

I wheeled on the desk and found him leaning against the back of the enormous ivory leather sofa.

He smirked at me, his muscled forearms folding across his cut chest, his posture relaxed. My gaze darted toward his large, powerful hands. Luna's prediction about the size of a dude's hands determining the size of his cock burned in my head. Omg, Killian had a big cock. But then I'd known about it already, hadn't I? His massive cock had pounded into me relentlessly in that dream walk of his.

But it hadn't been real! I pulled my lips back in a snarl to expel the memory and my throbbing need. I'd only make a fool of myself if I hadn't already. I'd never land a blow on him with my pussy damp with liquid heat.

I charged him again. This time, I didn't dive toward him directly like I had done when he was behind the desk. I needed to be smart about it since he was too damn fast. I would feign the move, so I could spot where he actually went through the corner of my eye, following the blur, then I would pounce on him mercilessly.

I shot to his left, a foot away from him, and I struck.

A hand slapped across my left buttcheck. When I turned with a hiss, Killian had moved away, leaning against his desk, his forearms across his chest again.

He'd fucking spanked me!

My plan had been good. What had gone wrong? It dawned on me that he was faster than me. How could it be possible?

"Now you royally pissed me off, asshole!" I shouted, my face flushing in anger.

"You don't disappoint, Barbie. I'll give you that," he purred, laughter in his eyes. "Your ass was nice and firm and felt delicious when my palm landed on it. But tell me, did I spank the left or the right? I'm sorry that I didn't pay attention. If I spanked the right, I'll have to spank the left next. I don't like things unbalanced. Do you?"

He was fucking toying with me! Hadn't he humiliated me enough ever since I'd had the misfortune of catching his eye?

"You'll regret this, sir!" I hissed.

"Promise?"

I lunged toward him like a lightning strike.

This time, I attacked him from below.

I dropped to the ground and rolled in a blur. I'd practiced the move to perfection to counter predators much bigger than me. I would kick my feet up with my back on the ground and boot his nuts while he was least expecting it.

Let's blue his balls and see if he could still laugh when he wouldn't be able to fuck a goose's tight ass for a week, as Cade had once put it so nicely after I'd kicked Javier in the balls.

I reached Killian in no time, my legs shooting toward his groin. But then, I found my legs being pulled wide apart.

Killian grabbed my shins, lifting me as if I weighed nothing, and pulled me toward him, my groin slamming right into his. My pussy hit his bulge, rock hard and huge. If the fabric hadn't been separating our flesh, his cock would've thrust between my thighs, impaling me brutally.

And deliciously, Sy added excitedly.

My eyes widened in shock, my lips parted, and my breath came in pants.

The prince's eyes grew hooded.

Just as I was about to take advantage of it since a man always thought with his dick, Killian tossed me across the room toward the sofa. Yet he underestimated what I could do. While I was airborne, I twisted my torso in a complex acrobatic move and shot toward his desk. The tip of my boot landed on the edge of the wood, and using the touch point to bounce back, I leapt onto his back before he could wheel toward me, my legs clamping around his waist to prevent him from shaking me off.

His body started to vibrate against me. I blinked in confusion until I realized that he was laughing. He laughed so hard that his hands squeezed my thighs from beneath.

Laughing at me even when I landed on his back, about to do some damage?

He didn't think much of me, did he?

Enraged, I pounded my fists on his upper arms rapidly.

"Good girl," the prince purred, then groaned in wicked delight. "You know I need a good massage, don't you? A lot of stress lately."

His rich, deep voice was so sensual that I felt the front of my pants start to soak through. Part of me hoped that he didn't feel the dampness on his lower back, and the horny, vindictive part of me wanted to rock my hips and smear the wetness all over him.

Sy voted for the latter. So predictable.

I, however, was about to go for the third option. I raised both fists, ready to ram them into his ears. But then, my fists halted in midair. I might want to put him in his place, but it wasn't in me to truly inflict great pain on him.

Sy wouldn't have this bleeding-heart issue. She'd be eager to eat him.

I would never eat Killian! Sy said.

Frustrated that I'd gone soft, I grabbed a handful of Killian's hair to drag his head backward. Still laughing, he spanked me in retaliation.

"Quit it!" I yelled.

A sting of pain and pleasure radiated through me at the spank, and more liquid heat pooled between my thighs. Before I could make a countermove to show him my displeasure, Killian flipped me over and slammed me onto his desk after dealing me another spank.

This had been his plan. He'd left his back open, baiting me to jump on him, just so he could pin me down on the desk.

The fucker got off on humiliating me.

I yelped at the impact and stared up at Killian's laughing eyes. For a full moment, I was dazed by his masculine beauty that no mortal or other immortal could ever compare to.

"*Baby, are you still having the best fucking day of your life?*" he taunted.

The door flew open. Cami, Rock, and Archer charged in, their eyes wide at the scene—I lay on my back on the wood, my eyes spitting fire, my golden curls still bouncing from the landing, and Killian was laughing his ass off with his large hand pressing hard against my stomach, fingers widespread.

Killian turned slowly to look at them, his laughter dropping, his team still darting their stunned and confused glances between their prince and me.

"Shouldn't you knock?" He frowned at them, not happy that they interrupted his sick, twisted fun.

"Your Highness, we thought—" Cami started, then stopped cold, her gaze glued to my hand that had lashed out to grab Killian's wrist and shove it away from my stomach.

The others saw the same thing she did, horror in their eyes, as if they all expected something terrible to happen.

What was going to happen? Bite me!

If Killian was going to make another stupid move, I'd make sure he lost face! My knee bent, ready to jam into his nuts. This time, I wouldn't miss.

The band looked even more shocked when nothing happened and Killian just dropped his hand to his side casually, as if that was the most natural thing to do, as if he hadn't pinned me on his desk.

The band traded a puzzled yet loaded glance before dropping their eyes to pay respect to their boss.

"You thought I couldn't handle a girl?" Killian cut in smoothly, yet his tone held a harsh quality, as if he was trying to hide something from me as well.

"Handle me, sir?" I hissed. I knew I shouldn't hiss like a kitten, but he riled me up!

"We apologize for disrupting you and your *fun*, Your Highness," Cami said. "We heard loud noises, and we just wanted to make sure no thieves snuck in."

Rock and Archer fought not to laugh now that they got over their initial shock. Archer coughed into his fist.

"I was training Barbie and showing her the ropes," Killian said. Sure, why not? By slamming me onto the desk and laughing his ass off! "I need her to survive the coming Bride Trials."

The band traded another cautious, dark glance with one another.

And they'd just confirmed that the Bride Trials were a deadly game, just as Pucker had said.

Shit!

"Next time, do not interrupt us when we're in the middle of training," Killian said. "Now go. Barbie still has a long way to go to get into fighting shape."

"We can train her, Your Highness," Cami offered. "You don't need to concern yourself—" She paused at the prince's sharp look, then sighed. "Actually, cousin, there's another matter that needs your immediate attention."

Killian scowled.

Cami darted a glance at me, then back to her prince.

"What is it, Cami?" Killian asked impatiently. "Go ahead, Barbie here isn't going to derail anything, despite others' low opinions of her."

My hackles rose again.

Cami took a deep breath before she spoke. "The king summoned you to the court. He wants you to depart right away. Queen Lilith, your betrothed, has left the Underworld. She'd love to see you at the court tonight, Your Highness."

Killian stilled, his face darkening, even though he tried to keep a blank mask on.

The air in the room shifted; the temperature dropped several degrees, and I had no idea if it was the prince or me. If it was me who did it, I probably sucked a drop of magic from everyone when a fit of rage shot through me at the idea of Killian and his fiancée hooking up soon.

Something coiled in me, like a rattlesnake wanting to strike at anyone who got in my way, especially the queen of great beauty. Sy snarled, backing me up, sharpening her claws.

I needed to get out of here before I lost my shit and put everyone and myself in danger, even though I wanted to hear more of Killian's plans regarding meeting his betrothed.

"Will you excuse me, sir?" I demanded indignantly. "I was forced into an unexpected, long, and tough training session on an empty stomach. The last thing you want is for me to pass out due to low blood sugar, and then you'll blame me for the inconvenience of having to carry me back to my room. Now I gotta catch dinner before everything is gone!"

Just like that, I broke the spell in the room, and everyone appeared relieved.

"Always worry about your next meal, don't you, Barbie?" Killian said.

Rich boys had no idea how much hunger could hurt!

"You should know that you'll never go hungry in my house," he said.

"Yeah? Prince Louis said the same thing before he jumped me to drink my blood," I said.

Cami frowned. "He did?"

Killian's face hardened. "Louis will never get his hands on you again!"

The prince offered a hand to pull me up, but I ignored it and rolled off the desk, forgetting the chair on the other side. Before I tumbled onto the armchair and possibly bruised myself, Killian caught me.

His arm snaked around my middle, lifted me, and parked me on my feet by the desk.

My face flushed. "I got this! I wasn't going to fall."

Rock chuckled. "You can never fool His Highness, Barbie, even though you fooled everyone else."

"From now on, when I'm not training Barbie, the three of you will take over," Killian said. "She'll find many excuses not to show up or make you run around in circles. You'll have to stay vigilant when it comes to Barbie."

I gave them a baleful look before shooting out of the room. I was so distracted and distraught—my chest aching at Killian going to see his woman, my pussy throbbing in need, unfulfilled, and my stomach twisting with hunger and anxiety—that I didn't see the door swing back at me.

Killian reached me like a flash before I got hit, holding the door open for me.

"I was just about to warn you not to let the door hit you in the face on your way out," Killian chuckled.

Then everyone was laughing at my expense.

I was out of the door like a bat escaping hell, especially when I neared the Queen's Suite.

"Make sure Barbie gets her food, Rock." Killian's voice overlapped the eerie voices that whispered my name from behind the red door, chasing me down the stairs.

21

Barbie

"Barbie!" Pucker bellowed in my ear.

"Not again!" I released my hands from hugging my chest for protection during sleep and tossed the spare pillow at the ghost guardian while burrowing further into the pillow beneath my face.

Ghosts didn't understand that the living needed shut-eye time.

"You gotta wake up, Barbie!" Pucker urged.

He hung out in my room a lot more often now, haunting me and taking his new role as my familiar seriously. He'd reported back that there was no Shrieker activity so far, which was good news. Giving away some of my energy to get him out of the house to patrol for me turned out to be a decent investment.

"Why?" I whined. "You know I didn't sleep well last night."

"You never sleep well at night, so it can't be used as an excuse," he said. "Despite being a three-quarter goddess, you're afraid of the dark like a little girl!"

"Shush!" I hushed him sternly, but I was grateful that he never bugged me about who my parents were. He mused about it and kept it to himself. Not all old men were terrible and insufferable. Pucker hadn't lost all his common sense.

"No one can hear us. No one is around in the suite! Your roomie Cami accompanied Prince Killian to the court to see his betrothed, remember?"

That instantly put me in a bad mood. It'd been a day since Killian left! I doubted he'd want to come back. Who knew what he'd been doing with Queen Lilith? Like I gave a damn! But then my stomach soured even before I had breakfast.

"Don't pout, Barbie!" Pucker said cheerfully. "You're getting a hot date too! Prince Rowan is coming. And if you manage to say the right things, you might even get laid!"

I sat up, blinking my sleepy eyes open, and saw my ghost familiar rub his hands excitedly.

"Why is he coming?" I scowled.

"Your date with Prince Rowan is today!" he said. "I rushed here to inform you before he rings the bell. You don't want to be seen not ready when he gets here. Insulting an heir never ends well."

It came back to me then that I'd picked Rowan as my first date when the princes set out to punish me. I hadn't expected the fae prince to be serious and even follow up. I'd forgotten about it as soon as Killian had put a stop to me dancing on the heirs' table in Jubilee Haven.

"Tell him to cancel it," I said, throwing myself back to the bed and burrowing my face into the pillow. "A girl needs her beauty sleep."

Two strong hands yanked me up into a sitting potion. Pucker could go solid now if he chose to, as my familiar. I blamed myself for creating a pest whenever he inconvenienced me, like now.

"You can sleep as long as you want after your date with Prince Rowan!" Pucker said.

"Then I won't have time to do laundry."

"Unbelievable," he said, shaking his head in disgust.

"I know. Laundry isn't going to do itself. I'm running out of school uniforms to wear."

"You're incorrigible," he sighed exasperatedly. "How can anything be more important than going on a hot date with a prince? Other bride candidates would weep with joy for such an honor—"

"It's not an honor," I protested. "The prince punished me for—"

"—and spend three hours just doing their hair!"

At the mention of hair, I ran my fingers through my messy, soft curls, shaking them a little and letting them bounce. "There, done!"

Pucker raised a finger at me sternly. "Get up and go clean up quickly and nicely. One of us has to be the responsible one."

"Talk about being responsible? You're a poltergeist and an identity thief!"

"And I was a gay!" he yelled at me. "I did all the pranks because I was bored out of my wits, but that was before I met you! You can't fault me for wanting to be a better man. I now have something to live for, through you!"

Jesus!

He yanked me to my feet and shoved me into the bathroom.

"Don't make me take a shower for you!" he half-snarled.

"I don't mind taking one for the team, but sometimes it's just too much! I can't do everything by myself. I won't!"

I sighed as I freshened up quickly. When I came out of the bathroom, Pucker had already picked out a dress for me and laid it on the bed.

It was a gorgeous pink gown with a neckline so low that my tits would have nowhere to hide.

"Where did you get the dress?" I asked.

"Who cares where I got it," he said. "The only thing that's important is that I obtained it for you."

"Tell me!"

"From Cami's wardrobe," he said with a shrug. "She won't know it's missing until it's too late. Anyway, she has hundreds of gowns. Now, put it on," he urged, fondling the silky material in admiration. "It's screaming your name since it fits you better than it does Cami. I bet when Rowan sees you in it, he'll have a hard-on right away, so bad that he can't beat it back. And that's what we want to see."

"I don't want to see that!" I said. "Seeing the vamps fuck around was more than enough. No way am I going to put myself in that gown, even if it's mine. Don't you know the dating rules have been updated? It's no longer about dressing to kill, and you don't want to appear too eager since you'll come off as desperate, which is a sure way to turn off your date. The current trend is to dress down."

"That stupid rule only prevails in the mortal world." He gave me side-eye. "Mortals have a short lifespan, so trends change fast. We're immortals. We stick to tradition."

"You aren't an immortal," I pointed out. "You're dead." Then over his crestfallen look, I sighed. "I'll let you live through me then. Just fetch me a simple shirt and a pair of pants. Hopefully, we can find a clean pair of jeans."

"You don't want to look like a bum, Barbie!" He raised

his voice again, offended at my taste, a vein throbbing on his temple. "That's the line I won't cross. Even though I might not be among the living, I still have standards! And you're forbidden to wear pants unless you're training, remember?"

He phased into my closet and brought out a dress. "Wear this one then," he said. "This is the only compromise I'm willing to make!"

It was a flowery blue sundress, and I liked it.

Pucker then dragged out a pair of dress boots that Cami gave me yesterday. She'd worn them only once and then she no longer wanted them. She was size seven and I was six. But whatever. It was better to have a size or two bigger than a size or two smaller. At least I didn't need to bend my toes when walking.

"I'm heading out to see where Prince Rowan is now," he said. "We'll make this date perfect!"

I narrowed my eyes before he phased out of the window. "You act like it's your date."

"It will be." He beamed. "I'm going with you."

My lips twisted into a wince.

"I'm your chaperone, Barbie. As your familiar, I can go wherever you go even out of the school grounds."

"I don't want you to tag along, Pucker. It'll be too weird."

"It won't be weird," he said. "I'll just observe and give you tips in a timely matter."

"I don't need tips from a d-dude!" I swallowed the word "dead," not wanting to make him all sad again. For a ghost who had been dead for so long, he was sensitive.

"C'mon, Barbie! I haven't had much going on for two centuries confined in this house. Don't you even have a single sympathetic bone?"

We don't, Sy said firmly. *Send him away.*

Maybe it wouldn't be too bad to let Pucker tag along. If

the date went terribly wrong, Pucker could scream bloody murder at least.

You have me, Sy snapped. *I'm the one who's always watching your six! You don't need anyone else.*

She'd been mostly quiet ever since she'd learned about my date with Rowan, and she hadn't been thrilled that I'd bonded a familiar.

"THERE SHE IS! BARBIE! BARBIE!" Rowan shouted as soon as he caught sight of me, fighting to extract himself from the bride candidates who surrounded him, with Medea in the lead, trying to engage him in conversation.

The fae prince wanted me to rescue him?

Sy seethed, wanting to come out and claw at every female close to her fuck buddy.

"Yeah, sir?" I asked, standing atop the marble stairs outside the door of the violet building of House of Chaos, not willing to move any closer to the she-coyotes in heat.

"We have a date!" he shouted again. "I could've sent for you, but I wanted to be a gentleman, so I came to pick you up in person. The leyline is close to Killian's house anyway."

Now he didn't think it was a good idea to be a gentleman coming in person, did he? The fae prince made himself a convenient target, especially since he hadn't even brought his entourage and guards. He'd let the romantic concept get into his head, and now he was reaping the reward of every candidate wanting a piece of his ass.

Medea snapped her head toward me, her hair turning to snakes, hissing at me, as if she thought her strong ill will could make me back out of the hot date.

I smiled sweetly and waved at Rowan, calling from a safe distance, "Lead the way, high sir. I'll follow you from here."

It was best to play it safe, as I didn't want the candidates to tear me apart.

Rowan gave me a disappointed look, then glanced at the aggressive candidates around him and nodded to Medea. "Princess, pardon me. I have a date," he said and shoved through the mob like an arrow wading through murky water.

Silas was a brute, Louis was merciless and had no care for his reputation, and Killian was feared by all. But Rowan appeared the most reserved among the princes and preferred to show his gentlemanly side in front of the ladies, and that was what got him into this situation.

Just look at what he was wearing—a white tunic of the finest material that befitted a fae prince. He dressed like a scholar, hiding his savage side that he probably only showed to Sy. Compared to Sy, who was all fangs and claws, I definitely looked a lot more delicate and meeker, but the handsome prince didn't need to know that I was meaner than Sy when I wanted to be.

Rowan had also seen how I'd been subdued by Killian on the ice in front of thousands, and I'd danced for the princes as they'd demanded. Making me go on a date with the princes one by one was a game to them. I wasn't foolish enough to believe that they actually wanted to date me when they hadn't even officially asked out the most elite candidates, like Medea, America, Cami, and Dixie among other royals and nobles.

All right, the princes were playing a dangerous game; I just didn't know what kind of game they were playing, but I'd make sure not to get burned first.

While Rowan looked all gentleman, he was only playing

a part, the intro. I'd play along, as it took two to tango, and I knew all the steps.

First, I was going to test if the powerful fae prince could see Pucker. So far, he hadn't spared a glance at the ghost guardian, who stood beside me, rubbing his hands excitedly like a kid about to get his candies and giving Rowan an appreciative slow-burn onceover.

No one had reacted to my familiar. No one could see ghosts except me.

The fae prince waded toward me, his elbows shoving away grabbing hands that needed some man-love.

As soon as he cleared a path, it sealed as the candidates behind the frontline rushed toward him, wanting his taut ass as well. The members of the House of Chaos were putting their reputation of rousing chaos into practice. A couple of chicks gripped the handsome fae's butt to test its firmness and let out satisfied sighs. Rowan turned to single out the offenders with a scowl on his face.

Even guys didn't appreciate having their butts grabbed without being asked.

"Ladies, ladies!" the fae prince chided.

"Your Highness, we'd like to invite you to..." the candidates insisted and wouldn't take no for an answer now that they'd gotten Rowan.

Now's your time to shine, Pucker. I let out a low chuckle. *Give the prince a hand since we don't want to stand here the whole day just waiting for him to get to us.*

Pucker waved his phantom wand as if conducting a symphony. A gust of violent wind carrying leaves and dirt swept over the horny crowd, followed by a wave of hail. The guardian had channeled my energy to revive his magic. His element was ice and wind.

Very nice. Very dramatic.

Pucker looked mightily pleased with himself as he watched the candidates scatter. Rowan seized the opportunity to charge through the cleared path while putting up a shield around himself to stay dry under the assault of Pucker's hail. He didn't extend his shield to any of the ladies, including Princess Medea.

So much for being a gentleman.

In the wake of the hail, Medea and her minions were all soaking wet even though they'd tried to shield themselves. None of them was as powerful as the fae prince, so they were unable to fend off a ghost's magic that channeled the power of a demigoddess. Too bad Pucker wasn't a fire mage.

The bride wannabes turned to glare at me. I smirked, spreading my arms to show them that it wasn't me. It was common knowledge that I could only neutralize magic as an Echo and I was still training.

It didn't matter though. Tomorrow there would be hell for me to pay, since Medea and her gang would make sure of it.

Pucker flashed Rowan a big grin, ready to receive thanks, but the fae prince only saw me, flashing me a wide smile and showing his white teeth, fangs hidden.

"Shall we get on with our date, Barbie, and not waste the rest of the day?" he asked.

"Certainly, sir, after you." I smiled back.

Pucker sighed happily and floated to Rowan's other side. I wondered how Rowan would react if he knew a ghost was tagging along as the third wheel. Pucker needed a good time to compensate for the years he'd been confined to the House of Chaos. And I'd put in some effort in making this date a success and let my ghost familiar feel the joy of life.

That was the least I could do.

22

Barbie

"So, Barbie, did you date a lot?" Rowan asked as we trekked through the valley that bordered the academy grounds.

"Oh yeah!" I lied without a blink. At least, Sy fucked a lot, and that should count.

The fae prince screwed a lot too. All the princes did, except for Killian. Well, the chaos prince fucked a lot, according to his reputation, before he got himself in a pickle by getting engaged. Was he fucking his betrothed right now?

I shoved the taste of bile and rage and smoke down my throat and fixed my attention on the fae prince.

Sy hadn't been her usual self since Rowan had shown up. All of a sudden, she was absent from making lewd comments about this sugar man or riding his big cock. But she was paying proper attention.

"Tell me about your dates," the prince said.

"What dates?"

"Your past dates."

"Why do you want to know?"

He smiled. "I want to learn what you like and dislike."

A privileged prince cared about what a female liked? Or did he just want to use what he learned against me?

"For a start, you can feed me," I offered.

He laughed. "That's been arranged. There'll be hors d'oeuvres, freshly made."

"Do you have a menu that I can review? I'd like to have some input, if you don't mind."

"You don't need a menu, Barbie. You just need to bring your mouth. You can be the critic after you taste them."

My eyes sparkled. "Then we should get there faster, sir. Race you?"

I looked over my shoulder at the ivory tower in the distance. We weren't on the academy grounds anymore. Half of the valley ahead of us was concealed in the mist. I had never come to this part of the region, as I hadn't had a chance to venture out of the school except for the south side, where the Veil was.

Rowan shook his head, chortling. "What kind of date would I be if I didn't provide suitable transportation for a lady?"

He whistled sharply, and a large pumpkin carriage driven by two stallions appeared out of the mist, heading toward us.

I blinked. "This is wicked!"

Sy, your fuck buddy got us a pumpkin carriage, like in a fairytale! I exclaimed.

Whatever, Sy said passive-aggressively.

Sy had been moody. Then it clicked why she wasn't thrilled. She was taken with Rowan, yet it hadn't seemed to cross his mind to ask her out. He'd only been fucking her. But wasn't that what Sy wanted? In the past, she'd only cared about sexual feeding.

"What is this place?" I asked, not wanting to deal with Sy's mood when I had intel to gather.

"A leyline leads to various destinations," Rowan said. "Only the royals of five kingdoms are allowed to travel through it."

I held my breath. "What various destinations?"

"You don't need to be concerned with that," he said dismissively, obviously not wanting to reveal more to someone who wasn't included in the big boys' club.

The stallions paused in front of us.

Rowan helped me into the carriage like a gentleman before he ducked in and settled himself on the bench beside me. Pucker phased in, but there wasn't enough space, so he was about to sit on my lap. I shoved away his ghost form, a bit too forcefully, and Rowan snapped his attention to my movement.

"I push my hand up a lot when I'm impressed," I said.

He smiled. "I aim to impress."

Pucker offered me an affronted look, phased out, and parked his ass on the back of a stallion. The animal bucked and neighed.

"Where are we going, sir?" I inquired, dragging Rowan's attention to me.

I should've asked about our destination earlier, but I was overwhelmed. This was my first date ever, though I wasn't dumb enough to believe Rowan held noble intentions, despite all the fancy designs and the promise of good food.

I wouldn't let my guard down though, and I had Sy and Pucker to watch my back.

"To my fae realm," he said. "I presume that you've never seen the realm outside Shades Academy?"

"No, sir," I said. "But I plan to, sir."

There were five houses in Mist of Cinder—House of Vampires, House of Shifters, House of Mages, House of Fae, and House of Chaos. Each house was ruled by a king. There was also an unclaimed region called CrimsonTide, where the most dangerous outlaws, rebels, rogues, and the exiles dwelled.

If things didn't work out for me, I'd venture into the neutral zone. I could live with criminals. I doubted they'd be more cutthroat than the bride candidates.

"It'll be my pleasure to be the first one to show you around," Rowan offered.

My eyes went wide as the scene transformed to starlit desert, then in a blink, we were out of the mist.

"Almost there," Rowan said, smiling.

The carriage stopped in front of a wooden bridge far above a clear lake, a school of goldfish leaping above the surface before diving in again. At the end of the bridge, a trail with stone stairs led to a three-story glass house atop a green hill.

"Welcome to my villa in the fae realm," Rowan said, climbing out of the pumpkin carriage and offering me a hand.

"Shit, it's beautiful!" I sucked in a breath at the wonderous sight.

Rowan smiled again at my awe, pleased.

We strolled across the bridge. Pucker jumped off the stallion and bounced off behind us. The horse looked relieved that the ghost was gone.

We climbed the broad stone stairs. Rowan let me soak in the beauty of the rare blossoms and fairy-like trees that I hadn't seen anywhere else. The air smelled like wine, blooms, and spring rain. It was so pure that I inhaled deeply and gratefully.

We entered the grand house on the green hill. Rowan brought me to the top floor. I looked around; all three sides were thick glass windows. The prince opened the French door and led me onto the terrace that overlooked the lake, ancient trees, and a splash of rare flowers over the flourishing shrubs on the other side.

Designer outdoor chairs were arranged artfully on the spacious terrace. On a handcrafted wooden table rested a pot of steaming tea with two delicate teacups. Everything here was elegant, expensive, yet not flashy.

The fae prince was treating me like a lady, so I restrained myself from darting forward to snatch an appetizer. I recognized cheese soufflés, tarts, and cream puffs among other treats. They were all my favorites!

"Enjoy, Barbie." Rowan nodded with a smile, seeing the glint in my eyes.

I beamed. "Thank you, sir. You're a better sir than the other sirs!"

I took the seat designated for me while the prince took the other across from me. From our table, we could both eat, enjoy the beautiful view, and gaze at each other.

Rowan poured tea for me. I thanked him again, taking a cream puff in a hurry and biting into it. The cream was so rich and fresh that I nearly moaned.

"The butler will bring in Coquilles Saint-Jacques, Escargots à la Bourguignonne, and more hors d'oeuvres," Rowan informed me.

I gave him a thumbs-up while I went for a soufflé.

Coquilles Saint-Jacques and Escargots à la Bourguignonne are delicacies, Pucker said telepathically. He'd made himself at home while inspecting and sniffing at the appetizers. *They go mighty well with a glass of bubbling wine. What I wouldn't kill to be able to taste them again, but I never can, even after channeling your goddess essence and going solid for a few minutes. I'm still and always will be a dead man!*

I nibbled my bites. *It sucks, man, but could you refrain from whining while I eat? I don't want to enjoy the delicious hors d'oeuvres and feel sorry for you at the same time.*

It'd been a bad idea to let him tag along.

"How do you like the soufflé?" Rowan asked.

He hadn't touched any of the appetizers but only drank his tea, which made me appreciate him more.

"You know I like them!" I exclaimed. "Do you have a five-star French chef here? Prince Louis's chefs aren't very good, since the vampires don't eat much solid food, so the kitchen staff, who are snobs, don't have the proper motivation to cook better for the human servants. They also complained about me a lot. Louis probably got them cheap and didn't offer them any health insurance. He did the same to me. Prince Silas's cooks aren't impressive either. They were all Americans, Texans, and cowboys. Their specialty is barbeque ribs since shifters are all about meat. They have no tastebuds for delicacies."

"I'd love to hear more of your food critiques," Rowan said. "But I have a couple of questions for you first."

My chewing slowed as I kept my face blank. My alarm shot up, reminding me to tread carefully. No matter how nice the prince heirs pretended to be now and then, they were predators in their bones.

Pucker straightened up too, leaning against the rail and staring at the fae prince with rapt attention.

"I see that you have some talents," Rowan stated.

I would play dumb until I couldn't. "What talent, sir?"

"You know exactly what I'm talking about," he chided lightly.

"I don't know what you're talking about, sir. I'm not the sharpest tool in the shed. I'm just a simple girl who has a healthy appetite."

"Could've fooled me," he said drily, "if everyone had still believed you were but a simple *servant boy*."

"That wasn't by choice, sir," I said. "Prince Louis assigned me the role of a squire, and it wasn't a servant's place to correct a master vampire. Sir Louis could snap my neck with his bare hands!"

"Could he?" Rowan studied me. "Louis did mention that you could always come up with clever excuses. Well, I didn't bring you here to give you a hard time. I want you to have a good time, Barbie. But I also think you can help me out. I've been looking for someone, a fae girl."

Instantly, I knew whom he'd been looking for. He thought he could fish it out of me. There was no doubt that he felt my connection to Sy, but he couldn't pin it down, and that didn't sit well with him.

I evened out my breathing to calm my wild heartbeat. I could never let him find out my double identity.

I blinked again. "A missing person, you say?"

He winced. "Kind of. Last time, I was tracking her, and I thought she ran into Underhill. You were bathing at that time when Killian and I entered the dark forest. You said you caught a glimpse of her."

Sy stirred, peering at the fae prince with lust and longing. If I let her, she'd shout at him, "Here I am, Houston! Fuck me!"

I frowned. "I don't recall much of that night."

"Somehow, you remind me of her," Rowan drawled with an undertone of suspicion.

"Why?" I blinked hard as if trying to focus on remembering. "I was a little sleepy when you and Sir Killian charged in, startling me, and then I was busy covering my b-boobs, you know. I might've caught a glimpse of a fae chick running and vanishing—wild, tall, toned, with silver hair, right?" I patted my forearm to show him that I didn't possess those taut muscles. "If anything, I'd say that chick whom you're looking for and I are opposites."

"It's your scent," Rowan said. "You have a similar scent to her, yet somehow different. Her scent is darker and spicier, and yours is like the open sky, with complexities that no one can name since it's constantly shifting. I've never scented anything like you or her."

My heart skipped a beat, and Sy moved to the front seat, utterly intrigued. Rowan inhaled again, and I shoved her down with brutal force and an inward snarl. She snarled right back.

"I apologize if I smell bad, sir," I said. "That wasn't my intention, especially on an awesome date like this. There isn't any deodorant in this realm. Oh, Dove deodorant was on sale, last I heard. Basically, they knocked a dollar off!" I shook my head in dismay that I couldn't get my hands on the discounted product. "And I didn't get to take a shower in the morning when you arrived, but it wasn't my fault. There's been a hot water issue in the House of Chaos. I bet that Princess Medea and her bootlickers used it all. If you can mention it to Sir Killian casually during one of your chitchats, good sir, I'll be in your debt."

He stared at me as if I was utterly ridiculous.

"I don't follow you, Barbie," he said. "What I want to know is—"

Just then, the door banged open, and obviously, someone strutted toward us with a cocky gait, as if he owned this place. But it couldn't be. Rowan owned this glass house.

"Saul, is that you?" Rowan called. "I didn't ring for you to bring the next appetizer! I'm in the middle of a conversation with my date, and we shall not be disrupted!"

Saul must be his butler.

Rowan and I turned toward the French door at the same time, annoyance on his handsome face that promised chastisement. As I said, none of the princes would be nice for too long. As soon as things didn't go their way, they pounced.

A giant of a man with the face of a golden god came into view, his storm-blue eyes sparkling with wicked delight, darting between Rowan and me, his sensual lips tugging up in a mischievous grin. His face brightened instantly at the sight of me.

My heart missed a beat, then pumped so hard that it hurt. Joy filled me.

But wasn't he supposed to stay longer in the court of the Chaos Kingdom to entertain his lady, Queen Lilith? But in all honesty, I was glad he was here. I'd missed him, though I'd never admit it to myself.

His sleeves were rolled up to reveal his muscled forearms, his designer gray shirt stretching across his cut chest. His slacks hugged his strong legs. His every line was powerful.

Sexiness rolled off him. This male was so carnal that he was definitely built to fuck. And just like that, the air was sucked out of my lungs at his presence.

Killian carried a beautiful plate, styled with hand-painted swirls and trailing leaves. My gaze snagged on the creamy round of brie with pesto on top of it.

Rowan stared at the prince of the House of Chaos as the uninvited guest flashed perfect white teeth in a grin. It didn't work on the fae prince though, since he growled, not amused at all.

"What the devil—" Rowan's shout disturbed the electrified air current flowing between Killian and me.

The moment Killian had appeared and locked gazes with me, everything seemed to swirl to life between us. Now that the spell was broken, I quenched the glint of glee in my eyes and put on a scowl for show, trying to be a united front with Rowan. I was his guest, after all.

"Relax, man. It's just me. Not the devil." Killian flashed another easy, charming smile.

Rowan appeared uncharmed and unmoved as he narrowed his eyes at Killian.

"Brie with pesto! How delightful," the chaos heir said, making a show of inhaling. "Fresh herbs! Hand-picked and grown in the fae realm. The anchoïade dip has a nice balance of olive oil, vinegar, and anchovies, but it needs more garlic. I guess you don't want to smell strong garlic in your mouth and ruin the perfect date, Rowan? Don't worry. A bottle of aged wine will do the trick and cover any smell. I sent your butler to your wine chamber to fetch us an excellent wine. I told him that I prefer the 1666 vintage."

23

Barbie

Rowan had a sour look on his face, as if he'd bitten into the sourest lemon.

"I don't remember inviting you, Killian!" he said, tossing his signature politeness out of the window, clearly done with playing the gentleman.

Killian winked at me and turned to frown at Rowan.

"You didn't?" the chaos prince asked, his brows furrowed. "That's rude."

"How did you get here?!" Rowan didn't tone down his aggressiveness.

"By horse," Killian admitted. "You know I'm fond of horses, but I don't have a fancy transport like yours. It takes time to enchant a pumpkin carriage. I parked Jigsaw, my stallion, right beside your pumpkin. Hope that's okay. Hard to find a good parking space here."

"How did you even find out I took Barbie here?" Rowan demanded. "I didn't tell that many people!"

"Too many questions, Rowan." Killian placed the plate of brie with pesto on the table and pulled a chair up to join us. "You don't want to bore your date."

"You know this is my date with Barbie, right?" Rowan half-snarled.

"Is it?" Killian looked confused before letting out a sigh. "Fine. Pretend I'm not here."

For a second, his gaze darted to Pucker, as if he could see exactly where the guardian was—leaning against the railing, enjoying the view, and listening to our conversation with a judgmental look on his ghost face. Killian's gaze lingered a moment too long before he turned to look at me, his face unreadable.

I dipped my gaze to the table and reached for the brie with too much interest.

Get out of here, Pucker, I urged silently.

Pucker took off right away, fading into a drift of cloud hovering over the water far beneath. And then he was gone from the scene. He didn't want the chaos prince to find out anything about him and our deal either.

One bite of the brie and I tried not to moan. The chaos prince watched me as if he wanted me as his appetizer.

"This is a date for two, not for three!" Rowan grated, looking between me and Killian. "I hate to be rude, but you must leave, Killian!"

"That's a dick move, Rowan," Killian said. "You're never a dick, unlike Silas. It took me a lot of effort just to get here."

"You should never have come here to crash my date in the first place!" Rowan said. "Will you have respect for others for once in your life?"

"You know I respect you more than I respect any others, probably except for Cade," Killian said. "That's why I also took the liberty and invited the rest of the heirs on your behalf. This will be a great opportunity for all of us to get together since it's a shame we don't see each other often anymore. They're all excited and will arrive soon. They can't wait to see you."

"I see them often on the campus!" Rowan said. "They can see me again tomorrow!"

"But why wait? They miss you already."

"Unbelievable," Rowan murmured. He was giving up on the fight.

"I came a bit earlier to scout and smooth things out," Killian confessed. "Also, I need to make sure Barbie isn't taken advantage of."

"Are you for real?!" Rowan lost his temper again.

Killian nodded solemnly.

"Taking advantage of her?" Rowan blurted. "I fucked so many bride wannabes in your house before, and you never even raised a fucking eyebrow!"

I hissed. Actually, Sy hissed through my lips. I clamped my mouth shut to prevent her from making another noise to expose us.

Rowan snapped his head to me, a little startled. He obviously recognized Sy's hiss.

Double fuck!

"I see my error now," Killian said ruefully. "That's gotta change. Starting now and starting with Barbie, I'll have to protect every gullible girl in my house. No one should screw around anymore, unless mutual consent is written on paper for me to review first."

My eyes widened. "There'll be a lot of paperwork then."

"That's the burden I'm willing to carry," Killian said. "I

must protect those naïve girls when they can't protect themselves."

"Naïve? They all have fucking claws and fangs!" Rowan retorted. He'd had his taut ass grabbed by those chicks today outside the House of Chaos. He turned to me with a regretful look on his curvy lips. "I apologize for cursing in front of a lady. I was just trying to point out how absurd and outrageous it is for the heir of the House of Chaos to play chaperone and act like a control freak this time when he never cared who was fucking whom before. And he has no fucking business coming here!"

"I get your point, man," Killian said, drinking from *my* teacup and nodding his thanks at me. I pulled my plate closer to myself in case he went for my bites as well. "But you can't blame me for being suspicious since you've never brought anyone here before. Why Barbie? Why couldn't you have a date on the academy grounds? What's your hidden agenda, Rowan? What's your true intention toward Barbie?"

"Do you hear how crazy you sound, Killian?" Rowan growled. "I'm having a hot date. I have the right to take my date wherever I want! Living on the campus is like living in a glass fishbowl; even the movements of my eye twitching will be recorded!"

If he thought that Sy wouldn't get wind of our date if he whisked me away to his remote haunt, he'd be in for a big, nasty surprise. Sy was hitching a ride wherever I went. As for the fae prince's intentions that Killian had demanded to know, I wasn't worried about his intentions toward me but his intentions toward Sy. The fae had brought me here to find out about her. It'd be a disaster if the two ever got attached.

I shook my head in dismay. Yeah, they'd shared two good

fucks, but it couldn't be so good that Sy would risk everything.

More than two fucks! Sy corrected me. *We fucked multiple times outside Underhill, fiercely then tenderly, then fiercely again.*

"I keep wondering why you're acting out of character this time!" Killian snapped. "Barbie is new to this game and thus the most vulnerable member of my house. Who else will protect her interests, especially when we all know your reputation of luring unaware females?" He gestured at the poetic sight of clouds floating through the blossoms, the crystal lake flowing serenely beneath the bridge, and mist surrounding us for mysterious effect. "Look at the fabulous views that are set to seduce an inexperienced girl. That's stage one." He waved a hand at the table. "The delicacies? Second stage. Women buy into all this romantic bullshit. It dazes them. I doubt Barbie will be immune either."

"Unfuckingbelievable!" Rowan shook his head in disgust. "And you haven't counted the fairytale pumpkin carriage ride, asshole!"

"Wait a second!" I shouted, glaring at Killian. I usually didn't like talking when eating. I wanted to enjoy my food in pure bliss. But I'd had enough. "I'm not dazed. I'm not naïve or gullible! I'm a chick with my own mind. And I'm not going to sleep with anyone after just one drink!"

I wasn't as dumb as Sy. She didn't even ask for a drink first. Sy bared her fangs at my criticism.

"I like how you think, little dagger," Killian purred. "But I suggest not jumping into anyone's bed even after more than one drink."

He was messing with me, getting my blood racing and my core heated. He might just palm my pussy under the table since that was the image he put in my head with a sensual purr. My body responded pathetically to his look, his voice, his heat, and his scent. I had to put my shield up to cover my scent of arousal and try hard not to squeeze my thighs together.

From across the table, he inhaled subtly, and I cursed him silently. I was only thankful and relieved that Rowan seemed to be oblivious to the tension between Killian and me, as upset as he was. I sympathized with both of us that the date was going downhill.

Before the fae prince could collect himself and salvage our date, a rush of footfalls sounded on the stairs, accompanied by laughter and banter. The other princes had arrived.

Rowan clenched his teeth. "Great! Just great! It can't get any better!"

Killian grinned at him. "I agree. This date is a blast, but you might want to cut short the party after a while and be firm about it, or they'll never leave."

"Wow, look at the view!" Cade poked his head out after opening the French door just wide enough for him to squeeze in, so Silas and Louis would have to put in their own labor to widen the gap for themselves. The heirs always tried their best to undermine their rivals instead of lifting a finger to help each other.

The mage prince stepped onto the terrace and grinned at me. "Hiya Barbie. Lo, Rowan, good man!"

Louis slid the door open wider and followed Cade. His hungry gaze landed on me right away. I knew that he wouldn't have a chance to sink his fangs into my neck with everyone around, but I still shivered at his dark intention.

He'd lost some weight. I bet it had to do with longing for my blood but being unable to get it.

"Barbie, good to see you," he said with fake cheer. "How's your date? Did Rowan treat you right? I always treat my date like she's the queen."

"Your mother is the queen!" Killian narrowed his eyes on Louis as if he were a scorpion. They were usually on friendly terms since they had a common foe in the shifter prince.

Silas joined us last, training his alpha stare on me and aiming to put me under his authority before he gave Killian a hostile glance.

"Thank you for the invite, bro." Silas nodded at Rowan. "Cade told me all about it since the heir of the House of Chaos forgot to mention it. As usual, he tried to exclude me, but here I am."

"That's unfortunate," Killian said. "But I don't believe that I have any obligations to include you in anything."

"Dudes!" Cade yelled, signaling a timeout. "Let's just enjoy the bash Rowan went to the trouble of throwing for us. It's not often that all of us can get together these days."

"For a start, it's not a bash," Rowan grated. "It's my date, and I didn't invite any of you! Killian got all of you here so he could crash my date. And thank you all for joining him to ruin it!"

"You don't mean that, man," Cade said with a charming smile. "You're the uncontested gentleman among us and the most gracious host!"

"Don't bullshit me, mage," Rowan said. "I meant exactly what I said! I won't have you taking advantage of my good nature. I hate to say this, but I have to cut this gathering short!"

"Why?" Louis asked. "We just got here! We haven't had any refreshments yet!"

At the mention of snacks, the vamp prince darted his hungry gaze at me again. I pulled my chair a few more inches away from him, as if that would help.

"Saul! Bring all the goodies!" Cade yelled. He knew

Rowan's butler by name, so he had obviously been here before. "We got six people here."

"Rowan has a 1666 in the wine cellar," Killian informed him with a grin. "I told Saul to bring it."

"Saul, good man!" Cade barked again. "Where's the 1666?"

I wanted to know what was so special about 1666, but I didn't want to sound ignorant and unsophisticated in front of everyone, so I bit my tongue.

"Coming! Coming! Highnesses," Saul answered. A second later, he pushed in a trolley with a variety of desserts on beautiful plates and a bottle of nicely wrapped wine in an ice bucket.

Rowan eyed the dessert apathetically, not eager to please anyone.

Saul bowed and laid the snacks, desserts, and wine on the table. He also brought plates and wine glasses for the heirs.

I hurried to drag several desserts onto my plate to secure them as the princes descended on the hors d'oeuvres like a pack of hungry wolves. Killian piled his plate high then pushed it to my side. Rowan gave him side-eye.

"It's a tough date," Killian said. "You'll need all the energy for this, Barbie."

Rowan shook his head. He'd given up battling the chaos prince, probably knowing from experience that he wouldn't win.

I wasn't going to reject food, so I dug into the plate offered by Killian first in case he wanted to take it back. I also beamed at him, knowing that this type of smile, unlike Sy's savage one, usually disarmed powerful people like the chaos prince.

"Yummy!" Cade said with appreciation after taking a couple of bites of a cheese puff. "I need to replace my chef."

"Not bad!" Silas agreed as he finished half a pie. "I just hope there'll be more meat!"

Louis wasn't interested in the cakes. He darted a few stealthy glances at my neck, and I had to lean a bit further from the table while reaching for another plate. The vamp prince shook his head, his blond hair flowing down his shoulders, as if he was trying to shrug off a daze. To distract himself from his need for blood, he picked up the wine bottle, regarding it.

"This is indeed 1666!" Louis said with delight.

"Yeah, enjoy! Why not?!" Rowan said sarcastically, brushing off the other heirs' thanks. "But know this." The dark promise of retaliation laced his cool voice. "Your dates with Barbie are coming, and I'll be there."

"We look forward to all the dates, don't we?" Killian patted Rowan's shoulder, and the fae prince shoved his elbow to shrug off the chaos prince's hand. Killian chuckled, not offended at all.

The princes weren't paying attention to their host's dark mood, as they were all eager to drink the 1666 that Saul had poured into their glasses. None of them thanked Rowan's butler, but I did when he offered me a glass too. I had more manners than the princes.

They sipped the wine in delight. None of them had swayed the glass or stuck their noses into it to sniff the scent before taking a swig, as mortals did at a wine tasting event, as if they were cool and knew their shit.

The princes laughed, drank heartily, and told Saul to pour another glass.

"Selfie time!" Cade whipped out a tablet and gathered everyone around me, squeezing me in the middle, just when

I had my eyes half-shut in the middle of a food orgasm. He flicked his wand, and the tablet floated a few feet away and snapped a picture of us.

"Send to Spinchat," he voice-commanded.

It was a bad idea, but it was too late to stop the mage.

Killian didn't go for any snacks, like the vampire prince. The two finished half the bottle of wine.

Our gazes met. Killian arched an eyebrow. "Is there a reason you keep staring at our hands, Barbie?"

"What?" I flushed furiously, realizing a bit too late I'd been staring at his muscled forearms and traced them to his large, powerful hands. "You're mistaken. I wasn't staring!"

Cade smirked. "There's this rumor going around amid the bride candidates that the size of a male's hands determines the size of his cock."

"No way!" I cried my innocence. "Who'd say such a stupid thing? And how could they know?"

Killian studied me, his elbow on the table, his hand cupping his chin, his eyes laughing. His heat radiated to me.

I scowled. All I wanted was to dig a hole and hide in it. This whole situation was making me uncomfortable. And to my horror, I started to feel my coming arousal in front of all the princes.

"We all have big cocks." Cade winked at me. "The five of us shared the royal bathhouse quite often in our first year at Shades Academy. It was never a secret that we used to share females as well. In case you're wondering, Barbie, the sizes of our cocks are in the same category, though Killian's might be a little longer."

"Too bad now the chaos heir has to keep his fly zipped at all times." Silas chuckled with an undercurrent of viciousness.

Killian turned to look at him, his eyes colder than ice, and the temperature on the terrace dropped.

"Well, well," Cade said. "Let's not go there. Let's just try to get along with each other for once, at least in Rowan's haunt. He was generous enough to invite us all here."

"How many times must I say that I didn't invite any of you?" Rowan snapped.

"So, Barbie, have I done a good job answering your question and satisfying your curiosity?" Cade asked.

I frowned at him. "What question?"

"Whose cock is bigger," he reminded me.

"I'm not curious about whose junk is bigger at all!" I spat, then lied, my voice turning husky, as I recalled my days as a boy. "I've never heard the saying of the size of the hands showing the size of—whatever!"

"No need to be defensive, Barbie." Louis chuckled, leering at me. "At least you saw mine, didn't you, on many occasions?"

Cade shook his head, still smiling. Silas narrowed his alpha stare on me, as if I were a whore and a vamp-lover whom he detested. Rowan regarded me, expecting me to explain, and a storm rolled through Killian's eyes while his face remained unmoved.

They all thought Louis had screwed me, as he'd intended to insinuate to discredit me or to rile me up for rejecting him. They focused on the orgy part, not even bothering to check the fact that Louis hadn't even found out that I was a girl. So how had he fucked me?

Dudes thought with their dicks.

"That reminds me, sir vampire," I said. "You still owe me a week's pay as your former squire, and I demand reasonable compensation for having to endure hours of watching the free porn that involved you and your blonde bimbos on five occasions, which was traumatic for me, since I'm still a virgin!"

Technically, I was!

Shocked silence slapped the princes in the face. Saul halted his steps as he brought more freshly baked cupcakes. Now everyone was staring at me, heat radiating from the princes. They all desired me, drawn by my power or Sy's pheromones, even though they hadn't figured out why. None of them had met my kind. Well, I might be the only one of my kind.

I lowered my gaze, regretting that I'd blurted it out like a fool. I especially refused to meet Killian's intense gaze.

Good moves! Sy applauded. *Get them all hooked!*

"You should've come clean when you were in my house!" Louis said, thinning his lips. "And I'd have treated you otherwise."

"Just pay her, Louis!" Killian snapped.

"Pay her, Louis, or you won't be invited to my parties anymore!" Rowan insisted as well. "Barbie is a virgin, a lady! Think of what she had to go through in your house. We aren't barbarians!"

"What the fuck?" Louis said.

"Barbie won't let this go. Ever." Cade gestured for Louis to go ahead and pay me. "She mentioned it to me in private as well. She told everyone who's willing to listen. Just pay her and get it over with, Louis."

I stared at Louis, my jaw clenched stubbornly.

The vamp prince pulled out a handful of gold coins from his pants pocket and slammed them onto the table. "Take it!" he barked with a bad attitude. "That's all I have with me at the moment."

Killian stared at the pure gold on the table, intrigued. The rumor was that he had a dragon inside. I bet that his dragon just peeked out, and dragons loved to hoard shiny things. Faster than a flash, I snatched a linen napkin in a swan shape beside a plate, snapped it open, and swept all the gold coins into it and then folded it, all in one swift move.

I dropped the linen napkin with the coins safely trapped inside onto my lap, beaming now. I was finally earning a living wage. I'd count every gold coin when I got back to my room.

"Uh, Sir Silas also owes me a paycheck from when I was his squire," I said. I didn't mention the minimum wage that his beta had promised since I might get more.

Silas glared at me. Louis nodded his encouragement to go after his nemesis.

"Aren't you a firecracker, Barbie?" Cade laughed, drinking his wine.

"Do a striptease for me and I'll pay you more than your worth," Silas said.

"Keep your fucking money then," I said flatly.

"Do you know the consequence of even looking at a prince wrong?" Silas rose to his feet, a savage grin on his face.

I tilted my head like a bird, a diabolical smile on my lips. Snarling, Sy pumped her strength into me, supporting me all the way. There was no fucking lying low anymore.

Several moves played in my head. I'd jump onto the table and kick his face for good measure when he swung his fist at me.

"Fuck off, Silas!" Killian rose, tossing away the table that I'd planned to jump on. I watched a dozen cupcakes fly over the railing of the terrace with regret.

Louis reacted fast enough to pick up the wine bottle.

There was one-third left. He smiled, waiting for the shit to hit the fan.

Killian placed himself between me and Silas.

Cade ran his hand through his reddish hair. "Not cool, man."

Rowan gestured for Saul to move anything valuable from the terrace. The butler burst into action gingerly, carefully staying out of range of Silas and Killian. With an exasperated sigh, Rowan flicked his wrist, vines shooting out of nowhere and ferrying away the dishes to the indoor table.

"Pick on someone your own size," Killian told Silas coldly.

"I got this, sir," I protested. "And my size is fine."

"I see how you look at your little pet, but you'll never get to fuck her," Silas said with a nasty smirk. "Everyone knows you can't touch any other woman except Queen Lilith. Your betrothed won't be happy if she gets wind of you showering your affection on Barbie; she'll end up just like the others."

"There were never any others." Killian's knuckles turned white. "But be careful what you say next, Silas. You don't want me as your immortal enemy, and eternity is a long time."

Silas snorted through his nostrils. "I'm already your enemy, brother."

Why did he call Killian brother? They couldn't be related, could they? Or was he also Killian's stepbrother, like Medea was Killian's stepsister?

"You two can't be in the same room for two seconds, can you?" Cade chided, spreading his arms. "This might be the last time I try to glue everyone together!"

Both Killian and Silas ignored the mage prince.

"I, however, will get into Barbie's pants eventually, now that she's a bride candidate," Silas bragged, intending to rile

Killian up more. "She'll crawl to me just like any other woman. Who doesn't want to land a prince heir? If you care to know, Killian, she'll be on my menu soon. I'm next in line to go on a date with her." His lips twisted into a cruel, lewd smile. "The first thing she'll do is dance on my lap before sucking my cock."

"Ha-ha. Ha-ha!" I let out a high-pitched giggle to get on Silas's nerves, my fingers grabbing Killian's sleeve before he could lunge at the shifter prince. It seemed that he was about to punch Silas in the jaw. After Silas had backhanded me when I was his squire, even horny Sy wouldn't fuck him. "You probably think you shit rainbows, sir shifter. Or maybe you do, so those candidates hope to see rainbows when they roll in your bed. I might be a nobody, but I want no fucking 'rainbows' that smell like shit near me. I officially and respectfully decline your demand for a date, and I'm absolutely fine with the committees or councils or whatever non-profit beauty pageant organization removing me from the pool of the Brides Selection as a result."

I tossed a small slice of tart into my mouth. "If you insist, sir shifter, it'll look bad. You don't want to be seen as the only prince who can't get a woman and has to resort to forcing her. Desperation doesn't smell good, not even on a prince."

I knew if I wanted to keep playing it safe, I should never ridicule him in front of the other princes. I didn't care much that he talked shit about me, but what he'd said about Killian set me off. I'd pulled the chaos prince back from launching a physical attack on the shifter prince, for I knew that often words had more power than fists, and my ridicule would hurt worse.

Even so, I was a little taken aback at my primal protectiveness toward the chaos prince.

You're defending your man! Sy preened in pride.

Killian isn't my man, I said.

Keep telling yourself that, she said. *One day you'll come out to swing for real to claim him. No one, not even a queen of great beauty and power, can take him from you!*

I noticed the shift in her tone and the words she chose. She no longer referred to Killian as *ours.* Sy was adapting and evolving. She also talked a little differently now, and I wasn't sure if I should be pleased or worried.

Cade, Louis, and Rowan stared at me, as if truly seeing me for the first time. Killian contained a smile, his desire and pride radiating to me, the connection between us vibrating.

"Damn, I should've recorded that and shared it on Spin-chat. That'd be a riot!" Louis chuckled. "She's the first candidate to ever turn him down, and she did it so mercilessly and brilliantly. Cade, let me borrow your tablet! I forgot to bring mine."

Silas trained his alpha stare on me, his amber eyes glowing now, and the other princes tensed. His power couldn't take on the other heirs since they were just as powerful, but Saul bent a knee at the shifter prince's power and panted in panic.

"Just let it go, man," Cade said in disapproval.

Killian growled a warning at Silas. Rowan didn't look pleased either. I took a cupcake from a plate that I'd saved when the chaos prince threw the table and bit off half of it while I stared back at Silas, unflinching and unblinking.

I wanted to scream at him that this was getting really old! He should've known by now that he held no power over me. Why did people repeat the same thing but expect a different result?

"Barbie's got balls and also some weird-ass power." Cade

let out a low chuckle. "No wonder Louis called her Little Bob in the first place and led everyone on a wild goose chase until Killian called her out."

Louis glared at Cade, then rolled a shoulder. "She fooled you too with her weird power."

The vampire prince wasn't even a little surprised that I could counter Silas but gleeful to see his nemesis humbled. He'd known I was powerful since he'd drunk my blood and seen Underhill aid me, but he didn't know what I was. Since then, he'd been lurking everywhere, watching me instead of striking out.

Silas leashed his alpha power but thrust a rude, vengeful finger at me, either to mark me for half-death or try to bore me to half-death. "You have no fucking idea who you're dealing with, girl!" he said.

"It's *whom*, sir," I corrected him and showed him a hand sign of aloha, which I borrowed from Cade, and the mage prince immediately returned the favor, so we got two alohas.

"This is getting fucking boring," Killian said. "Is your date with Barbie over, Rowan?"

"It was over when you got here," Rowan grated.

"Then we should be on our merry way," Killian said. "It's time for Barbie to return to my house. She has homework to do. I don't want her lagging far behind. I am responsible for every member of my house."

"Are you now, Killian? That's new, isn't it," Louis said tartly, his hungry gaze drifting to the veins on my neck again, "this controlling thing?"

Let the lovely vamp prince have a sip. Sy nudged. She'd missed the pleasure his feeding had brought and the free porn he starred in.

24

Sy

"How did your *hot date* go, princeling?" I sneered, stepping out of the black tree guarding the entrance of Underhill and narrowing my eyes on Rowan as he stalked closer.

I'd left a trail of scent for him, knowing he'd track me down here.

Instead of the tunic he'd had on when he was entertaining Barbie, he was clad in a trench coat with a dark red shirt underneath that showed off his broad, taut chest. He had gone for a wild boy impression rather than a gentleman scholar. The light of the moon streaked through his silver hair, and his silver eyes roamed over my every inch with hunger, as if he had missed me.

While his exotic, masculine beauty took my breath away and made my pussy slick, I controlled my urge to jump on him and ride him. I needed his cock in me badly and wanted to feed from him greedily, yet I held back.

I hadn't treated him like my usual targets—fuck them fast and furious to sip the energy I needed and then take off without sparing a second glance at them. Rowan wasn't just a target, as I wanted him more than any other male.

I was royally pissed at him for courting Barbie. I loved my other half more than myself, and I'd die for her any second of the day. I'd felt privileged to take most of the pain for her when our father had sipped and nipped on her essence. Barbie was more magical than me, but she was also more vulnerable. She could barely tolerate any pain.

For the first time, I didn't want to share Rowan with any female, not even with Barbie. I hid this from her though. She couldn't know all my thoughts, and I'd been practicing for years to keep some of my dark intentions from her.

There were sparks between Rowan and Barbie, like the sparks between every prince and her, since they were help-lessly drawn to her goddess power without knowing why. But the sparks weren't enough to bond them. It was nothing like the link between Rowan and me.

Plus, Barbie had eyes for only one male, even though she insisted on not fucking him. Unlike her, I had no rules or boundaries. What I wanted, I took, and damned the consequences.

But I wasn't entirely irresponsible, so I'd lured Rowan to Underhill so Barbie could get inside the dark forest if I made a mess for her.

"So, you heard about my date then," Rowan purred with a smug smirk on his curvy lips.

My heart fluttered while I also wanted to punch him at the same time.

"You wanted to get into the pants of that short girl with bouncing golden curls, didn't you?" I narrowed my eyes, my nostrils flaring. "Did you succeed?"

"If I intended to get into her pants, I'd have set the date at night, like now with you," he said, strolling closer.

I put up a hand. "I'm not pleased with you, so don't come any closer!" Yet my body begged for him not to listen to me. I wanted him to throw me to the ground, push my skirt up to my waist, and pound his massive cock into me.

I wasn't wearing underwear for a reason.

I'd try to fight him off half-heartedly to spice it up, and then I'd flip him off and ride his hard length brutally. I'd take what I needed! He could beg for mercy, but I wouldn't give it to him.

And that was my style!

That's savage, Barbie chirped.

Rowan has the best cock I've ever seen, I told her.

She rolled her eyes. The whole night she'd been sulky and kept yawning to ruin my mood. But she hadn't prevented me from luring Rowan here. It was better to let me sex feed than eat something or someone raw—less blood and gore and less messy. I'd taught her a lesson or two for going against my will.

"Now you want me to stay away?" Rowan smiled. "Last time, you were all over me and couldn't get enough of me, and I thought I might never get away."

"Get away?" I squinted at him in displeasure.

I'd never let him get away if I put my foot down! I wasn't the kind of girl who would take no for an answer!

We don't do non-con! Barbie barked at me furiously while I was engaged in a heated conversation with Rowan.

"Not that I want to," Rowan said, his smile widening.

"You know I can't stay away from you. That's why I came to seek you out."

My fierce jealousy seemed to only turn him on. He dug crazy chicks, and I wouldn't disappoint him. I was an expert at leveling up craziness.

"But I don't want your dirty cock getting into me if you fucked another chick not long ago," I said haughtily.

Barbie was cunning. I could be too.

"What other chick?" Rowan growled. "I haven't fucked anyone since I fucked you!"

"You courted Barbie. The short girl's name is Barbie, isn't it?" I taunted, and Barbie bristled.

"Are you going to stay mad forever?" Rowan sighed. "It wasn't courting. It wasn't even a true date. It was a bet among all the heirs when it came to Barbie. I went along with it, hoping to draw you out once you heard of my fake date."

"What bet?" I asked at Barbie's urging. She'd been suspicious of the princes' intentions. She was the paranoid type. She just didn't know how to relax.

"It doesn't concern you, Sy," he said.

"But I want to know," I said. "I barely know anything about you. Am I just your fuck buddy?"

With Rowan, I wanted more.

"I want to know more about you, too, little monster," he said. "I want to know your ancestry, your history, and where you live."

He could never know any of that. Maybe I could never have what I wanted. Maybe all I could have was a few nights with him, not even a full night. Between me and Barbie, she was the primary; I served her. I would never have my own life. I wrapped the sorrow tightly within me, so Barbie wouldn't know. It was the way it was, no matter how unfair it was.

I tilted my head. "Tell me about you and your life, starting with the bet, so I know that I'm not just a pussy to you."

"You know you're never that. You're much more," he sighed. "Fine, I'll tell you, but you can't share this with anyone else, Sy. The other heirs are like my brothers, though we don't always get along. We were raised together as children, so there'd be no war between the houses. But somehow, the tensions between houses keep rising lately."

I nodded, pretending to understand the realm's politics.

"We can't afford another war while magic in the realm is fragile and the wild magic from Underhill refuses to replenish the rest of the realm. Old magic won't return unless one of the heirs, me included, produces the prophesized One. And now there's this dark force coming toward Mist of Cinder. We don't know much about it, only rumors here and there. But we've encountered the abominations that murdered our kind brutally and seen the blight right outside the Veil with our own eyes."

Barbie stirred. Nothing shook her like Ruin and his Shrieker army. We'd thought that we no longer needed to look over our shoulders after we got into Mist of Cinder, but some Shriekers had found our trail. A couple of them had gotten into the realm and slaughtered a few supernaturals. We hoped that we'd killed all the Shriekers that had followed us here. If Ruin got wind of where we were hiding, a large horde of his agents would be coming to this last magical realm that Barbie and I now called home.

Barbie would never allow our father to harm this realm. She'd do anything to stop him, including going down with him to protect this land. I was ready for that, too, but I wanted Barbie to live on. We had never really lived, until we came here.

"Also, our associates in the mortal realm have informed us that there's been great unrest in their corners," he continued. "The Federal Republic is falling apart. Humans' regional wars are going to expand to a global war. Their numerous bombs and technological pollution can weaken the Veils that separate our realm from theirs. Just another thing to worry about."

I liked him talking to me and sharing his worries with me, as no one had treated me this way before. I leaned into his touch, not realizing when he'd come closer, stroking my cheek.

"What do the wars have to do with Barbie?" I pursued. I didn't care about the world, but I wanted to make sure Barbie was unharmed. "And you still haven't told me about the bet. What is it? What's your intention toward her?"

"I have no intention toward Barbie whatsoever, but the other heirs placed a bet on her," he said with a sigh. "Whoever deflowers her will be the winner, and the winner takes it all. They set out to bend her. Tame her. They have to. It's a matter of house honor. No other female and no other bride candidate has ever challenged them except Barbie. We're princes. We can't let things like that slide. We can't allow any defiance. When she posed as a boy, she turned both House of Vampires and House of Shifters upside down. I almost accepted her into my house. I dodged a magical bullet!" He smiled, pleased with himself, then shook his head. "That girl attracts trouble like no other. Anyway, my intention was to get to you. I knew you would hear about the date and come running to me. You came, didn't you?"

I growled, showing my fangs, and he showed his too, grazing them along my neck. I shivered in fury and pleasure at the same time. When Rowan's hand palmed my bare pussy, my need to feed overwhelmed me.

Not now! We need more intel before you go straight to fucking, Barbie barked in a nasty mood, cursing the princes and their bet.

"So the courting and dates are all but a ruse to get to Barbie?" I hissed while propelling my hips to ride Rowan's hand.

"It's their little game of revenge," he said, smiling. "They want to set an example. They plan to court her with whatever they have and whatever it takes, until she falls for them. Then they'll set up a scene, get her to drop to her knees to suck their cocks, and record it for all to see. They aim to utterly ruin her and make her damaged goods even before the official Bride Trials."

My golden eyes glowed with a dangerous light.

"And you'll join them?" I drawled.

"Jealous?" He smirked, then added over my growl, "I have no intention of bedding other women, as long as you remain available to me, my monster."

"Does the prince of House of Chaos know about the bet?"

"We have to keep it from him, or it'll be an issue," Rowan said, regarding me, his silver eyes flashing. "Are you friends with Barbie? You seem to worry about her a lot, and I keep confusing the scents of you two."

I laughed savagely. "That's your excuse to try to get into Barbie's pants as well?"

His eyes flashed with dark light. "I told you that I had no intentions toward her."

"Then why don't you tell me about the date so I can check out if you're telling the truth or not."

"Fae can't lie, but we've mastered the workaround very

well," he said smugly, his hand rubbing my pussy roughly. "You sure you can tell lies from truth?"

I sucked in a gasp. "Do you want to get laid or not?"

No matter what I threatened him with, I was going to get laid.

He studied me, his eyes hooded. He'd give anything to have his cock in me. I could see now that I wasn't just any female to him. Our stars had aligned.

"Before it even started," he said, his thumb brushing my clit, and a moan tore out of my throat, "Killian crashed it and turned it into a farce! He was drastic even when he was a kid. If I'd known how the date would turn out, I wouldn't have bothered putting a lot of effort into entertaining Barbie. I don't want to badmouth her, but she's a certified she-devil, despite her act of batting her pretty eyelashes innocently. She outwitted Louis, then Silas. I bet she and Killian can play each other like fiddles, and not in a good way. It might be interesting watching them if those two don't exhaust everyone."

Even as Rowan complained, he didn't sound bitter now that he had me in his arms. His expression grew thoughtful as he pondered something. "There's something strange between them. Killian is insanely possessive toward Barbie, as if he has a right to her. Entitled prick! But then I have to admit that there's a mystic thread between them, as if they're true mates in a sense. I caught a glimpse of it before it was hidden. The other heirs can't see what I see, or Silas would use it against Killian. Even Silas, though a brute who believes power, position, and violence can solve everything, has spied the chemistry between Killian and the new girl."

"Wait, why are you the only one who can see the thread between them? Is there really such a thing as a mystic bond between fated mates?"

"I'm a powerful fae," he said. "Fae are pureblooded magical beings compared to other species. Shifters, mages, vampires, and other creatures all have a strand of human DNA, more or less. But we're a completely different species than humans, and thus we're closer to nature and elemental magic."

I guess his opinions wouldn't be popular among the other princes.

"Barbie and Killian are unlike others." Rowan shook his head, confusion darkening his eyes. "If they want to find out if they're fated mates or not, they'll have to try it out, but Killian is already bound to the Queen of the Underworld. He won't be able to touch any other woman without burning them since Queen Lilith has staked a claim on him. She's very powerful. Three females suffered severe burns when they tried to touch him." He frowned in distaste. "In a way, Queen Lilith has put an invisible chastity belt on Killian."

Barbie held her breath. We both did. Killian had touched her without hesitation, as if he knew instinctively that he could touch her however he wanted. Now that Rowan had mentioned it, I recalled the shocked looks on the faces of Rock, Archer, and Cami when they saw their prince pinning Barbie down on his desk and Barbie grabbing his wrist without being toasted.

Whatever curse Killian carried, it had no effect on Barbie. But then, Barbie ate curses like lemons. She only winced a little.

"What if Prince Killian makes a move on Barbie?" I asked.

"It'll end in disaster. Only if Barbie is his true mate will he be able to fuck her without blowing them both to hell. That would mean that Queen Lilith isn't his true mate.

Either way, I don't envy him. Enough talk of Barbie and Killian!" He growled, thrusting a finger into my pussy, eliciting a gasp of shocked pleasure out of me. "I don't like to talk about other men when I'm with you. Let our bed be pure with just you and me, and no one else!"

"There's no bed, princeling," I said breathlessly between moans as his finger thrust in and out of my tight heat.

He didn't need to know that Barbie would always be in bed with us no matter if he and she wanted it or not. And Rowan would utterly freak out if he knew that I had hitched a ride on his and Barbie's date just this morning. Now the roles were reversed, as Barbie was hitching a ride and peeking out at us moodily.

Do a quickie and let's get out of here! she urged.

"Let me take you to my place," Rowan offered. "Sleep in my bed tonight."

My heart fluttered in excitement before Barbie poured a bucket of icy water down my head with a furious growl. *No bloody way!*

"Just fuck me! Right here, right now!" I snarled, not sure if it was aimed at Barbie or Rowan.

"Be nice about it, little monster!" Rowan growled back and spun me, slamming me against the black tree. I wiggled my ass to get him going. I liked to get fucked from behind ever since Rowan had first taken me.

I gazed at him over my shoulder, grinning, as I watched lust distort his handsome face. He was starting to lose control, needing to get his dick wet. With a snap of his fingers, his attire vanished.

I stared at his glorious full frontal. There wasn't an ounce of fat on him. Every muscle was steel hard, every line beautiful. And he was not hairy like the shifter prince. Rowan was silky steel, all smooth, which I appreciated.

My gaze fixed on his cock—long, straight, massive, and rock hard. A bead of precum formed on his smooth crown. At my rapt attention, his cock jerked aggressively.

"I need to take you fast and hard for the first couple of rounds," he said, his voice rough with lust.

"Promise," I purred, my heart pounding.

"Did you think of me when I wasn't around?" Rowan asked uncertainly.

"Get your cock in me and fuck me good, and I'll tell you," I crooned.

"Aren't you a bit aggressive, my horny monster?" He chuckled, pushing my legs wider and grabbing my butt cheeks before he shoved his cock between my folds.

His hard shaft drove into my molten depths, filling the aching emptiness inside. Without giving me time to adjust to his size, he pounded into me, hard and fast. My breasts slammed into the trunk at his pounding, and I giggled at his rough play. I'd return the favor soon.

He leaned forward, his fangs grazing along the column of my neck.

"You're so wet for me, Sy," he said. "Let me bring you to my house. Stay with me."

"Be careful what you wish for, fae," I purred.

Yet the idea of staying with him and cuddling with him all night in his bed sounded like music to my ears, more enticing than anything else. No other male could feed me like he did, and I'd never go hungry by his side.

Could that life be possible for me? I propelled my ass toward him, fucking him back fiercely, so I could ignore the ache in my chest at the impossible dream and just get my fix in full today.

"One day, you'll know this body belongs to me; this

pussy is mine to fuck only," Rowan rumbled, impaling me with his cock again and again.

I cried out as I arched my back, taking more of him, all of him.

"Good girl," he said. "Not many can take all of me!"

My pussy gloved his shaft tightly and possessively.

"You are so fucking hot and tight around my cock. I feel like I want to come right away." He groaned in pleasure as he thrust into my core, seating himself to the hilt. "Your juice coats my length, just the way I like it!"

My inner walls clamped down on him, sucking him in deeper.

He chuckled. "You gotta let me move, little monster."

He drove into me, the feel of his every inch inside me delicious.

"Did you fuck other women like this?" I growled.

"Different," he offered. "You want to watch me fuck other women?" He pulled me to him and lowered me to the ground while we were still connected. And then I was on all fours. He gripped my hips and rammed into me from behind again. "Like this?" he teased.

Before I could curse him, he pumped his cock into me hard, so hard that I fell forward, but he caught me, then pounded into me even more brutally.

He plunged into me with dazzling speed, sending me his energy, feeding me. I threw my head back, giggling in delight as I fed greedily. He inhaled my scent deeply, soaking in my energy as well.

"You taste divine, Sy," he said. "I've never met any female like you."

I knew that Barbie and I tasted like nectar. Monsters especially loved our taste and smell, especially Barbie's, since she was purely magical. Once anyone truly had her, he would and could never let her go.

Rowan's thumb went around to rub my sensitive clit as he fucked me harder and faster. I thrust my ass back to meet him beat for beat. We fucked like wild beasts, panting. For a long minute, neither of us spoke but fucked relentlessly while drinking in each other's energy.

This was divine! I wanted to be fucked like this to the end of time. I wanted to feel connected like this and be cherished. Rowan tunneled in and out of me, bruising my pussy. I exploded around his cock.

As he rode my climax, he also arrived. His cock jerked, growing harder, then he pumped his hot seed into me.

Before I could drop my belly to the grass to take a break, he pulled out of me. Lightning fast, he flipped me around and made me lie on my back with him kneeling between my thighs. I watched his cum still shooting out of his cock, landing on my stomach. It was the hottest thing I'd ever seen.

He stared at my bare pussy in fascination, lust distorting his face. Before my hand reached for his cock to play with his cum, he nudged the crown of his cock at my entrance and shoved it in while he was still coming.

"I'm going to fuck you for the whole night," he promised.

My legs wrapped around the small of his back as he drove into me, the sound of flesh slapping flesh erotic and thrilling. I moaned breathlessly, my fingers raking across his back.

"You're driving me mad, little monster!" he hissed, hammering into me ruthlessly. "I want to see your face when you come! You'll wear my scent everywhere, which will warn off other males."

I giggled and heaved up my hips to fuck him back.

The scent of sex permeated the air, and I drank it in, filling my well.

As he kept pounding into me mercilessly, a new wave of orgasm crashed into me, so hard that I howled. I lifted my torso, my fangs sliding out and piercing the skin between his neck and shoulder. Rowan roared as we came hard together.

Barbie screamed at me.

And then my other half did something unforgivable.

25

Sy

*S*hut up! Have him shut up too! Barbie screamed over our roars of satisfaction. *What did I say about not attracting attention? Are you going to put me in danger again?*

I giggled, ignoring her, but I extracted my fangs from Rowan's skin delicately and licked the tiny wound there with fervor.

Shadow beasts growled from the depths of the dark forest, and wolves howled from the other side of Underhill. They must've heard Rowan's and my roars and answered in challenge.

How glorious! I felt so free. I hadn't felt so amazing in all my life. With Rowan, I tasted the delicious side of life and saw what the future could be for me.

The shifters will run this way to investigate, Barbie huffed in warning.

Don't worry, I said, grinning at Rowan as he grinned at me too. His cock was still hard in me. No one fucked me like him, and I knew I could never get enough of him. *I'll have one more round. Only then will I stop.*

Wrap it up! I'll give you time to say goodbye, Barbie ordered. *Your well has been filled, brimming over actually. Do not indulge in this frolic when we can't afford it.*

You indulge yourself all the time, I countered. *Why can't I? Am I lesser than you? I'm my own person too, and I should have my own life. When you had a date with my man, you didn't cut it short. You enjoyed it to the fullest, ate all the delicious goodies, and flirted with the princes. And now I'm having the best fucking night of my life, and you demand I quit it. Nope, I'm going with him to his house and sleeping in his bed, no matter the cost.*

Now you sound not only crazy but stupid, Barbie hissed.

She'd never been so angry with me. A hollow emotion hit me, but I pumped strength into my heart and hardened it. I gotta be dominant. This time, I aimed to take the reins, or she was going to walk all over me, as usual. I would have a say in how things should run from now on. And I was sick and tired of her being so judgmental.

Do I? I sneered. *You're just jealous! I can fuck Rowan, but you can't fuck Killian, even though you drool over him every second.*

She was silent before she went all cold. *Leave him before it's too late.* She issued another order. *The shifters are coming, and they'll discover you.*

Will I always be your dirty secret? I said, equally cold. I must fight for the life I wanted and deserved, and what better time than now? She needed to learn to back off! *You don't get to order me around anymore, Barbie. Even if the shifters come, what can they do? It's not like they've never seen fucking before. They group fuck all the time! They'd appreciate seeing Rowan fuck me.*

He isn't like any fae! He's the fae prince! Barbie shouted incredulously, as if I was the unreasonable one. She could be such a bitch; no wonder so many supernaturals were against her! *Word will get around. We don't want others seeing you!*

Why not? It's time I show my face! You aren't the only pretty one!

You'll jeopardize us! she snarled.

I snarled back. *You always use the same excuse to suppress me, making me lesser than you. All these years, it's you who has lived! I won't let you do it to me anymore.*

That was never a life. Not until we came to Mist of Cinder!

Exactly! Now I have a chance to smell the roses and feel the sunlight too. Why don't we share and split everything from now on? You do daytime, and I do nighttime.

You're ruining this, Sy, for what? For a cock? For a few seconds of orgasm? She hissed in disdain. She always looked down on me. *I won't allow you.*

Not just any cock, Barbie, I purred to provoke her, ready for the battle I knew was coming, *and it's more than a few seconds. I could go for a whole minute or two. Didn't you feel it? Oh, you couldn't feel the full impact of the pleasure I experienced, and it's killing you that you don't get it from Killian. You should quit being a prude. You should just go to his room and beg him to fuck you. Take initiative and be aggressive. Take what you want!* Yep, I had enough contempt for her as well, so now I was lecturing her without reservation. *We're predators, but you're soft. You're weak! You cower from others but treat me like a pushover. Hell shall freeze before I continue to let you treat me that way. You won't allow me?* I snorted. *Try me and see how it'll work out for you.*

Barbie looked like I'd hit her face with a brick. I knew I came off strong, but I was pissed that she'd tried to poop on my fun. It wasn't just fun. I was falling for Rowan, and I was addicted to this feeling of falling as well. So no, I wouldn't let anyone spoil it, not even Barbie, especially Barbie. That ungrateful bitch forgot how I'd watched her six all these years and how I'd taken her agony into me when our father tortured her and ate her essence.

Now things were different and the tide had turned, all she cared about was having a full life for herself while treating me like dirt.

"Are you okay, Sy?" Rowan asked, pulling me up with me sitting on him. "You've been quiet." He studied my face with possessiveness and concern. "You look mad. Did I hurt you?"

He cared about my feelings. He cared about me more than my other half.

"Never better, princeling." I smiled at him, and he leaned in, his fangs grazing along my neck. "You give me joy and pleasure no one else can offer me. I won't allow anyone to ruin this between us."

He smirked. "Glad to be of service, my lady."

He treated me like a lady!

Rowan bucked his hips up and pounded into my needy depths. His powerful thighs slammed into my bottom.

"We'll try every position," I moaned breathlessly. "Let's fuck the whole night!"

Barbie attacked. She grabbed me, trying to drag me off Rowan.

Nope, nope! You should never try to get between me and my man! I punched her right in the eye. She jerked her head back, shocked. I'd never gone violent on her, but I had to. She had low tolerance to pain, and I wanted her to feel it and suffer through it, so she'd learn her place. She'd stay down. *Think you're stronger? Think you're more dominant than me? Don't kid yourself, little girl! I let you think like that when I let you win. You aren't the shit you think you are.*

You turned on me for a dick? she asked bitterly.

See? Always criticizing me!

Not just any dick! I smirked and rammed my fist into her jaw while she was still shocked. *Back off, or I'll maul your pretty face with my claws. You know when we fight like this, it manifests physically. You don't want Killian seeing you like that, and you won't even be able to explain it to him.*

She kicked my knee, as if that would make me bend. How pathetic! I laughed at her.

I'll take what I'm owed, I said. *I own this life and this body! From now on, I'm taking the reins. You'll still get half of the share since I'm not as selfish as you.*

I grabbed her bouncing golden curls, which had grown long enough for me to grip, and dragged her down. I pinned her and slammed her head to the hard ground twice. She stared up at me, dazed, while trying hard not to cry at the pain. Barbie was the sensitive kind. While she felt every inch of the pain, she could also feel pleasure tenfold more intense than others. Her pain radiated to me, but I couldn't afford to be merciful.

This was a duel of wills between her and me, the outcome deciding our new dynamic. I finally chose me. I dug my toe into her face. She struggled to turn her cheek to the other side, as if she couldn't bear to look at me.

I laughed, showing her that I had no such sentiment. I was more of a survivor than her. I was tougher and stronger and wilder. I'd call the shots.

Tell me you understand, I purred cruelly, knowing that I

was always capable of it. *Tell me you'll live by my rules, and I'll let you up.*

She remained silent.

Claws slid through my toes, slashing across her cheek while I didn't miss a beat riding Rowan. The pleasure from my fae male and satisfaction from defeating Barbie made me feel high. I wasn't soft. I didn't do weak.

No pain, no gain.

I quietly hummed the song Barbie had performed for the princes while I let her bleed—

"Baby, I'm having the best fuckin' night of my life
And wherever it takes me, I'm down for the ride
Baby, don't you know I'm good? Yeah, I'm feelin' alright—"

I POUNDED into Rowan like the wild thing I was—gliding along his hard length, twirling and slamming down. He hissed in pleasure.

You're wrong, Sy, Barbie said, a tear rolling out of her green eye, yet her sapphire eye remained dry.

My heart skipped an icy beat. I'd never seen her like that. We'd fought for dominance before, but it had never been this bad. I clenched my jaw hard. I was fighting for my future. I had to show her brutality!

Surrender, Barbie! Last warning! I removed my foot from her bleeding cheek and crouched next to her. My claws lashed out and elongated, ready for the kill. *The bleeding is just a taste of what's coming.*

She stared at me passively.

This is your doing, I said mercilessly, my claws slashing toward her golden face. *You made me do this!*

Her hand struck out, lightning fast, and caught my wrist, the tip of my claws leaving a shallow blood trail across her jawline. I swung my free fist toward her lips, but she caught it as well and wrapped her fingers around it.

I snarled, trying to break free of her grip, but she held on with her death grip, her strength surprising me.

Her two-toned eyes glowed in rage.

A blink and my strength left me. Just like that. All the energy I'd reserved emptied, and the new energy I'd harvested from sex with Rowan flowed to Barbie.

All these years, you don't even know who I really am, she said icily, as if talking to a stranger. *You thought you were the monster. I just never truly let mine out. You can never dominate me. No one can. Not even our god father, not even when he bound and chained me.*

To my horror, I saw myself start to fade. My skin turned grayish, A lock of my lush hair fell out and landed on Rowan's taut chest.

I paused in the middle of hot sex, freezing on Rowan's hard length as I screamed and thrashed to break free from Barbie to no avail.

Leave while you still can, Barbie ordered, ice and steel in her green and sapphire eyes as they both glowed crimson. A terrible realization dawned on me that Barbie was ready to drain me, even kill me, if I continued to defy her.

One more second on Rowan's lap, and Barbie would make me wither. I'd look like an old hag in front of Rowan, for whom I'd started this fight against Barbie.

With a sob, I flung myself off Rowan.

"I have to go," I told him, my heart breaking in two.

Not only did I know now that I could never have a relationship with him, but I also had a hard reality check—my other half was more than me, more than I could ever be. She was the true top predator and carried the goddess gene. If I pushed her across the bridge, there'd be no turning back.

Barbie would turn off her humanity and finish the job. Finish me.

I'd prided myself on being brutal and merciless; I had just never really stared into Barbie's face. She'd put a veil over it, concealing her dark essence, afraid of looking at it as well.

I was never her equal; I was her pale shadow in every way, every sense, and every universe. She was the primary, the one who was allowed to live a full life.

"What's wrong, Sy?" Rowan asked. "Don't leave! Come with me—"

"I'm sorry." I fought back tears as I sprang into a run.

I couldn't give him what he wanted, unless Barbie also chose him, and then we'd share him.

Rowan gave chase while he was still naked. Dark wind shot out of Underhill, preventing him from getting to me. Barbie had called her ally, and the wild magic listened to only her.

Another point she'd just proven that she was the shit!

As darkness bound Rowan and concealed me, Barbie surfaced, took over, and tossed me away. She strode into the dark forest of Underhill like she was coming home. The wild magic twirled around her like an overexcited puppy, responding to her wild goddess energy.

Utterly humbled and defeated. I sank into the depths of the icy abyss to accept my exile as Barbie commanded the shadow beasts to safeguard the entrance of Underhill and to allow no one in.

The forest shifted and brought her the lake, accommodating her every whim. Barbie dove into the icy water, fully clothed, to scrub off the remnant of Rowan's and my scents on her skin.

Barbie

I bit my shivering lip as I headed toward class the next morning. I didn't want to go, but I also didn't want Killian's men to show up at my door. Killian's circle, except for Cami, all treated me like some high-maintenance chick due to their prince's attention to me. They whispered about Killian and me among themselves. I wanted to know what that was about, but I didn't want to send Pucker to spy on them. Every scrap of information cost me. In order to get as many sips from me as possible, the ghost guardian always held back intel to trade for favors.

After I'd bathed in Underhill and made sure to erase the scent of sex that Sy and her lover had smeared on me, I returned to the House of Chaos. Pucker had slanted me one look and decided wisely to stay away for the rest of the night.

I hadn't felt this terrible since we'd escaped Ruin's lair.

For the first time, Sy and I truly turned against each other. That hadn't been a fight for dominance; it'd been a bid for survival. The loser diminished and the winner took it all.

I didn't claim victory, but Sy still sank so deeply that I could barely feel her now. I had never felt so alone, but I did not seek her out. All these years we'd been on the run, we'd just tried to get to the next town, find the next meal, and hope to stay alive and free the next day. And now when we could have a life, she wanted to be the one who lived it.

It'd started with a good fuck, then she got addicted to the fae prince. I could barely rein her in when her need for him was consuming her, especially while my own unfulfilled lust for the chaos prince nearly undid me. Every time I saw Killian, my pussy throbbed with such raw need that it turned into physical pain.

I sympathized with her need and want, even related to it, but I couldn't allow her to throw everything away just so she could sleep in the fae prince's bed every night. We all wanted something we couldn't have.

But Sy didn't understand the complexities of gritty reality. She was too primal. So I'd had to talk in her language and resort to brutal violence to settle our differences when she set out to usurp and replace me.

Now she'd finally peeked at the dark secret I'd kept from her—I could consume her, like a twin eating the other in a shared womb. I'd felt her fear of me, like her fear of Ruin, when it sank into her that I could unmake her.

If I erased her, she wouldn't have anything left. Not a soul. Not a consciousness. Not a trace. She'd be gone like she'd never existed. But if I killed her, part of me would die forever, and I'd never feel whole again.

I replayed our brutal fight, my footsteps leaden, my

breath shaky, and my chest tight. I trod the cobbled path amid a cluster of small buildings and trees and passed by the sculptures that represented the five houses safeguarding the tree of magic.

White blossoms drifted in the air, falling on my golden curls. I sighed. Nothing lasted forever. Everything faded, even the strongest bond.

I was in such a black mood that I didn't even go to breakfast. Giving the orange dome with the shimmering letters "Pathfinder" on the façade a dull glance, I entered.

I climbed to the third floor, made turns, and jogged toward the end of the corridor, where the divination class would be held, according to the map on my tablet.

The classroom could hold over two hundred students. I halted by the door to see if there was a trap, which had become a routine ever since Medea and America had started this campaign to make my academy life as difficult as possible. I had to look over my shoulder at every turn, which was totally fine, as this life was still a paradise compared to the life of captivity and torture in my father's brutal hands.

No trick. No "Carrie" stunt either. But I wouldn't put it past the bullies to come up with something else.

As soon as I stepped in, every head snapped to me.

Shit! It seemed all my foes from different years were here, their eyes boring into me with hate, disdain, or something like jealous fury.

Medea and America took the center front seats with their minions, including Javier, Bellona, Imelda, Fake Blonde and her fae boyfriend, among others, surrounding them.

Cami and Dixie were in the class too, but they sat in the center of the middle rows with their circles.

My gaze skipped all of them quickly, not wanting to invite crap. In my current mood, I had less control. I spotted Bea as she stood up from a far corner, waving at me. I smiled, ignoring the heat and hatred coming my way, and made a beeline toward my loyal friend.

A couple of supernatural geeks sat in her corner. I was glad of the one percent of friendly force, as I needed this support more than ever, especially as I no longer had Sy to cheer me up and watch my back.

I tried to banish my devastation and dark feelings as I slumped onto the seat Bea had reserved for me.

"Do you have something to eat? Candies, energy bars, or even a handful of pumpkin seeds?" I asked hopefully.

No matter how black my mood was, I needed to eat to quench the hunger. I was most dangerous when I was hungry and depleted.

A geek girl from the chaos house turned from the row in front of me and tossed me an oatmeal cookie. "I'm Jinx, by the way."

Jinx had ashy hair, a broad forehead, and intelligent gray eyes that said not to trust anything that moved.

"Much appreciated, J." I smiled at her, biting into the cookie and finishing it in a couple of seconds. "I'm Barbie."

"Everyone knows who you are," Jinx said with a shrug.

I blinked. "No shit!"

A guy behind us laughed. He handed me a burrito that was still warm.

"Have it," he said. "I was keeping it for a second breakfast, but by the looks of it, you need it more than me."

"I do, but if you give it to me, you'll have no second breakfast," I half-protested, biting into the burrito before he could take it back, and he let out a chortle.

"The eggs and cheese in it were cooked to perfection, man!" I told him in appreciation.

"His name is Wyatt," Bea said.

"Which house are you from?" I asked after I finished his offering in a few bites. Wyatt blinked at my eating speed. I was trained to swallow food down my throat in record time, since I'd always had to brace for a fight at any time while replenishing my energy. "You aren't a vampire, a shifter, a fae, or even a mage."

"I'm first year, but no house wants me," he said, crestfallen. "I was hoping to get into the House of Chaos, like you."

I gave Wyatt another look. His hazel eyes were bigger than Javier's. Green strands streaked his ink-black hair. As I sniffed, I could sense some demon blood in him. Anyone with demon blood was mostly shunned in the realm.

"I'm half-human, half-demon," Wyatt volunteered, waiting for me to turn away from him and shun him too. When I shrugged, he added, "I don't eat people."

"No one is perfect," I said.

Jinx laughed.

"Listen, Wyatt," I said. He offered me food, so I wanted to return the favor. "I can talk to Pucker on your behalf to consider letting you into the House of Chaos."

"Who's Pucker?" Jinx, Wyatt, and Bea all asked at the same time.

"The dude ghost guardian in the House of Chaos," I said. "I haven't seen the old chick guardian for a while."

"Isn't he a poltergeist?" Jinx asked.

"He's misunderstood," I said, waving a hand. "Like we all are."

"But they say his name is Luther," Jinx said.

"So when anyone calls him Luther, he doesn't need to answer," I said.

"You can talk to a ghost?" Bea said. "You never told me that."

"Well, yeah," I said, not willing to tell even Bea that one of the ghost guardians of the House of Chaos was now my familiar. I had enough shit to deal with already. "Pucker is a good listener. Anyone in the house just needs to tell him what they want, and he'll happily oblige."

You shouldn't have said that, Barbie! Pucker's voice suddenly growled in my head. His phantom form appeared on the sidewall next to me. *It's my reputation on the line! I don't happily oblige those little shits! On the contrary, I don't give a fuck what those brats want. I often give them the opposite. I only care about what I want!*

I looked around in alert to see if anyone else had spotted him.

No one can see me except you. Pucker thinned his pale lips. *Or probably Prince Killian can when he concentrates.*

Why are you here? I demanded. *Didn't I send you to patrol the Veil?*

There was nothing going on there, he said. *I got bored.*

I told you not to follow me to class since I want to learn instead of being distracted.

You've been in a bad mood since last night. I was concerned.

I'm fine. You should go.

Whatever, he yawned. *I'll go back to the house and have a nap. Classes are boring anyway. But do take care not to spread rumors about me again. I might be your familiar, but I still need to tailor my image and keep it the same as before.*

You'll let Wyatt into our house, right?

If you offer me an extra sip, he bargained.

I shook my head in disgust. *Fuck off!*

He let out a low laugh, and then he was gone.

"Even if Guardian Pucker can be agreeable, Prince Killian might still deny my case," Wyatt said. "He turned me down last time, and I bet it's because of my demon blood."

"Actually, there're a few half-demon half-fae or half-demon half-warlock in the House of Chaos," I said. "I can talk to His Highness for you too."

"You can't just talk to His Highness," Jinx whispered. "He doesn't talk to anyone, not even Princess Medea."

"He's actually easygoing when he isn't in a mood," I said.

Jinx laughed. "Good luck catching His Highness in a good mood."

"Prince Killian is the opposite of easygoing. He's the most terrifying—" Wyatt said, then stopped mid-sentence as America headed toward us with Bellona, Javier, Fake Blonde, and other nameless minions in tow, all of them with bulldog expressions.

Medea perched her royal ass on the desk, watching. After the show of her open conflict with Killian, she now preferred to be the mastermind behind the scenes, so nothing could be pinned on her. Princess or not, if she got into a serious fight with Killian again, he'd kick her out of his house, like he'd done to Bellona, Imelda, and a couple of their pals.

Rumor had it that the House of Shifters had offered Bellona asylum. Of course, any foes to Killian and me would be Silas's allies.

"You need to see this, Barbie!" Bea said, shoving her tablet under my nose. She'd whipped it out a while ago, anxious to show it to me, but I'd been engaged in a chat with Jinx and Wyatt. Bea wasn't the rude kind who liked to interrupt anyone.

I squinted at Spinchat, the supernaturals' major social

media site. A picture of me squeezed in the middle of the five prince heirs on Rowan's terrace took up the center page with thousands of comments already.

Fuck! I had my eyes half-shut as if I was having an orgasm. If anything, that had been a food orgasm!

Bea scrolled down the screen expertly to show me more comments and hashtags, something like: #Dirty-CuntBarbie'sFirstDate #FakeOrgasmShameless #LittleBob-DirtyDickSecrets #TheHeirsPulledoffHerPantsToExposeDirtyBarbie #WeDon'tWantBarbieWhore...

I didn't have the heart to read the rest of the comments that grew nastier and lewder.

That was probably why America was now marching her minions toward me. They'd learned their lesson about chanting insults at me after I'd turned it against them in the dining hall. I'd wound up getting a date with a prince, the most enviable thing to all the bride candidates.

And through Sy and the fae prince's unholy coupling, I'd learned about the princes' true agenda at asking me out.

What Cade had done by posting the selfie on Spinchat was the first step.

Those assholes spoke sweet lies to my face but carried cruel intentions toward me. Deflower me? Seriously? Who still used the word "deflower"?

They'd never intended to court me. All the dates were their revenge game aimed at bending me and ruining my reputation, even though I'd never had any reputation to begin with.

I doubted that anyone with my kind of background would give two fucks about reputations, or things like that. But I still didn't like public humiliation, as I was a girl who was shy in her core.

"Dirty whore!" America stopped by my desk in the aisle, her manicured finger pointing at me.

I made a show of looking around before turning to her, my one eye shut while the other squinted at her. "Me?"

"You!" she hissed. "Don't pretend!"

"Do you have proof, My Lady America?" I asked innocently.

She whipped out her tablet and flashed me a video clip on the screen. Unfortunately, I was featured again. It showed me sweeping the gold coins from the table onto the napkin, but no one knew the context—Louis had paid me under pressure from the other heirs.

I had a hunch who had filmed it. Silas was most eager to destroy me. Under the photo, the hashtags said: #Barbie-GotPaid #LousyPerformancePoorEscortService #LowtoZe-roCustomerSatisfaction

Comment 1 chimed in: Ask money back!

Comment 2 played: I'll still bang her! She's got nice tits!

The clip that went with the photo of my food orgasm did put me in a bad spot.

"You opened your legs for them to screw you, and you got paid afterwards!" America accused in fury, and the pack of coyotes flanking her glared at me, eyes full of righteous fire.

I nodded and pried open my other eye. "It was an eye-opening experience."

"You're only good at lying on your back and spreading your legs, dirty bitch whore!" Bellona shouted behind America.

I gave the minions a sweeping, curious gaze. "You all think so?

Their glares threatened violence. However, no one seemed to want to toss spells or offensive magic at me. One, they wouldn't work, and two? Their spells and magic would hit them back. They knew that now.

They might not like me, but I was the bitch queen of the domain when it came to anything magical.

"It's amazing," I nodded with an appreciative smile, "that you all think I'm good at something. I can teach you all for a fee, fifteen percent discount for friends and family."

"We aren't your friends!" Fake Blonde yelled.

"Then you'll have to pay the full amount for the technique," I said ruefully. "Only after you master it will a prince come to knock on your door and ask you to spread your legs wide for him. Word travels, and you don't want to be labeled as a lousy lay." I winked at her. "You know what I mean?"

After I'd called her out as Fake Blonde in front of Cade, she had dyed her hair to silver.

Angry and shocked gasps rippled across the classroom. A few students who weren't included in the ranks of the minions snickered. They hadn't dared to have an attitude before, but they'd seen me fight back all the time and somehow, I "prospered" and ended up securing a date with a prince. Now the underrepresented had started to grow balls.

I needed to seize this opportunity to rally the underdogs behind me, so it'd be us against them instead of me against everyone. My days of living on the streets had told me about the numbers game. I needed to think like a lady boss of an organized criminal organization. Why did the mighty Superman fall? He fought alone.

"That wasn't a compliment!" Bellona shouted. "Whore is an insulting word, and no one wants to be a dirty whore!"

"Are you sure, my feisty giant friend?" I winked at her, then turned to wink twice at Medea to include her. "The difference between you ladies and me is that you offer dirty sex for free since you aren't whores. That's very generous of you all. I applaud you, but I can't afford to give myself away for free, so there's a price. Unlike you, I'm expensive and very picky."

Now more than a few students were chuckling. Yep, I was hilarious.

"But a hashtag said LowtoZeroCustomerSatisfaction!" some dude from their ranks yelled.

I arched an eyebrow at that boy. "You're even dumber than you look. Didn't they tell you not to believe fake news?"

Some students had started recording this entire exchange. The good days of staying in obscurity were long gone with the booming of social media. For a long beat, I was profoundly sad that Sy didn't preen or encourage me to push my tits up, shake my golden curls, and strike my best pose for the filming. She'd seize any two seconds of fame or notoriety.

"You're a disgrace to the academy!" America shouted. "No whoring is allowed. You'll be expelled!"

I blinked innocently. "You mean I should follow your and your women's example by offering cheap sex for free instead of receiving gold coins, even after an exemplary service?"

She opened her mouth then shut it, but Medea took over.

"You're nothing but the princes' new squeeze toy," Medea said from her seat.

I had to admit that was the truth, but I shoved down my anger, as I refused to let my nemesis get under my skin.

"Squeeze! Squeeze!" I said, putting a hand under my armpit and pumping my elbow to make a loud *squark* sound.

"My brother won't always be there to watch his new pet, or even make sure she's fed," Medea added viciously. "He'll get tired of you in no time like he did all the others. And wait until his true mate, Queen Lilith, comes next month..."

Before I could retort, an alarm blared in me. Something chilled my bones, then dark, damp, and ominous fog filled my skull.

27

Barbie

S hit!

The druid glided into the class in his white robe. My heart pounded erratically. My mouth turned dry and tasted bad.

One time when I spotted him entering Jubilee Haven, I'd had to exit through the back entrance of the dining hall to avoid him. Usually, nothing and no one could make me skip my meals, but that druid dude carried a vibe creepier than a psycho serial killer.

The class froze at the sight of him, their voices dropped, and the room chilled. I wasn't the only one who got goosebumps. I was only glad that I was perched in the far corner with enough space between that creep and me.

My relief lasted two seconds as his inky black eyes snagged on me, trying to pin me like a fly.

What the fuck?

There were over a hundred and fifty students of mixed years here, and I was the newest of the first year! I wasn't even a noble chick. Shouldn't he fix his eerie attention on the princesses in the front, as was only proper in this realm?

Did he have to stare at me like a vulture? I didn't even have Sy to snarl at him.

I squirmed. How was I going to shake him off? I'd been unfortunate in catching his attention last time. He'd been trying to get his hands on me, intending to lock me up and experiment on me until he and his mistress could get every drop of the godly power they coveted out of me after he'd glimpsed my essence in his crystal ball.

Greed was indeed a cardinal sin in any language and realm.

His dark whispers to Ethel echoed in my head. "*...one of the original gods remains. The boy is more than meets the eye. He wears a glamour unlike anything I've seen. If he's the demigod we've been looking for...*"

He hadn't known I was a girl.

I darted a panicked gaze at his hands to check if he carried a crystal ball. Last time, he'd announced that the crystal ball couldn't pierce through my dark secret since I had the darkest aura around me.

My heart rammed into my ribcage as I spotted a large toolbox in his hand. The ball must be inside. Maybe I should create chaos and find a way to destroy his crystal ball once and for all.

America and her minions turned to stare at the druid in apprehension.

"Isn't Professor Tallulah supposed to teach the divination class?" America murmured.

"Professor Tallulah is being replaced," the druid said coldly. "From now on, I lead this class."

Shit! Shit!

Instinctively, I knew that I was the reason that he took over the class. He was going to gun for me.

He hadn't been able to get his hands on me, so he and Ethel had created this opening.

"Return to your seats!" the druid said with authority. "I won't tolerate any disorder or disrespect. This is a class, not a social club."

America and her army fled to their seats. Even Medea dropped from her perch on her desk and remained subdued in her seat.

I sank lower, trying to get out of his line of sight.

"Barbie!" the druid barked amid the silent classroom.

I pretended not to hear him but stared beneath the desk.

Wyatt patted my shoulder from his desk behind me. "Barbie, the professor was calling you!"

"Barbie, stand up!" the druid called again.

"Uh?" I looked up. "Why?"

The druid stared at me with that unnerving vulture look of his.

I stood up, my shoulders slouched. "Are you wearing the same robe as last time, Professor Druid?" I inquired. "Do you do laundry like others? Sorry, I meant if you have your servants or your acolytes do it? It's not acolytes but apprentices, right? You aren't exactly a priest, so—"

"To the front now, Barbie," the druid ordered and waved two students seated in the first row to relocate to the back. "You'll sit here with Lady America."

"But—" America and I protested at the same time.

"I'll allow no nonsense in my class," the druid said. "You'll help me keep an eye on Barbie, Lady America. She derailed everyone last time, so she can't be trusted even in my class."

The minions let out a gleeful shriek, happy that the druid had me as his new target.

America brought her school bag to the designated front seat, puffing her chest out.

Bea and I shared a worried look. Bea squeezed my hand to offer me sympathy and encouragement, and Wyatt tried to punch my shoulder to congratulate me as I rose reluctantly, his punch landing near the top curve of my buttocks.

"Sorry," he whispered at my frown. "Go get them, tiger!"

I jogged toward the front while watching carefully for any feet sticking out from the aisle to trip me. I didn't have Sy to watch my back now.

All eyes fell on me, and I regarded the druid's toolbox on the podium warily then glanced at the door longingly.

The druid had shut the door.

"Uh, Druid. Professor Druid," I said. "On second thoughts, I believe this class is too advanced for me. I'm only a first year. I'll see myself out."

A purple wind lashed out from him, shoving me toward my seat. His wind couldn't make me move, though it was strong. As it brushed me, I felt dirty and violated, since it also carried the intention of invading my body and mind. I strengthened my shield in case he threw another unwelcome gust at me.

"Stay, girl!" the druid barked, as if I were an ill-behaved puppy, impatience flashing in his inky black eyes.

"Are you sure, Professor Druid?" I protested, my eyes darting around frantically. "I'm too dumb for this advanced divination class. I'll bring you and the class shame."

"You'll only shame yourself," he said matter-of-factly.

America giggled in vengeful delight, and all the minions joined her. I stood by the seat I had been assigned and surveyed the class. Only Bea's corner and Cami and her circle didn't join the mocking laughter.

I bit my lower lip, half out of my wits, my hands clasped in front.

"Sit down!" The druid bellowed his order, a vein throbbing in his temple. He was losing patience with me. It was obvious that he considered himself a great druid, and great men barely had patience for anyone. "I especially required you to be enrolled in this class!"

"Why would you do that, Mister Druid?!" I cried out in panic, feeling like a trapped little spider. "I think it's best I talk to the head of my house, which is Prince Chaos—no, it's Prince Killian of the House of Chaos—about the wisdom of my attending a super advanced class. It might not be legal, to my understanding, since I'm very low in the hierarchy. I was a former servant! And Prince Killian warned me seriously not to be a laughingstock and shame his house!"

"Headmistress Ethel personally assigned you to my class," the druid snapped. "One more improper word out of your insolent mouth—"

"—and I'll get expelled, as My Lady America kindly informed me earlier?" I asked hopefully.

America glared at me.

"One more word out of your uncouth mouth," the druid drawled, "and I'll dole out severe punishment personally, and you won't have food for two days, as everyone knows how much you love to eat!"

Medea, America, and their minions giggled in delight.

"Barbie is a glutton!" Medea said.

I opened my mouth, then shut it. I wouldn't get out of here anyway, and it'd be dumb to risk the druid's wrath. I slumped into the seat next to America.

"Sit up straight!" the druid ordered, and everyone sat up straighter.

I sighed, unhunching my shoulders. This was going to be a fucking long day.

"Today!" The druid scanned the class before landing his vulture stare on me again. I was his sole interest. "We'll start with the divination of the tarot cards. Find your partner. You'll read each other's cards."

The class clamored as students moved around to pair with their friends. I jumped out of the seat, ready to spring toward Bea.

"You stay where you are, Barbie!" the druid said. "I've assigned Lady America as your partner."

America looked dejected too, her lips pulling downward.

"We're stuck with each other, My Lady America." I offered her a grin, trying to make the best out of the situation. "Too bad we can't shake off this love-hate relationship between us."

"There's no love between us!" she snapped.

"You just don't know it yet," I said, smiling.

The druid waved a hand, and a deck of tarot cards appeared on everyone's desk.

"Each student draws two cards only," the druid instructed.

America shuffled the deck, pulled out the first card, and frowned at it.

It was a sword card.

She handed the card to me. "Okay, this card is for you. I'm going to draw a new one for myself."

"No, thanks. Keep the stabbing card yourself." I didn't want her bad luck.

I pulled a card from the middle and stared at a golden-haired girl pinned down by seven swords. In fact, all the swords pierced her back.

A dark feeling swirled in my middle at the bad omen.

"Fine, let's exchange," I said, handing her my card. It was better to be stabbed by one sword than by seven. "You can have mine, and I'll have yours."

"No way!" she shouted. "I don't want your Seven of Swords!"

"I got The Lovers!" A chick a few desks away squirmed.

Not all lovers were good. Hadn't she learned?

America reshuffled the deck, placed it down carefully, and took a deep breath.

"If you're going into labor, let me draw first," I said.

"No, I'll go first, as it's my right!" she said, her hands hovering over the deck to prevent me from taking a good card.

She picked the second card from the top, and I went for the bottom one. We flipped over our cards.

She stared at mine. "Eight of Swords is also a bad card!"

What was with all the swords? So violent! I'd have to pretend to be sick to get out of the next divination class.

"Yeah?" I shook my head. "Yours is worse, My Lady America. You're going to be hanged."

She glared at me. "That's not what The Hanged Man means!"

"What does it mean then?"

"When The Hanged Man card shows up, it can mean high crimes in some cases," she said, musing for a second before scowling at me. "Why am I even telling you this?"

"Before I guide you to interpret the arcana cards, I want you to read them on your own," the druid said. I clasped my hands in front of my cards to block his sight, even though it was futile. "Now pick up your partner's cards and let your magic feel their intentions."

Problem was that my magic wasn't like any other's, and I had yet to find a way to unlock my core power spellbound by a god. But I couldn't let anyone find out about it, so I snatched America's cards and bent them.

"Don't ruin the cards like you ruin everything!" America snapped at me while she gripped my cards as if by doing so, she could inflict harm on me.

Well, only if she knew that my father was called Ruin...

I smirked at her. "Shouldn't you close your eyes, let your fae magic out, and read the cards properly? You don't want to do it wrong and get a low grade from the scary-ass druid, My Lady America."

"Don't tell me what to do! You're nothing compared to me!" she snapped, but she shut her eyes.

I stuck out my hand, stole the chocolate in her pocket, unwrapped the silky cover, and tossed the chocolate into my mouth. It melted right away on my tongue.

America flashed open her eyes before I could smack my lips at the excellent flavor of her chocolate.

"So soon?" I frowned at her.

"I got it!" She glared at me. The fae chick had a lot of anger issues. "The combined two cards of Seven of Swords and Eight of Swords you drew for yourself predict your impending future. You're in danger, and they're coming for you soon!"

"Who? Which sucker is coming for me?" I snickered. I already felt menace creeping up toward me, which had to do with the druid hovering nearby. "Could you be any vaguer?"

"Listen!" she scolded. "If you know what's good for you,

you should get out of the academy and never come back before terrible things happen to you!"

"Nice try," I said.

"Eight of Swords symbolizes 'taken.' You'll be taken," she said viciously. "If you want to avoid that fate, it's best you leave Shades Academy!"

My heart skipped an icy beat. My father's agents could come and try to take me anytime, but I didn't think that it had anything to do with the cards.

"Queen of Swords spells dark plotting, Princess." Bea's voice carried from a couple of rows away. I snapped my head toward her. Somehow, she'd ended up as Medea's partner. "Your second card, The Moon, bears a hidden message. You're aware of the intruder getting between you and your love interest, so you're cooking up a dark scheme to put down your rival..."

"Don't tell me that you can't even read the cards!" America demanded, jerking me back to our session while I pondered if Medea might mistake me as the intruder.

America was right about my failure in feeling the cards, but even an idiot could read those two cards she'd drawn.

"Let me tell you your future," I said, pumping confidence into my voice. "You've been warned, My Lady America." I flashed the cards in front of her face dramatically before tossing them on the desk. "If you keep stabbing others in the back, you'll be hanged, like that dude in the card."

"I'm done!" America shouted for the druid to hear. "You have no talent and no magic." Her face darkened, and a warning flashed in her blue eyes. "You don't belong here. You need to leave!"

While she was still yelling at me, a nauseating feeling swept over me, so strong that I felt like throwing up. I turned my head, my gaze snagging on the druid's crystal ball on the podium.

The nasty druid had brought a bigger crystal, made by dark magic harvested from human sacrifices. I could hear the terrible screams of the souls that fueled it. Rage burned in my eyes. The druid had proved to be a problem. He must die!

A trail of smoke emitted out of the crystal ball before it cleared. On its dark surface, Ruin emerged, his eyes peeking at me.

His beautiful face that outshone everyone else's showed his great recovery. How? He needed me to replenish the essence that he'd lost during the war of the gods. How had he managed to regenerate so fast in my absence?

His hair of true gold radiated light. His deep sapphires eyes held the mystery and power of the stars. His lips were carnal and cruel, everything pouring out of them lies or promises of death.

The most gorgeous man—no, god—stood tall, his form nearly complete, except his clawed, skeletal hands. He'd soon return to his full glory, and the world would be done.

I'd be done.

The apple of my eye, Ruin whispered, his hand reaching toward me in an offer. *Come home, Daughter, and the ones you cherish will be spared.*

"Motherfucker!" I cried out, burning ash filling my mouth.

Every student turned to me in surprise, not expecting my meltdown, their hands still holding the tarot cards.

"I gotta go, Druid!" I called out, forgetting to be respectful, as I was terrified by my father's phantom image in the crystal ball. "I forgot to turn off the shower this morning."

I bolted toward the door.

"Stop!" the druid bellowed, tossing a dark magical net toward me. "I order you, Barbie!"

I kicked the door open, and it tumbled down, the druid's net narrowly missing me.

I alighted on the fallen door, then zoomed away like a bat out of hell.

28

Barbie

I sat on the shore of the lake, looking out into the distance, brooding. I'd run straight to Underhill after escaping from the druid's class. I'd thought of swimming laps to cool myself down and calm my fear, but I changed my mind, so now I just perched here, my academy uniform pooled at my waist.

Wild magic brushed me, sending a delicious, comforting feeling across my body, but it couldn't lessen my apprehension. My heart pounded in cold panic. My veins iced over.

My father had seen me through remote viewing. He'd peeked out through the crystal ball and found me in a class. Had he truly seen me? Or was it merely an omen about my father's coming? Either way, it was bad. And I didn't have the nerve to find out which was true. The druid was bad news enough for me to stay far away.

I dipped my feet into the icy water, gazing down at my

reflection on the surface of the lake. I'd filled out nicely in Shades Academy. My cheeks were rosy, my eyes bright, my pink lips fuller, and my golden curls shone and bounced in the wind.

My breasts were like full blossoms, my tits so perky, as if ripe for...

My thoughts froze, my mouth opened in surprise as I turned and saw who strode toward me. My pulse raced, and my body was instantly on fire.

"There she is," the chaos prince's rich, sensual voice purred, making me shiver with need and delight.

He slid out of the copse of thick trees, gloriously nude. My gaze followed him. Broad shoulders to lean on when crying, check. Muscled chest good for a head to rest on, check. Eight pack delicious to lick, also check.

The prince's entire body was velvety steel, every line hard and seductive. Lust rained down on me.

My pussy started to throb with raw need, my molten core aching.

While my blood ran hot, my eyes roved over the tattoo of an emerald dragon sprawling from his left hip to cover his thigh before they glued to his massive erection. His silky steel rod jerked forward proudly and shamelessly under my scrutiny.

The magnificent sight would make Sy drool, croon, and urge me to jump the chaos prince, who was sin and pleasure incarnate.

Yet she hadn't stirred from the deep abyss. I was afraid that she'd never surface again. I bit my lip, but I didn't need to work hard to push away the sorrow, searing lust, and need seizing me at the approach of the chaos prince.

Had he just walked all the way here stark naked?

Shit!

What if anyone saw his butt, or worse, his massive cock? The entire school would riot, especially as the chaos heir had a carnal god's face when he displayed his sensual side. He should be more careful! Those supernatural chicks weren't to be tempted. They'd jump him and pin him down to ride him, even if he protested!

I'd give him a piece of my mind about that after I looked at him for a few more seconds.

The air rippled. The lake swayed, turning from translucent green to radiant blue. Right in front of my eyes, Underhill transformed. It was still the dark fairytale forest, but it was now a different version from the original.

Starlight spilled into the forest like a dream. Tiny winged fairies flew out of the ancient trees, darting through the gold and blue blossoms and gliding over the lake.

Killian had dream-walked into my reality again. Wild magic dashed to him and chased him merrily. Dream or not, Underhill had let him in again. Then it dawned on me that water was the medium that helped him get to me. Last time, I'd been in the bathtub when he'd teleported me to his gold and marble jacuzzi.

"You do have a knack for attracting trouble, don't you, little dagger?" he said, his storm-blue gaze pinning me.

"I don't know what you're talking about, sir," I said.

He arched a brow, his eyes sparkling with dark amusement. "Are you the one who kicked down the door to the formidable druid's divination class?"

Shit!

Bad news traveled fast.

"The druid left me with no choice," I said, which was true, considering that he might've been the one who had conjured up Ruin. Though it was also possible that my father showed up on his own in the crystal ball when the arcane channel provided an opportunity.

"So you came all the way here butt naked to scold me?" I hissed, changing the subject and going on the offensive. "Or did you come here to watch me bathe? What will the most beautiful and powerful queen, your betrothed, say about that?"

His storm-blue eyes darkened, yet the hunger in them remained, and my blood heated.

He growled. "I wonder what else that mouth of yours can do."

My heart leapt at the suggestion. Despite everything, despite the fact that he was forbidden fruit, I wanted to taste him more than anything.

He might be bound by Queen Lilith, but nothing was strong enough to shackle him, at least not in this reality created by his power of dream walking.

The haze of my fury receded, my need for him burning hot and bright. I needed to be lost in his embrace and feel safe in his starlight, especially while roaring panic still coursed through me after I'd seen my father in the druid's crystal ball.

"Why don't you come closer and find out?" I purred my challenge.

I sucked in a breath as he was suddenly in front of me in a blur, his cock a couple of inches from my face. Lust boiled in me.

But I should scold him for his boldness before I let myself have a little fun. I opened my mouth, and he nudged the crown of his cock between my lips, urging me to open my mouth wide.

I wasn't exactly thinking, so I did his bidding until he invaded my mouth.

What the fuck?

What the fuck had just happened? And it all happened so fast!

My words died in the back of my throat before they had a chance to come out.

I widened my eyes and gazed up at him. I had to open my jaw a lot wider to accommodate the girth of his cock.

Shit.

His shaft was huge and rock hard!

Killian pushed his cock further into my mouth and started to thrust.

This was one of the biggest misunderstandings!

I wasn't inviting him for a blowjob when I parted my lips. But then his cock was deep in my mouth now. What was done was done. So I might as well just enjoy it while it lasted.

"Good girl! Aren't you zealous?" He chuckled, thrusting deeper. "Take my full length!"

The head of his cock pushed down my throat, and he hissed in pleasure, pounding into my mouth while I was still stunned.

"No other woman can take me like that, little dagger," he purred in approval. "You're made for me."

That was nonsense, but with his cock cramming into my mouth, I couldn't voice my opinion. I made a cooing sound, which he interpreted as an eager agreement.

His fingers threaded into my thick golden curls and pulled my head backward, not so gently, as he watched in fascination how he fucked my mouth vehemently and how my full lips gloved his cock.

"I crave you more than that damned vampire craves your blood, little dagger," he said, and alarm shot into me at the mention of blood. If he was also into getting me to donate blood to him, he was in for a world of hurt.

The chaos prince propelled his powerful hips forward, his cock pushing deeper down my throat. It was so long and large, he could only get half his length in. I might be able to accommodate his entire shaft by combining my and Sy's strength and altering my jaw a little, but I refused to do so at my expense.

Anyway, I wasn't a man pleaser. I gotta protect my own interests so I had something to fall back on if things didn't work out.

"I've craved you since the first time I had you in my sight in the woods before that fucking vamp whisked you away. I almost got into a life-and-death duel with him over you that night, but I reined in my beast. I tried to forget you for your own good, but I can't. So I forged this dreamland for us, little dagger. It costs me, but it's worth it to keep you safe."

I didn't get most of what he was saying, but then I had a cock in my mouth, thrusting eagerly. I doubted any woman would be able to think or talk articulately with a cock down her throat.

I rolled my tongue beneath his shaft and let it sweep over his length before I let my teeth play a little too. He growled in pleasure, his eyes rolling back. The chaos prince liked a little pain mixed with his pleasure.

My fingers traced the dragon tattoo on his thigh and froze when I felt a pulse of flame warming my hand. I gazed up at Killian. His eyes had turned deep sapphire with golden rings like fire radiating in them.

If I didn't know better, I'd say a dragon was peeking out of his eyes, assessing me.

A new scent of brimstone, burning flame in an open sky,

and snowy mountains joined Killian's signature scent of powerful male and pine.

A sense of danger, uncertainty, and urgency washed over me. I wouldn't put myself in a vulnerable position when a predator came out to play. Instinctively, I reacted. The tip of my tongue slammed into the crown of his cock just as Killian thrust in again. With my goddess strength, I shoved his cock out of my mouth. Clamping my lips together, I stared at Killian in defiance, irritation, and desire.

Killian arched an eyebrow. "What's that about, little dagger?"

"Next time, you'd better ask before you stick your dick into my mouth!" I snapped with a bit more fire to show him that I wasn't the kind of chick who tolerated fooling around.

He blinked. "But your delicious mouth invited me in."

"That wasn't an invitation by any means!" I said, my face flushing. "I was about to give you a piece of my mind. I opened my mouth to talk, not to ask a cock to fuck it!"

"Hmm, you didn't?" He smirked. "Interesting. My mistake then. But no matter, it turned out better than we expected, didn't it?" He held his cock, pumping its length. My eyes followed his moves while I tried hard not to lick my lips. I wouldn't give him another misunderstanding.

"You want to give me a piece of your mind? Go on, little dagger. I'm all ears and all yours."

I jumped up and tossed a leaf out of my curls, not leaving an opportunity for him to stick his cock into my mouth again while I was talking. Mostly because I'd want to run my tongue and teeth along it again, so I trusted myself even less than I trusted him.

We stood facing each other, his hand holding his heavy cock as he mused where he should put it next. I tried hard not to keep staring at his cock while I folded my arms across my chest in defiance and covered up my tits at the same time. Initially, I had thought of putting my fists on my hips to show more attitude, but then my perky tits would be glaring at him invitingly.

"Let's make ourselves comfortable and sit down," he suggested with a smile.

Instantly, Underhill shifted a tree to us, its low branch providing a perfect chair. The wild magic liked the chaos prince.

Killian nodded his thanks and lowered himself to sit comfortably on the branch chair, his massive cock jutting out between his powerful thighs proudly, as if it believed that every chick would worship it.

The shameless prince patted his lap. "Sit on my cock, Barbie."

"I'm not going to sit on your cock! How could you even say things like that? There should be some proprieties."

He grinned. "Like what?"

I didn't know, so I glared at him.

"It'll be comfier to sit on my lap than the hard ground," he offered. "I'll make sure my cock behaves, I promise."

That wasn't a terrible idea. I gave his cock a heated glance, then stalked to him, brushing his cock to press against his stomach to give me more room. He smirked in amusement as I parked my butt on his lap. He was large and I was petite, so it worked out just fine, and I was comfy as he'd promised.

He wrapped his arms around me, his cock sticking into my back. I shoved it away and adjusted my position to sit sideways, so I could watch what he was doing. Even though I was hot for him, I didn't like to give him my back, especially now that Sy wasn't watching my six.

Killian chuckled. His cock bounced to my side, hot and heavy and damn hard. It wasn't one to give up easily.

His large hand slid up to cup my breast. I stifled a moan at the pleasant sensation.

"I need information, sir!" I demanded.

"What do you want to know, little dagger?" he purred, not taking me seriously while kneading my tit and tracing kisses along my jawline.

I tilted my chin to give him better access, trying hard to gather my thoughts. I needed fast answers before his hand wandered down to palm my pussy. When it happened, I wouldn't have the presence of mind to string puzzles together.

"The myths say that only Hades's direct bloodline can dream walk," I started, cutting to the chase.

"So you've figured it out." He let out a breath. "No one else knows I can dream walk except you."

"Don't say the line 'I'd tell you, but then I'd have to kill you.' It won't work on me since I'm hard to kill," I said. "What are you to Hades? Do not lie to me because I'll know."

"Will you? And can I trust your discretion?" he purred.

My heart pounded. He was going to tell me his well-kept secrets.

"Who am I going to tell?" I leaned toward him, my hands gripping his shoulders. "The whole school is against me."

"Not the whole school," he said. "But I'm willing to put my secret in your hands, little dagger." He brushed his nose over the crown of my hair and inhaled my scent deeply, as if needing it for courage. "My mother is the heir and only daughter of Hades and Persephone."

Fuck! No, not fuck! This was good news.

The chaos prince was Hades's grandson! No wonder his

essence wasn't exactly of this realm. He was also a demigod, at least.

"Where is Hades now?" I asked in a shrill voice.

If Hades was around, if all the Olympian gods were still around, then maybe we could all get together and combine forces to take down Ruin, one of the remaining original gods.

It'd be super tough for me to unmake my father alone, even though I didn't mind all the hard work.

"He is gone, as is my mother. She left when I was an infant," he said, his face devoid of emotions, but his eyes were cold.

"Will they come back?" I asked hopefully while shivering.

He shook his head. "I don't think so."

Fuck!

"What about your dad?" I asked, a little subdued now. "He's the king of the Chaos Kingdom. Is he also a descendant of some godly bloodline?"

"No. That old bastard came from mixed bloodlines," Killian said, his body tensing at the mention of his father. I sympathized with anyone who had daddy issues. "He rose to power due to his cunning and brutality. He doesn't like the new generation—us."

I nodded. "Old dudes are all like that."

My father was ancient. He was older than anything and anyone on Earth. He was older than dirt. I wondered why he couldn't just retire for good, like the other gods, faded or slumbering for eternity. What was there in this world for him even after he rose to his full power? Why must he still make trouble for the world like other power-hungry old dudes? But then, he wasn't one who was going to listen to anyone's counsel. He was the eater of the world. He consumed everything.

A revelation about Ruin almost slipped from the tip of my tongue. I wanted to tell Killian this piece of my dark secret after he'd shared his. But then, being Hades's grandson was one thing. Being what I was?

I bit my lip, then blurted out, "Are you also a dragon?"

I'd felt the flame inside Killian when I traced the dragon tattoo on his thigh. I'd felt the beast peeking out at me. For a heartbeat, the chaos prince's eyes had turned from storm-blue to deep sapphire and gold, like the color of a galaxy.

He gave me an unreadable look, then the corner of his lip tugged up. "Want to know all my dark, dirty secrets, don't you, little dagger? Why don't we trade? No one knows anything about your true origin, and you've been tight-lipped. Your innocent look can fool almost anyone."

I swallowed. I couldn't allow anyone to find out that I was Ruin's daughter. Ruin and my origin were my deepest fears. They haunted me in my dreams and in my waking hours. But maybe I should tell Killian about the god without revealing his relation to me? I'd dropped some hints about Ruin and his Shrieker army to other princes, but it wouldn't be enough when my father came calling.

Nothing and no one could prepare for his invasion.

A wave of anxiety slammed into me. My blood turned to ice.

I pressed my hands against Killian's cheeks. "Will you give me oral pleasure?" I pleaded, needing his heat. I needed to forget about my father and my doom a little longer.

"I thought you'd never ask, little dagger," he crooned, pleased by my urgent need for him.

I was suddenly bare, my uniform gone. Killian laid me

on the branch that shifted to a flower-strewn bed at Under-hill's command. It was invested in our coupling.

"Beautiful, my little dagger," the chaos prince said as his heated gazed traced my every inch and snagged on my bare pussy. I was all bare and golden there, as I was born that way. I knew a lot of chicks had bushes. Sy had a thick bush.

"When I see you, I want to fuck you," he growled. "When you aren't around, I dream of fucking you fast and hard. I want to pump every drop of my cum deep inside you."

"That's the dirtiest thing I've ever heard!" I said, shocked, yet liquid flame tongued my aching pussy at his dirty talk, my blood heating with lust.

"Until the day I can fuck you in every way for real," he promised roughly, "you'll beg me to be dirtier. The pleasure will be ten times more intense than what I'm giving you now."

"Let me have a sample taste," I challenged him, wiggling my ass, "so I'll know if you mean it."

His eyes shifted between storm-blue and deep sapphire with golden flame. I could feel his dragon peeking out again, staring at my pussy in dark fascination, and I opened my legs wider for him to view.

The vamp prince's question suddenly pinged in my head. *"Is it true that your dragon will come out only when he recognizes his fated mate? Are you even a dragon?"*

The air pulsed with rising heat. Killian swallowed and growled, as if he was fighting to rein in his beast.

"I crave this lovely pussy like no other!" Killian lifted my hips, dragging me toward him, and wrapped his mouth around my sex.

Fuck!

My legs jerked at the incredible sensation before I rested

my ankles on his broad shoulders, a moan escaping my lips. Killian buried his gorgeous face between my thighs, feasting upon me.

His wicked tongue licked my slit skillfully, up and down. Up and down. Then it did a clockwise full circle before it lapped at the peak of my clit.

Holy fuck!

I let out a gasp before moaning breathlessly at the intense pleasure. And he'd said if we fucked outside the dreamland, the pleasure would be even more intense.

Was he serious?

Killian let out an amused, sensual chuckle before his tongue thrust into my heated channel with force, tasting my juice and sampling me.

He knew his shit!

I pulled my torso up and threaded my fingers into his thick mane, grabbing a few strands to anchor myself as the pleasure became too intense.

He darted his tongue out of my heat, and I protested. He smirked and moved his mouth to wrap around my sensitive clit and sucked brutally.

"Oh, fuck! Fuck me!" I cried out, my body vibrating from the stimulation.

"Easy, little dagger." He lifted his lips a couple of inches from my pussy and chuckled in pure male satisfaction at my rapt responsiveness at his every touch. "I promise to fuck you soon, so hard that you'll beg me to stop. I might if you're a good girl."

My blood heated at his promises, yet Sy remained absent. She didn't even stir. I'd hoped Killian's potent sexual energy would draw her out. She needed feeding, but it was like she'd checked out for good. A hollowed-out feeling haunted my chest while ice coursed through my veins.

Killian licked my bundle of nerves, bringing me back to him, pleasure like fireworks hitting my nerve endings.

I wanted to lose myself in the pleasure Killian brought to me in this dreamland more than anything, yet a tidal wave of grief, pain, and guilt crashed into me like a tsunami, drowning me and filling my chest with ice shards.

Sy was gone, like amber buried by ashes. I'd snuffed out her spark.

A few more erotic strokes from Killian's skilled tongue, and I'd have one of the best orgasms. I wanted it badly, yet part of me felt dead inside without Sy. I was indulging in lust and pleasure. I hadn't allowed her to have more time with her lover, as I'd always put my needs above hers.

She'd never been created as my equal, a cold truth that I'd never shown her until she'd crossed the line. I'd offered her an illusion, so she'd always protect me or take the fall when needed.

All these years, she'd thought she was my equal or even my better, so she'd rebel once in a while and fight for dominance half-heartedly. But this time, she'd given it her all when she fought me, and I'd shown her my true face and brutality. And now she knew that I could unmake her at any time I chose.

I'd crushed her hope and spirit, and she'd withdrawn and sunk into a deep abyss. Without Sy, I felt dead inside.

Tears burned behind my eyelids while pleasure from Killian's tongue threatened to undo me. Then, a fit of rage and grief surged with the wave of pleasure.

I lashed out.

"Why are you pleasuring me when you have another woman at home, Prince Killian?" I asked viciously.

The chaos heir froze, then blinked, as if he thought he'd heard it wrong.

"I'm not your plaything," I said, holding back bitter tears. "I'm no one's little bitch."

"You aren't and never will be," he growled.

"Then what are you doing here? Doing this to me? You're bonded with a powerful queen and a great beauty, but you still fool around with some girl who's barely one step above a servant. Aren't you going to get married right after your graduation, which will be less than a year from now?"

A twist of agony flitted across his handsome face before his expression shuttered. Coldness slid into place, turning his face to icy marble.

In truth, I didn't care too much that he had another woman, especially after today's encounter with my father, which still left me shaking and reminded me that I was living on borrowed time.

Even if Killian was a free man, I couldn't truly have him either. He was the future king of the Chaos Kingdom, and I was a nobody. Even the school uniforms I had belonged to Shades Academy, paid for by Killian's house.

I wouldn't have a future with him or anyone. And that was the ultimate cold truth for me and for Sy, but she couldn't see it or had long forgotten about it.

Killian extracted himself, cold air filling the gap between us.

It hurt.

A blink, and he was fully dressed, as was I.

He held my gaze. "It won't happen again, Barbie," he said. "You have my word."

I felt a crack form in my heart, frost sliding in and filling my chest.

I was losing him as well.

"Return to the house before it's dark," he said mildly. "Your safety is important. When you come back, you need to tell me what freaked you out so much that you had to kick down the door to the druid's class and run all the way here."

The air rippled, and Killian vanished like a dark star blinking away.

The wind blew past, leaving a pungent and bitter taste in its wake.

29

Barbie

I dragged my leaden feet along the trail toward the glass and steel building of the House of Chaos, my mood darker than the dead of night. I chose this less traveled track as I didn't want to encounter anyone.

I planned to sneak back into the house unnoticed and throw myself into bed with the cover pulled over my head, dead to the world. When I woke up the next morning, things might just go back to the way they were, before Sy and I had turned on each other.

I'd need to hang a "privacy" sign on the door, so Pucker would get the hint. These days, he took the liberty of charging into my room like it was an open bar. If he whined and nagged me for another sip of my energy tonight, I might explode and do something regretful to him.

The waxing moon was gone, the starlight faint. It seemed most of the stars were absent tonight. Maybe it was just my dark mood talking. It didn't bother me much to traipse in the dark alone, but then I'd always had Sy to watch my six.

We called ourselves the creatures of the night and darkness, pun intended. Without her presence, my senses were dulled.

Regret brewed in my middle. I'd hurt Sy, then I'd lashed out at Killian, driving him away as well. Maybe I was indeed my father's daughter, a poison, an eater of the world, and a ticking bomb that could go off at any time.

Sy was a savage, but she was the bright light in me while all this time, I thought I was the lighter one. I'd shown her my true dark side when we fought like enemies.

What would Rowan do when he could no longer find Sy? What would become of Killian and me after tonight? I craved him, aching for him, burning for him, yet I was afraid of seeing him.

I'd never thought that the threads of my life could get any messier, but this was still the best fucking life I'd had. So no, I wouldn't wallow in self-pity. I'd face this new adversary without breaking my stride.

I hummed my favorite song, my footsteps lighter.

"Don't got a lot, but that's enough for me, yeah
'Cause I'm good, yeah, I'm feelin' alright—"

I STOPPED cold as a dark wave of wrongness rolled over me. Something bumped into me the next second.

"Watch it—"

A dozen figures slid out from behind the trees, their feet silent, their intentions vile, as they cut off my escape route.

My heart skipped with dread. This bunch looked like assassins, and they were dressed the part—they all wore black and had masks that exposed only their eyes and part of their cheeks with blood-red war paint.

I wheeled. I was closer to Underhill than to the House of Chaos, so I'd run back to the dark forest, and Underhill would help me deal with the assassins.

But a dozen more stepped out of the trees, blocking my passage to Underhill.

Fine, fight then. I needed to vent my fury and grief anyway. Too bad I didn't have Deathsong with me. But then, I'd been afraid of carrying the arcane blade to the divination class and risking exposing myself.

Instead of throwing out dumb whimpers like, *"Why are you doing this?"* or *"What do you want?"* at the bad guys, I lunged at the nearest ninja wannabe, my boot jamming into his throat.

He went down in a heap before he could shout a complaint, not expecting me to react so fast. Some professionals!

Before I alighted, my elbow rammed backward toward another enemy's face and made solid contact, crushing a bone. Damn, that'd hurt.

A rough hand grabbed my wrist, but I twisted mine in his grip and grabbed his, using it to anchor myself and leaping up. My legs kicked out in a roundhouse style.

It seemed that not just amateurs liked to underestimate me. Yet in the back of my mind, I had a foreboding feeling that this whole setup was off. It unnerved me to register that there was only one magic user in this wild band. It took me another second to realize that magic user was a woman and a ringleader. She hadn't attacked me. In a fight like this, magic users usually attacked first to disable the person of interest quickly, but this one seemed to take care not to broadcast her magic but shield it.

After I maimed a few more ninjas, I'd tear her shield and eat her magic, then use it against her underlings and bring them to Underhill. After I got the intel out of them as to who had sent them after me, I'd offer them as a nice gift to the shadow beasts.

The beasts didn't venture out of the dark forest, as per the terms of the truce between Underhill and the rest of the realm, or they'd help me clean up right now.

"Now! Before she uses it!" the magic user barked urgently.

"Now what?!" I snickered. "You want some passionate kisses?"

They rushed me at once, swarming me. I kicked and punched wildly while training my focus on the magic user. I broke down her shield in two seconds, which might've set the record in her book, judging by the shock in her unmasked eyes.

I stretched a hand to suck her magic into me, and it flowed toward me.

"Pom-pom, your light's going out!" I shouted. "And I'll get home just in time for a late dinner."

But then, everything stopped as if in slow motion—her train of magic bounced back to her, relief replacing the terror in her eyes. A cold metal bracelet clamped down around my wrist, clicking sealed.

Instantly, I felt my power being muted.

Fuck!

That shit could bind me!

Nothing had nullified my power before, but that bracelet seemed to be specially made to subdue me. Chills rose, filling my chest. Someone else here knew a lot about me. Someone understood my origin. And he or she had set up a special op to deal with me.

To my knowledge, only my father could forge a weapon to bind me, yet the bracelet didn't have his signature.

Sy! I screamed, my eyes on fire.

She would answer me, wouldn't she? She wouldn't abandon me when enemies surrounded me, cornered me, and overpowered me like this, would she? We might be fighting, but it was always us against the world. That hadn't changed, right?

I needed her now more than ever. I needed her strength and her claws to cut off my hand that had the fucking bracelet on. It was built to unmake me!

The silence seemed to last forever, until Sy came roaring.

Relief and gratitude swam in my chest. But before she could surface, the spells flared from the bracelet, tossing Sy into the void. I watched in horror, screaming for her. Yet before she'd been banished, she'd sent me all she had, leaving nothing for herself. With Sy's power, I partially shifted, one of my hands turning to blade-like claws.

Instead of hacking at my enemies, I slashed toward my hand to be free of the bracelet, the only way I would escape a terrible fate. The metal bracelet was already draining my energy and weakening me by the second.

I braced for agony, and still the excruciating pain rendered me senseless as my claws cleaved my own wrist. I bellowed as my severed hand dropped to the hard dirt, my dark wind lashing out and spearing a dozen attackers. I seized the magic user's power and yanked it to me, and she howled in pain.

A blade that wasn't forged by this world slid between my ribs, burying deep. I cried out and gasped to take in a breath, my power radiating out like hard waves toward my enemies, sending more of them tumbling down. But two hands wrapped around my neck just before my claws cleaved off a head.

I let out a croaked cry. To my utter horror, my strength was draining away again. A torque was sealed around my neck, replacing the bracelet that had dropped off my severed wrist.

Blood was everywhere, mine and my enemies', soaking into the dirt.

Agony bloomed from my bloody stump, and pain pounded in my skull from the torque, designed to restrain my power and stop me from siphoning any magic.

I screamed, slicing my remaining hand-claws at my enemies before the pack of jackals pinned me down with their sheer numbers. Then I was on the ground, face-planting into the hard dirt and grass.

Hands grabbed my curls to pull my head backward. I spat out a mouthful of blood, snapping my teeth to find flesh to bite, only to have an iron mask slammed down on top of my head until it covered my entire face, muffling my scream.

No one could hear me anymore. Not even Killian would come to me.

My world went utterly black while terror like nothing I'd known for a long time skewered my every bone.

I kept fighting frantically in the dark to no avail.

"This is the first trial of the Brides Selection, and you'll beg for death, *Barbie!*" a malicious voice said in my ear against the iron mask that had swallowed my head.

30

Killian, Heir of the House of Chaos

I jogged down the stairs of the House of Chaos, my hands in my pants pocket. My subjects in the courtyard bowed, and the bride candidates gazed at me with lust and longing, thrusting out their chests. I ignored them all.

Rock and his team followed me, but I shook my head at them. I had no need for bodyguards. A lot of times, having them around was just for show. Right now, the last thing I needed was for them to come with me to Underhill to pick up Barbie.

Underhill had taken a liking to her, which my men and I had kept under wraps. I didn't want her to draw any more attention or danger.

She hadn't returned to the house hours after I'd dream walked to her. I'd need to have a word with her, including the safety rules of the house.

She'd fought her attraction to me today, which was fine. I'd give her space, but it was time for her to come back. It made me restless to think she wasn't shielded.

My cold, dead heart started to beat again after Barbie slammed into my world, tumbling into my arms in the Windsong woods. She'd gazed up at me, furious and annoyed, and snapped at me to "watch it," her golden curls bouncing.

No one else had dared to use that tone with me, but she hadn't known who I was. Then she'd truly seen me, and her lips parted in surprise, her eyes lit up with lust. She blossomed right in front of me, radiant in the deep night. My cock that had been sleeping for a long time hardened right away. I'd never wanted anyone as I wanted her. Her scent had haunted my every dream and waking hour since then.

Bound by the powerful Queen of the Underworld, I was forbidden to touch any other, as my touch would burn them, no matter who initiated it. Only my true mate could overcome the curse. Barbie could touch me any time, however she wanted.

Yet she had no idea who she was to me, and no one would know what she meant to me. I must make sure of it. I knew I should stay away from her, but it was beyond me. I had tried. That was why I'd let her stay in the vampire house, then the shifter house, for weeks. But now I no longer cared if any house collapsed, or the world burned. I needed to be close to her.

She hadn't entirely forgiven me for ripping her clothes off in front of thousands of supernaturals to expose her as a girl. I did what I needed to do to get her to my house, where she would be shielded, but I hadn't expected my rivals to lay their greedy eyes on her and swim around her like fucking sharks smelling the most enticing blood.

I narrowed my eyes in displeasure. I needed to come up with a brutal plan to discourage them all, so the other heirs would quit the idea of courting her. None of them deserved her and they should fucking know that!

I was stalking toward the outskirts of Underhill when a blinding pain shot through my heart, followed by a stab of terror. I staggered in confusion. It took half a breath to stabilize myself, but the calm didn't return.

The string that connected Barbie and me coiled so tightly that I held an icy dread that it would snap. I growled and pushed my power of starlight to cocoon and shield it. The bond didn't break, but it vanished into the void.

I could no longer feel Barbie. My dragon roared with brimstone and fire.

Acid fear seared a hole through the pit of my stomach, an ominous feeling that something horrible had happened to Barbie haunting me, eating me up.

I saw death in the cards.

I broke into a run toward Underhill, as if hellfire was pouring down on my dark soul. I let it burn.

For our sake, for the sake of the fucking world, I prayed I wouldn't be too late to reach my true mate.

House of Shifters and Smoke
Shades of Ruin and Magic Book 3
Coming April 2024

DEAR READER,

Thank you for reading *House of Fae and Mist*. In book three, Barbie will start the first brutal bride trial, and you'll meet Killian's betrothed, Queen Lilith. Don't pout yet, since I've written a very funny scene for you, where Barbie goes on a speed date with all four princes, arranged by Killian and our ghost sidekick.

Don't we all need some good laughs these days?

I'll share Barbie's speed dating scene in my next newsletter. Subscribe to Meg's Newsletter if you can't wait until book three comes out in April.

You're the ones who keep the lights on! Love you!

xoxo Meg

An Exclusive Novel Just for You!

Join my Newsletter to receive all the latest books news. I usually send out a newsletter a month. As a thank you, you'll receive this book!

P.S. If you enjoy House of Fae and Mist, would you consider rating it or leaving a brief review on Amazon? Thank you!

Dear Reader,

Follow Meg on Amazon.

SNIPPET OF SHIFTER GOD

"Shifter City is the opposite of the vampire lairs in Washington State, which is all rain and cold," Shade said. "We picked the sunny state for a reason. No vampires like to venture into Nevada. Only a few very powerful vampires can survive the brilliant sun in our mountainous region."

My heart stuttered. "What about the Vampire God? Can he come here? He's powerful, right?"

"As I said, he's more like a myth," Shade said. "No one has seen him on this continent for a century. Though rumors say he was sighted in North America recently." He lowered his voice to a hushed whisper. "Even if he's hunting you, he won't get to you. We'll make sure of it."

"We're home," the driver, who was a bear in his animal form, announced happily.

A fenced city with high-rise buildings loomed ahead. Sparks jumped from barbed wire fences at its top, and a legion of shifter soldiers patrolled the walls.

"Are those watch towers?" I asked, pointing at one of the towers inside the gate. Four armed soldiers stood on the top platform beside a mounted machine gun.

"We have eight of those towers in the city," Shade said with pride. "We now have to rely on old-fashioned watch towers since the satellite era was over a century ago."

When War, the second horseman, had come to Earth, I wondered what had happened to him. Had he died, retired to his Heavenly home, or simply disappeared?

A chorus of howls from the city jerked me out of my trance. The shifter soldiers were acknowledging the return of their Alpha Heir and his team.

The leading jeep braked before the gate, as did the rest of the fleet. Sideburns jumped off the second vehicle and strode toward us. The strange thing was I hadn't missed him one bit, but as soon as he was in proximity, my core tightened, needing him and wanting him in a shameful way.

From the sudden heat rising in his hard gray eyes, I could tell he felt exactly the same and he didn't like it either.

The Alpha Heir tilted his chin toward the two other shifters sharing the jeep with Shade and me. The shifters bowed to him, left our jeep, and filed into a black van.

My heart pounded erratically, and my hand reached out to grab Shade's sleeve. The younger prince had convinced me that his older brother had promised not to put me in the retaining center, but what if the Alpha Heir changed his mind?

Sideburns glanced at my hand as it landed on Shade's arm, and his face darkened.

"I'll escort Pip to the Academy and make sure she settles in," Shade offered, his eyes on his brother.

"That's where I'm going too," Sideburns said. "You drive."

Shade flashed me a comforting smile before he moved behind the wheel. Sideburns slid into the jeep and took the seat beside me. I wanted to scoot away and put some distance between us, but I didn't want to be that obvious and get further on his bad side. Who knew how he would take it? It wasn't exactly a smart move to give him the wrong impression or even let him know about his effect on me. He'd warned his inner circle not to reveal that I was his fated mate, and I was more than happy to pretend I was ignorant about it after how he'd treated me.

I might have nothing, but I wore my dignity like armor.

The fleet rolled forward and entered the city through the vast, heavy gate. Soldiers saluted their princes, and some curious eyes lingered on me. I regretted not putting the ball cap back on. My lilac-blue hair stood out from the others with us. Other than that, I didn't even know how I looked or how old I was.

As we drove, I sat quietly beside Sideburns. Neither he nor Shade talked to each other. I was also glad Sideburns hadn't interrogated me again after that night. The silence was heavy and awkward between us, yet the heat and desire that radiated off the Alpha Heir was thick and undeniable.

He might have decided that I wasn't good enough for him, but the mating call harassed him just the same. It would almost have been fun to watch him execute his self-control by balling his fists at his sides so he wouldn't reach for me, if the mating heat didn't get a rise out of me as well.

I'd stay far away from him as soon as the next opportunity came. As I tried to take my mind off him, I worried about my unknown new life in a city full of strangers.

What if everyone hated me?

I had only one friend, but Shade wouldn't be around all the time, and I shouldn't demand he babysit me. I was so nervous, all things considered, that I was no longer in the mood to observe the broad streets, the buildings, and the people strolling down the alleys.

If Shade and I were alone in the car, I might be more relaxed. I might have enjoyed the rest of the ride. I had so many questions regarding the new school and Shifter City.

"Uh, revered Alpha Heir," I said, turning to him but lowering my gaze, as I'd learned that looking into the eyes of the shifter was usually considered a challenge or defiance. I had no need to rile him up now. "You really don't need to accompany a humble newbie like me to the Shifters Academy. I bet Canary can guarantee my safety and even make me behave."

Shade didn't comment back, but I could tell he was trying not to laugh.

"I'm not escorting you," Sideburns said in a scathing tone. "As you said, you aren't important enough to be worth my effort."

Oh, burn.

"I am going to visit Princess Viviane, my intended," he said, reining in his temper. I had no idea why he was even angry. "Princess Viviane is a well-respected senior student in the Academy. She's supposed to graduate early next year."

"Cool," I said. "So you two will get married and have children soon? Sorry, I meant pups."

"That's none of your business," he grated.

Wow, where did this sudden hostility come from?

"No pups then?" I asked. "You aren't shooting blanks, are you, Your Highness?"

Continue to read SHIFTER GOD

Excerpt of Cursed Kingdom of Dragons and Roses

In Elvey's old chamber, it was just him and me.

I took in the room that was devoid of any personality. It

had scarce furniture: a desk, a closet, and a bed that seemed no one had slept on for a while. Elvey had never seen Sihde as his home. He resented this place, having been a blood slave for centuries.

But now he was free, and he was with me.

Should I have a chance to rule in Sihde, I'd make sure to level the Red Palace. I would choose another high court and would make both Sihde and the Dragon Realm a home for him and for many others.

You're my home, he said in my head. Yet he still didn't come to me as I perched on the edge of the bed. His hot gaze locked with mine.

"You claimed me in your court," he said, heat and tenderness in his blue eyes that were full of the mystery of the stars. I was falling into them.

I'd fallen into them a long time ago.

My heart fluttered, and I was afraid the tiny wings inside would carry it out of my body.

I raised an eyebrow, trying to maintain a cool manner. "You didn't object," I said. "You want to object now?"

A slow, sexy smile spread across his masculine beautiful face.

"You'd better make it in truth then," he said, his voice rough with desire.

Fire sparked in my belly, spreading lower until it licked between my thighs.

Being with Elvey had a cost. He was a complicated man loaded with complications. But he saw me when no one else did. He'd seen me when I'd been the Fury beasts, when I was a dragon, and when I was Fae.

He'd been looking for me before I was even born.

I'd wanted him from the moment I'd set my sight on

him. Now I would have him, but at a steely price—my other three mates.

No, it wasn't because of Elvey that they'd chosen to leave me.

I shook my head. My heart was still broken, but—

Before I blinked, Elvey was on me in a flash. He pulled me up, crushing me against his hard chest, and his lips slanted onto mine.

He was gentle, and then he wasn't. He'd been hungry for me for a millennium but had been denied every chance to be with me. And now his passion unleashed with a vengeance.

Its force was staggering. The demigod's immense power infused into me. Powerful hybrid dragon and Fae or not, I wouldn't have been able to take it if I weren't his mate.

Already, my lips felt swollen, but I wouldn't let him go.

My lips parted for him, and his tongue thrust in with pure male dominance and demand. Oh, Elvey knew how to demand and dominate.

But he didn't just take as he ravished me; he let me taste a dream, burning stars and beyond. His scent of forest sunlight and faint pine covered me, trapping me in his blend of splendid illusion and harsh reality forever.

A mere kiss from him could undo me.

As I moaned, craving more, wanting more of him, all of him, he broke the kiss.

We panted hard with burning lust.

I stared at him, his eyes bright.

"Undress for me, woman," he ordered.

He wanted to play slow and sensual when he'd kissed me like that?

I smirked, but I found that I wanted to undress for him.

If he wanted slow burn, I would give him that, and we'd see who would burn up first.

I took time to remove my cape, tossing it to the floor. Then I bent forward to remove my boots, very slowly, wiggling my ass at Elvey. At some point, I believed that I swayed my hips like a horny maiden.

Cold air touched my bare skin before I reached for my other boot.

Every piece of my armor was gone—he'd used magic to strip me off in a blink of an eye— while I was still bent, my rear toward him.

I straightened and wheeled toward him, my face flaming.

Dark lust and amusement sparkled in his eyes. He trailed his intense gaze all over me, caressing every inch of my body without touching.

"It's unfair," I said. "You asked me to take off my clothes, and you just stripped me without warning. And you're still fully dressed."

"What about I let you strip me?" he said with a corporeal smile. "Will you still complain?"

I pouted. "I don't know how to use magic to undress."

"I'll teach you. For now, you can probably help me with your hands. I like your hands."

I stalked toward him, until we were mere inches apart. I pressed a hand on his chest through the fabric, his powerful heart beating rhythmically under my palm.

And my heart beat equally loud.

I started unbuttoning his shirt as I controlled my urge to rip it apart, so we could be skin to skin. I pulled it off his broad shoulders and pressed my palms against his hot, bare torso.

He sucked in a sharp breath, and I could feel his pleasure.

My fingers traced his muscled chest down to the hard plane of his stomach, and all the way down to his waist.

He watched my every move, the heat in his eyes fueling my fire and my desire.

Swiftly, I unbuckled his belt and yanked open his fly.

I stretched myself against him, my mouth finding his as my hand slipped into his trousers and half wrapped around his hard cock.

Gods, it was so big that I might need two hands.

I had always thought Elvey was the patient one, for he'd waited for me for a millennium and endured things no one else could. But at this moment, he wasn't patient. He didn't wait for me to completely undress him.

A breeze passed by us, and then his clothes were all gone.

Our bare skin pressed against each other, mine soft and supple, his hard and muscled.

I moved my naked body against him, and my nipples hardened at the contact, shivering in want.

Elvey pulled away from my lips, lowering his mouth to my breast and capturing my nipple between his teeth. He started to suckle me greedily. A low moan escaped my throat, and I threw my head back as pleasure rippled through me. He sucked my tit so hard—almost brutally—I had to lace my hand in his hair to ground myself.

"My rosebuds. Mine," he murmured as he suckled my other tit before tracing his lips down my body until they found my heated core.

He kissed it deeply, his tongue lapping and flicking my clit.

A hiss escaped me at the sensation. I jerked and moaned, my knees buckling as my fingers twisted his hair.

I begged for mercy. "Elvey!"

Here I was, bared before him, with not just my body, but my soul and my heart.

Take me, I said. I wasn't patient anymore. I didn't want slow burn or low burn. I wanted him to get his big cock inside me, penetrating me and filling me.

I wanted him to fuck me senseless.

But he pulled away again.

What was he waiting for? After all these centuries, he should no longer want to wait.

He gazed up at me, and I saw tears in his eyes.

"I never imagined I would have you and could be with you," he said. "But you came for me and gave me back my freedom, my beloved."

Emotion choked in my throat, and I couldn't even utter a word. If only I could have come to him earlier.

Elvey's mouth enveloped my pussy again, lapping at me like a starving man.

I shivered in pleasure and with burning need for him.

Elvey rose, swept me into his arms as if I were feather light, and carried me to the bed.

He laid me on the center of the sheet, and I watched him, waiting for his next move.

His gaze was full of desire and dark promise as it roved from my face all the way down, lingering on my breasts and my pussy the longest, then to my toes, inch by inch, before tracing back and staying at my pussy. I could feel it was slick and swollen with urgent want.

He placed his hands on my knees and parted my legs wide before he settled between my thighs.

"I won't be gentle," he warned. "I won't stop. I have to

fuck you hard. I've wanted to fuck you for ages. I've pictured this thousands of times. I've been desperately searching for you for centuries. Now you've finally returned to me. And you're in my bed."

He was my first destined mate.

He should have been mine centuries ago. We'd been robbed of our union for nearly a millennium because my evil aunt had done this to us. I wouldn't allow her to take anything from us again.

"Take me. Fuck me hard," I said. "Make up for the time we lost."

"I'll fuck you until you're sore. Until you bear my mark."

Read **Cursed Kingdom of Dragons and Roses complete series** on Amazon.

BOOKS BY MEG XUEMEI X

SHADES OF RUIN AND MAGIC: Brides Selection

House of Vampires and Flame

House of Fae and Mist (coming Dec 2023)

House of Shifters and Smoke (coming April 2024)

House of Mages and Ravens

House of Demons and Bones

House of Chaos and Gilded Dreams

MONSTERS AFTER DARK

Shifter God

Vampire God

Death God

UNDERWORLD BRIDE TRIALS

Playboy King

Rejected Queen

Hellfire Crown

Hidden Court

CROWN OF THORNS AND SINS: UNDERWORLD BRIDE TRIALS

Hunted by the Dragon

Ruined by the Dragon

HALF-BLOOD ACADEMY SERIES

Magic Trials

Magic Secret

Magic Fury

Magic Unchained

Magic Flame

DARK FAE KINGS SERIES

Book 1: Fever Fae

Book 2: Frost Fae

Book 3: Night Fae

Book 4: Blood Fae

THE WAR OF GODS SERIES

A Court of Blood and Void

A Court of Fire and Metal

A Court of Ice and Wind

A Court of Earth and Ether

COURTS OF UNDERWORLD SERIES

The Burn of the Underworld

The Rise of the Underworld

The Dragonian's Witch

The Witch's Consort

ABOUT THE AUTHOR

Meg Xuemei X is a USA Today and Amazon Charts bestselling author of paranormal and fantasy romance. She loves writing badass heroines and hot psycho alphaholes.

Sign up to Meg's mailing list to hear about her new releases and get newsletter only bonus scene and a special gift.

Made in United States
Troutdale, OR
04/17/2024

19243513R00162